THE CARTEL

THE CARTEL

AND OTHER COVER STORIES

WAYNE GRADY

Freehand Books gratefully acknowledges the financial support for its publishing program provided by the Canada Council for the Arts and the Alberta Media Fund, and by the Government of Canada through the Canada Book Fund.

This book is available in print and Global Certified Accessible™ epub formats.

Freehand Books is located in Moh'kinsstis, Calgary, Alberta, within Treaty 7 territory and Métis Nation of Alberta districts 5 and 6, on the traditional territories of the Siksika, the Kainai, and the Piikani, as well as the Iyarhe Nakoda and Tsuut'ina nations.

Library and Archives Canada Cataloguing in Publication
Title: The cartel, and other cover stories / Wayne Grady ; foreword by Margaret Atwood.
Names: Grady, Wayne, author. | Atwood, Margaret, writer for foreword.
Identifiers: Canadiana (print) 20260219606 | Canadiana (ebook) 20260219614 | ISBN 9781997534242 (softcover) | ISBN 9781997534259 (EPUB) | ISBN 9781997534266 (PDF)
Subjects: LCGFT: Short stories.
Classification: LCC PS8613.R337 C37 2026 | DDC C813/.6—dc23

Edited by Deborah Willis
Design by Natalie Olsen
Cover painting by Frantz Seimetz
Author photo by Leah Feldon
Printed and bound in Canada
FIRST PRINTING

FREEHAND BOOKS
freehand-books.com

Canada | Canada Council for the Arts | Conseil des Arts du Canada | Alberta Government
CERTIFIED CANADIAN PUBLISHER

FSC www.fsc.org MIX Paper FSC® C100212

For Merilyn, con amor y bugambillas.

CONTENTS

FOREWORD

WAYNE GRADY'S UNMISSABLE *The Cartel and Other Cover Stories* is not like any book you're likely to have ever read. Yes, it's a collection of accomplished, enjoyable, and intriguing original tales. But it's also an investigation into the nature of stories themselves: how are they constructed, what are they telling us and how? And what's in the locked room? Is it a lie? Is it an act of self-sacrifice? Is it a dead body, or an almost-dead one? Is it a paradox? Is it a passionate love that may also be a trap? Is it a betrayal? Or is it, perhaps, a dog? Curiosity being one of our predominant human virtues or vices, we read on, nor will we be disappointed: all of these are on offer.

In his introduction, Grady explains what he means by "cover stories." The term comes from music – musicians can "cover" another musician's song, by singing or playing their own rendition of it. Such covers are both tributes to the song and self-standing creations. It's the same song, yet not the same. The tempo, the key, the voice – all may be different. We are used to such metamorphoses in music, and especially in the theatre – there was a recent version of Macbeth, by Robert Lepage, that was done as a feud among Montreal motorcycle gangs, complete with motorcycles instead of horses, and black leather jackets with each clan's name on the back. In opera and ballet, such inventions are rife. But stories? Classically, there too. How many versions of the Bluebeard story are there? How many Penelopes, some of whom are not faithful at all? How many dragon-slayers, with dragons of all kinds?

So Grady is hardly out of line; it's just that we aren't used to seeing this done with short stories. During his series of high-wire acts (without a net, I note), Grady riffs on many well-known masters—Chekhov, Kafka, Gogol, de Maupassant – and shifts the stories in time and place, with characters that are and are not the same. Macbeth on a motorcycle! A lot of the fun is reading the original, then seeing what Grady has done with it.

At the end of each story, Grady thoughtfully provides a little essay about the process: not how he did what he did – that's a secret – but why he came to make some of the choices he made. For aspiring story writers, this can be very helpful.

The whole project might also be very helpful for those teaching the short story. Hey! You wouldn't even have to do any teaching! All you'd have to do is say, "Read the originals. Now read Grady's cover stories. Now read the little essays." And, for an extra, you could say. "Now try it yourself."

How about, for instance, Kafka's "Josephine the Singer, or The Mouse Folk"? Lots of scope there.

Go on. I dare you.

Margaret Atwood

INTRODUCTION

Each story in this collection was inspired by a story written at a different time, in a different place, by different writers. I think of mine as "cover stories," because although they are related to the original stories, they also have lives of their own, independent of the stories that inspired them. I have adopted the term "cover stories" from the field of music, but it also extends to the field of literature.

Elvis Presley's "Blue Suede Shoes" was released in September 1956 as a cover of a song by the same name that Carl Perkins wrote and released in January of that year. By April, Perkins' original recording had sold over a million copies; Presley later said he released his version to help Perkins, who'd been in a car accident while on tour and was unable to continue promoting his own record. Perkins' sales were beginning to drop, and Presley's cover repopularized the song and brought Perkins' sales back up. Scottie Moore, Presley's lead guitarist, later said that "Elvis wasn't thinking at the time that it was going to make money for Carl, he was doing it as more of a tribute type thing." But the release of Presley's cover did made money for both artists, and Perkins said he was grateful to Presley for the tribute.

Musicians view their covers more as homages than as rival or stolen versions. When k.d. lang released her album *Hymns of the 49th Parallel* in 2004, on which she sang songs originally sung by Joni Mitchell, Leonard Cohen, Jane Sibbery and other well-known Canadian singer-songwriters, the *Guardian* called it "her cover-version homage to her song-writing compatriots."

But cover versions can also be appreciated as important, even original works. When Ralph Vaughan Williams wrote "Fantasia on a Theme by Thomas Tallis" in 1910, he was both inspired by and honouring the work of the sixteenth-century church musician whose musical spell Vaughan Williams fell under while editing the 1906 edition of the *English Hymnal*. Tallis's work set to music the King James version of Psalm 2. Vaughan Williams echoed the theme of Tallis's original, but as his biographer, James Day, writes, his rendering of it was "unquestionably the first work by Vaughan Williams that is recognizably his and no one else's." Although Vaughan Williams's "Fantasia" was generally well received, cover versions are sometimes considered to be unoriginal. One critic called it "a queer work by an odd fellow from Chelsea." Psalm 2 begins with the question, "Why do the heathen rage, and the people imagine a vain thing?"

Anton Arensky probably had no thought of reviving interest in the work of Tchaikovsky when he wrote *Variations on a Theme of Tchaikovsky* in 1894, the year after Tchaikovsky's death. Arensky had been a student and later a friend of the great Russian composer; he composed his *Variations* as a tribute to Tchaikovsky's memory and an expression of his grief. The tribute did not make Arensky famous at the time – fellow Russian composer Nikolay

Rimsky-Korsakov predicted, accurately, that Arensky would "quickly be forgotten" – but his *Variations* has recently been revived, and has led to a new admiration for his chamber music.

In 2012, the classical composer Max Richter released *Recomposed by Max Richter*, a Deutsche Grammophon album subtitled *Vivaldi – The Four Seasons*. Richter's re-composition is a forty-four-minute work based on Vivaldi's forty-nine-minute masterpiece, which, Richter felt, had become banalized by overuse in shopping malls, elevators, and restaurants: Lydia Davis notes that commuters in New York City "may hear a little Vivaldi from the loudspeakers of the Port Authority Bus Terminal or Penn Station." Richter felt that everyone heard Vivaldi's music, but few actually listened to it. He wanted modern audiences to rediscover Vivaldi through his recomposition. In composing his version, he discarded three-quarters of Vivaldi's original music and overlaid what was left with his own work, which in fact brings Vivaldi's work so clearly to the fore that at times it's not clear which composer is controlling the musical experience.

"Richter's work is not an adaptation of Vivaldi," Daniel Hope, the solo violinist for the premier performance of Richter's work, said in an interview, "it's a recreation. The deeper you enter Richter's work, the closer you approach Vivaldi."

IN THE "TRANSLATOR'S NOTE" to her translation of *Empty Words*, a novel by Uruguayan writer Mario Levrero, Annie McDermott writes that Franz Kafka was an early influence on Levrero's writing, and that Levrero, who died in 2004, claimed that his first novel, *The City*, "was almost an attempt to translate Kafka into Uruguayan." *The City* is Kafkaesque in tone, but it is not a translation of Kafka. The narrator inhabits a city in which he is constantly becoming lost, even if he's only setting out for the corner grocery store, and every attempt to move in a given direction results in frustration and inertia. It's like Kafka, but not a word of the novel is from Kafka. When interviewed, Levrero called himself a "realist."

"Everything Levrero wrote," writes McDermott, "is instantly recognizable as his." In what sense, then, is *The City* "almost a translation" of Kafka? Perhaps in this: the deeper you penetrate into *The City*, the closer you approach *The Castle*.

Henry James's short story "Paste" is based on Guy de Maupassant's "The Necklace." James follows de Maupassant almost paragraph by paragraph, although each of James's paragraphs differs from de Maupassant's. Like Max Richter with Vivaldi, James recomposed de Maupassant's story. He wrote "Paste" with de Maupassant sitting on his shoulder, whispering things like, "Okay, now have her do this," and "Here the scene shifts to the jeweller's." There is much about "Paste" that approximates "The Necklace," but there is much more that comes from James. James was a different writer from de Maupassant — as different as England was from France, and as America was from either.

IN HER ESSAY "An Experiment in Modernizing Laurence Sterne's *A Sentimental Journey*," Lydia Davis discusses her reason for doing what at first seems to be an oxymoronic exercise: "translating from English into English." She undertook the task of modernizing *A Sentimental Journey*, first published in 1768, to make Sterne more accessible to contemporary readers, not so much because modern readers *couldn't* read Sterne in the original, but because, as she says, hardly anyone except scholars now *do* read anything older than Jane Austen. She found it odd, especially since many people still listen to eighteenth-century music and go to galleries to look at eighteenth-century paintings. She thought that if she "made some Sterne easier to read, perhaps a few readers would be drawn to the original." Which is something any translator working from any source language hopes to accomplish: to direct a reader's attention back to a writer they may not know or have not read, or whose popularity — like that of Carl Perkins or Antonio Vivaldi — has faded either from disuse or over-familiarity.

All art is transient, but of art's Three Sisters — Literature, Painting, and Music — Literature seems the most vulnerable to the passage of time. We know only approximately what the Homeric poets recited. Only seven of the ninety plays written by Aeschylus have survived. The colonialist practice of translating oral literatures to written texts does not guarantee that the literature, or even the language, will survive colonialism. Teju Cole, in "A Quartet for Edward Said," writes that he first heard the *Poco allegretto* from Brahm's Third Symphony in 1995, in the Tower Records shop in the below-ground section of the World Trade Center, in New York. Many years later, he was listening to the same movement in a taxi when he found himself "passing the site where the World Trade Center had stood: a remarkable coincidence. The towers, of course, were gone. But the music — music one would have thought of as delicate and helpless — was still blooming out, and it always will." Cover stories, even those in the same language as the originals, may be read as efforts to give to Literature the longevity enjoyed by its sisters.

Perhaps it was in this vein that Peter Carey wrote *Jack Maggs*, his recasting of Charles Dickens's *Great Expectations*, Percival Everett wrote *James*, a retelling of *Huckleberry Finn*, and Barbara Kingsolver wrote *Demon Copperhead*, which a reviewer in the *Financial Times* called "a contemporary take on *David Copperfield*" that "mostly mirrors the original."

STEVEN HEIGHTON'S 2004 poetry collection, *The Address Book*, contains his own poetry as well as his "translations" of poems by Rimbaud, Rilke, Émile Nelligan, Homer, Ángelos Sikelianós, Jean Takamura, Li Bai, and others. The poems are nearly but not exactly translations of the original texts, and Heighton doesn't call them translations: he names the section "Fifteen Approximations." In a note to his version of Li Bai's "A Song of Ch'ang-kan" (an eighth-century lament voiced by the wife of a merchant who has been away for five months), he thanks Gary Geddes for Geddes' "fine and faithful (compared to Ezra Pound's great and unfaithful) translation," but went on to create something different from either Geddes or Pound or, for that matter, Li Bai; he wrote a poem that acknowledged its debt to the original, but was identifiably his own. Here are three lines from Pound's version:

> The paired butterflies are already yellow with August
> Over the grass in the West garden;
> They hurt me. I grow older.

And here are the same lines from Heighton's approximation:

> The butterflies brought by August
> still flitter — two left — over grass in the west
> garden. Their passing grieves me.
> Waiting, I age.

Heighton took the notion of translation as approximation from Mexican poet José Emilio Pacheco, whose first book, *The Blood of Medusa*, was published in 1958 and, like Heighton's, included a section called "Approximations." Pacheco's "translations" of poems supposedly written by such well-known poets as Gérard de Nerval and Arthur Rimbaud, however, are in fact poems by Pacheco composed in the style of those poets, if we imagine those poets writing in Mexican Spanish in the 1950s. In other words, Pacheco's "approximations" were an elaborate literary joke.

Both Heighton and Pecheco make the same point. By calling his translations "approximations," Heighton acknowledges that no matter how faithful you try to be to the original, your "translation" will never be other than your own poem inspired by a poem written in another language. Pacheco takes the further step of saying that you might as well skip the pretense of making a faithful translation, and write your own poem. Because if you are any kind of poet at all, you will anyway.

IN 1962, Robert Lowell published "The Scream," a poem that he said was "derived from" a short story by his close friend, Elizabeth Bishop. The poem later appeared in Lowell's collection, *For the Union Dead*, where, in a prefatory note, he again acknowledged that "The Scream" "owed everything to Elizabeth Bishop's beautiful, calm story, 'In the Village.'"

The first paragraph of Bishop's story begins: "A scream, the echo of a scream, hangs over that Nova Scotian village. No one hears it; it hangs there forever, a slight stain in those pure blue skies, skies that travellers compare to those of Switzerland, too dark, too blue, so that they seem to keep on darkening a little more around the horizon. . . ."

And here is the first stanza of Lowell's poem:

> A scream, the echo of a scream,
> Now only a thinning echo . . .
> As a child in Nova Scotia,
> I used to watch the sky,
> Swiss sky, too blue, too dark.

Lowell picks up not only Bishop's words, but also her style, which relies for much of its effect on repetition: "a scream, the echo of a scream," "no one hears it, it . . ." "a slight stain in those pure blue skies, skies . . .". And Lowell: "a scream, the echo of a scream, / Now only a thinning echo . . ." "I used to watch the sky, / Swiss sky . . ." But he adds details of his own. Nowhere in Bishop's story does she say she grew up in Nova Scotia (although she did), but Lowell adds himself as a child in Nova Scotia, even though he grew up and lived most of his life in Boston, moving to New York two years before he wrote this poem. The poem owes a lot to the story, but it doesn't owe everything.

Why put himself in the poem? What was it in Bishop's story that made Lowell want to derive a poem from it? Most of the other poems in *For the Union Dead* – indeed a great many of Lowell's poems in general – are about his family, one of the old Boston families that traced back to the *Mayflower* and of which he was extremely, if complicatedly, proud.

Lowell suffered from bipolar disorder. Like Elizabeth Bishop's mother in the story and in life, Lowell was hospitalized twelve times between 1949 and 1964, usually for several months at a time, and was deeply ashamed of the shadow his illness cast on both his historical and immediate families. During Lowell's bouts of depression, the poet

Dan Chiasson wrote in the *New Yorker*, Lowell was unable to distinguish between metaphor and reality: "the symbols changed places with reality . . . the 'like' and 'as' of metaphor dropped out of his mind." Actually, metaphors don't use "like" or "as"; a simile says a glass of wine is *like* a poem, a metaphor says a glass of wine *is* a poem. When Lowell was sick, according to his friend Jonathan Ravan, "the metaphors took over," and Lowell "became, in his mind, Christ, Hitler, Napoleon, Dante, Milton, Alexander the Great, John the Baptist, and many others." Including, one suspects, Elizabeth Bishop.

But why that particular story? A possible answer appears early on, when Bishop's central character emits that silent, recurrent scream "because in Boston, she had not got any better, in months and months – or had it been a year? In spite of the doctors, in spite of the frightening expenses, she had not got any better." Lowell, too, had been treated for months and months, in hospitals in Boston (and in New York), and had not got any better. It seems likely, then, that when he read those lines of Bishop's, the distinction between metaphor and reality fell out of his mind, and he sat down to cover Bishop's beautiful, calm story with an agonized poem of his own. "The Scream" isn't *like* "In the Village," it is *his* "In the Village."

IN HIS NOVEL *Open City*, Teju Cole cites "directly" James Joyce's short story "The Dead," because he felt a kinship with the Irish writer and, despite the vast difference in their native cultures, responded viscerally to the story when he first read it. "In one paragraph," Cole writes in a later essay, "Epiphany," "I substitute rain for snow, and Belgium for Ireland, but otherwise make few changes to Joyce's original."

He says this is not plagiarism, because he has no intention not to be found out: “The lifting is obvious and unsubtle.” Nor was he simply being influenced by another writer. It’s more the case that other writers helped him define his own literary sensibility, and passages from their work flowed through his imagination and became part of his own vocabulary. As Elizabeth Bishop’s flowed into Robert Lowell’s. Teju Coles’s citing of lines from Joyce or Mann or Sebald, he says, constitutes an ongoing conversation with writers who have helped to shape his consciousness.

“Far from having any anxiety of influence,” he writes, “I am skeptical of an originality that does not place itself in conversation with antecedents.”

LA GORDITA

A TYPICALLY SWELTERING July day at the height of Mexico's rainy season. The Federal Army has withdrawn from the city of Colima, leaving it in the hands of two powerful drug cartels, Los Caballeros Templarios and La Nueva Generación Jalisco. Everything has shut down. The hotels and restaurants are empty except for cartel officers and their soldiers; bus companies have suspended normal operations; destination wedding arrangers have found other destinations; tourism is down to a trickle. Every embassy in Mexico has declared the state of Colima a high-risk, no-travel zone, advising any foreigners caught in it to avoid all non-essential forays outside their places of residence. Cartel soldiers lounge openly in cafés and on street corners, brandishing state-of-the-art grenade launchers and AK-47s, eyeing the young women on their mopeds, surveying the rooftops and doorways. They've seen the movies. Many of them are mercenaries, trained in the army before being recruited to work for the cartels for better pay. Everyone is on edge.

Cartels Occupy Colima, read the headlines. Mexico's armed forces have sent a total of sixteen thousand troops into the surrounding region, with helicopters, rocket launchers, and patrol boats, with the 51st Infantry patrolling the highways, the Navy blockading the port of Manzanillo, and still the government can't defeat the cartels. "We have secured the state," is the best the generals can say to the media, "no more cartelanos getting in, and no more drugs getting out." Which is patently untrue, and only makes the expats stuck in Colima feel as though they're locked in a hot car and the government is throwing in rattlesnakes.

When the last of the Federales have retreated from the interior of the state to regroup near Manzanillo, an uneasy calm settles over Colima, silent and deeply disturbing, like a dream from which no one awakens. Citizens wait anxiously in their homes, terrified that their garden tools and kitchen knives will be mistaken for weapons, and they'll be executed as members of the vigilante Grupo Autodefensa Communitaria. The streets are quiet. Life seems to have come to a standstill. Every so often an old man pushing a wheelbarrow or a woman carrying a shopping basket is seen scurrying down a narrow callejon, always on the shaded side, hurrying out one wooden doorway and darting quickly through another. The tiendas are open but deserted, most of the farmers having remained in the campo, out of the mercados, and the hotels have sent their cooks and maids home. Everyone waits without knowing what they are waiting for.

Before long, however, the initial fears prove unwarranted and a degree of normality returns to the city. The cartel soldiers are not indiscriminate killers. They relax in the cafés and talk with the locals about farming and football. They buy them drinks. In many cases, cartel leaders dine with local families in their homes, attend mass with them on Sundays, have their soldiers repair their washing machines or computers. Some of the mercenaries are well bred, university graduates, former army officers, and out of politeness express their regret to their hosts that the government has seen fit to send the army to settle what is, in fact, a civic matter, declaring this a war on drugs, which, secretly, the government does not want to win. The families appreciate these sentiments; one never knows when one might need the protection of a cartel officer, a high-ranking member of the Knights Templar or La Nueva Generación. Why offend someone upon whose good graces one depends? That isn't bravery, it's foolhardiness, and the good burgers of Colima are no longer as foolhardy as they were when, as vigilantes, they defied the cartels and took matters into their own hands. Those days are over. That was before the reprisals, the torched businesses, the flaming school buses, the narquebloqueros on the highways. In the end, the supreme accommodativeness of the Mexican people holds sway, by which it is perfectly fine for the mayor to be polite to criminals in the privacy of his own home, so long as he isn't overtly familiar with them in public. In the media, priests may denounce the presence of cartel men with whom, in their presbiterios, they remain on the friendliest of terms. Many are the cartel bellies warmed at night by a glass of a Colima family's mezcal or a priest's reposado.

Gradually things return to the familiar and comfortable. The shops reopen. Business picks up. The farmers return to their market stalls, the mariachis once again fill the Plaza with the sound of duelling trumpets and guitars. As for the cartel leaders, they become as familiar to the citizens of Colima as their own city councillors. When there is talk of members of the Sinaloa cartel coming into the city to join up with La Nueva Generación and the Knights Templar, no one is surprised. No one wonders how they will get in. No one asks, But what about the roadblocks?

Still, under the surface there remains a subtle and ill-defined anxiety, a strange, unacknowledged feeling, like a bad odour that has spread throughout the town, as if the sewers were backed up or a dog has drowned in one of the arroyos. It is the stench of defeat. Of resignation. Of subservience. Of collaboration. It's a familiar odour, and it rankles all the more for that. It infiltrates the dwellings and the public squares, gets into the curtains and the rugs, sours the food and turns the wine, and gives everyone the impression of being on a very long voyage in a dangerous and barbarous land, from which it is now time to think about returning.

The conquerors demand money, of course, lots of money, not from individual citizens but from the city itself, for protection. And the city pays up; it is the state capital, after all, a city of merchants and artisans, not rich but with a certain amount of pride and honour to maintain. The city leaders do not call it protection money. They think of it as tribute. The cartels do not need more money. They're shipping four tonnes of cocaine and four more of methamphetamines out of the state each month, unless the army really has closed down the drug-trafficking routes, which is unlikely. The government claims they have, the television stations and the internet, when it is working, are saying that almost no drugs are leaving Colima, and the cartels are becoming desperate. Could that be true after all? Are the rattlesnakes getting angry? If that is the case, is anyone safe?

These concerns are expressed privately, of course, not in the public areas, not in the Plaza or even in the cafés, where cartel members spend most of their time. But among the expats, those who have been caught in the city by the unexpectedness – the betrayal, which is what they call the army's withdrawal – there is little compunction about voicing their concerns. Expats always believe themselves to be exempt from local matters. Those in Colima look on the situation with a kind of bemused interest, like anthropologists observing the curious ways of a primitive people among whom they have temporarily taken up residence. To an expat, there is something provisional, something non-binding, about a permanent residency card. They have, after all, retained their American citizenship. All their money is in American banks. They can't vote in local elections. They have no say in whether the airport should be enlarged, or a historical street should be torn up and repaved, or a fine old building converted into condominiums. And they aren't anthropologists, of course, so Heisenberg's principle doesn't apply; they don't care if the fact of their presence influences the authenticity of the rituals they observe, they rather hope they do, in fact: it wouldn't be a bad thing if, because of their presence, the cartels were less brutal with the locals. But they don't feel threatened themselves, not really. They are other. Their lives belong elsewhere; their investments are safe, their families are back home, and although the bus companies have cancelled their services for the duration, there are still ways of getting out of the city if they have to. Surely the cartels won't want to bring the wrath of the United States down on their heads by preventing U.S. citizens from leaving the danger zone as quickly as possible? And someone is always willing to risk getting them out, if the right amount of money changes hands.

Accordingly, a handful of expats, having purchased United Airline tickets from Manzanillo to Los Angeles, speak to the owner of a private shuttle-service about getting from Colima to Manzanillo. The owner is an affable man who thrives on the business of expats and the wealthier tourists, and readily agrees to take them. He has a small, twelve-passenger bus that will serve the purpose. They will have to leave early, however, and take a roundabout route, since all the major routes are blocked either by the cartels, demanding money and sometimes even the vehicles themselves (but not buses, not to worry), or by the army, which checks every vehicle and its passengers for drugs, which could take hours. Also, the mountain roads are in terrible shape because of the rains. The expats agree, the owner sells a few more tickets to bring the total to ten, and early on a Tuesday morning, the unmarked vehicle, well provided with gas, oil, bottles of water, and a detailed road map for the driver, is ready for the journey.

Since the entire expat population of Colima is somewhere around ten thousand —Americans, mostly, but also Brits and Canadians — the departure of these few hardly represents a mass exodus. However, that is exactly how the media will characterize it if they get wind of it. "Foreigners fear for their safety, flee war zone." Which is why the shuttle-service owner insists they be on the road before daybreak. He sees himself arranging for all ten thousand expats to leave the city, ten to twelve at a time, at five hundred U.S. dollars per seat, and he does not want either the cartels or the army to shut down his operation before it even gets under way.

For some time now the rain has been making the roads around Colima all but impassable, which is partly what bogged down the army so decisively. The downpour let up over the weekend, and the shuttle-service manager counted on the roads being relatively dry by Tuesday. But at precisely three o'clock Monday afternoon, huge black clouds bore down on the city from the Pacific, bringing more rain, and a virtual monsoon fell without stopping the entire evening and continued all night. By four-thirty Tuesday morning, when the travellers gather in the lobby of the Hotel Aldama waiting to board the small bus, the sound of rain pounding on the paving stones and the bougainvillea in the courtyard beyond the glass doors is almost deafening. They are still sleepy, and shiver with cold as they pile their luggage onto the bellhop's cart. The hotel manager, who is also the shuttle-service owner, wrings his hands. There seems to be an awful lot of luggage. And it is unreasonably heavy. What are these gringos taking with them? The passengers can see little in the darkness beyond the doors, and they consider that a good sign. The rain will cover their escape, not that they think of their departure as an escape. It's more like a strategic withdrawal. Two of the men, both Americans, are acquainted with one another, and a third, a Brit, comes over to speak with them. "We're bringing everything except the furniture," he says. "So are we," says another. "Me, too." The first adds: "We're not coming back to Colima. If the cartels try to take Manzanillo, we'll fly out of Guadalajara." They nod. All are of the same mind.

The bus waits in the courtyard. A flashlight, carried by a hotel employee, comes out of one dark doorway and immediately disappears into another. Still the bus sits there, rain bouncing off its roof. Eventually the driver, a young, heavy-set, confident-looking man whose name is Manuel, comes into the lobby. He looks briefly at the passengers, counts them (they think he's nodding at them, and they nod back), then walks through the automatic lobby doors and out to the bus. Because of the darkness and the noise, the passengers can't tell if the bus is running or not, but they murmur their approval when a hotel employee pushes the luggage cart outside and begins loading their bags into the back of the vehicle. All they can see are his feet below the open back door, with the water in the courtyard flowing up to his ankles, but no one remarks on it. They stand in the lobby, stiff and immobile. Manuel comes back into the lobby and disappears behind the reception desk. Feet tap, watches are consulted. Sheets of falling rain obliterate shapes and distort everything. The sound is like that of a gigantic waterfall, and standing in the lobby is like being in a kind of floating blankness, caught in an intermingling of tiny atoms that seem to have tired of filling space and are now intent on filling the earth.

"We can't go in this," says one of the expats, speaking to no one.

No one answers.

The driver reappears behind the reception desk. "Why don't you get in the bus?" he says. "We'll be leaving in a few minutes."

They hurry to comply. The seats are arranged in three rows of double seats on either side of a central aisle, with overhead shelves for small packages and hand luggage. The six expats settle in the back with their carry-ons, which they arrange in the overhead bins; the others mill about and finally take their places without a word being spoken. Water drips off the men's hats and the ladies' handbags, which they put on the floor under their seats. One of the men fiddles with the heat controls in the ceiling, and soon a fan is blowing warm air into the rear of the bus. For several minutes they speak among themselves in low voices about the apparatus' advantages, as if a heater were an amazing technological innovation. "What make is this bus, anyway?" one of the expats asks. "General Motors," replies Manuel, whose English is excellent. "Ah, good." "But assembled right here in Mexico."

Finally, when the windshield wipers are going and the front fan has cleared the condensation from the windshield, Manuel turns and asks if everyone is aboard. From the back comes the reply, "Yes." Does anyone need to use the bathroom? "No." Manuel puts the van in gear, and they begin to move.

They make slow, slow progress through the dark city. The wheels are up to their hubcaps in water; the bus creaks and groans under the weight; the engine roars and throbs alarmingly as the driver changes gears, turning sharp corners and weaving around parked cars, straddling the deeper rivers that course down the centre of the streets. Only the sound of the wipers going full speed can be heard above the engine and the splashing of the tires.

And slowly the day dawns. The rain stops when they are a few minutes out of the city, and the grey light filtering through thick, dark clouds shows the blackness of the countryside, the sodden ploughed fields, the distant lines of large, fully leafed trees, with now and then a tiled rooftop amid a riot of foliage. The passengers can now make out the image of the Virgin of Guadalupe on a postcard Manuel has pinned to the sun visor with a paperclip. Dogs bark at the slowly moving vehicle from behind sagging wire gates, roosters crow from the tops of ramshackle sheds. Few other vehicles appear on the road — an ancient pick-up truck with a heavily dented cab, its box filled with avocadoes; a small, blue, bumperless Nissan; a larger American sedan with its roof sawn off above the rear seat, upon which is tied a stack of yellow, plastic chicken cages. The bus carrying the expats is practically brand new, and stands out from these rustic conveyances like a diamond on a tray strewn with pebbles. No one intent on robbery would stop a truckload of vegetables; maybe they should have taken their chances on the highway.

At the back of the bus, on the driver's side, Barry and Carol Anderson sleep leaning against each other, their heads rolling back and forth in unison as the bus lurches through the mud. Anderson is a retired advertising executive from New York, specializing in online accounts. He told his fellow expats in Colima that he was the one to come up with the Amazon logo; no one believed him, but no one cared. He wears a battered baseball cap with the orange Amazon smile prominently displayed on the front. He's known for his lively wit, and can be counted on to say what he thinks without worrying about anyone's feelings. His many friends in the expat community rarely mention him without adding, "That Barry, he can be priceless." He and Carol owned a house in Colima, still have a condo in Manhattan that's rented out when they come to Mexico, and have a summer home somewhere in the south of Portugal. He's tall and thin and a bit gangly, he likes to loom over a party, and has the beginnings of a paunch surmounted by the soft, florid face and unfocused eyes of a habitual drinker. His wife is correspondingly short and soft-spoken. Her family is from Albany, New York, a good family but not a wealthy one. Her father was a business professor, and she studied art and design before marrying Barry. It might well have been her who designed the Amazon logo. But she seems happy enough; her main concern now is how they are going to get their paintings out of the country without paying the exorbitant art-tax demanded by the government.

Across the aisle from them, on a higher, more rarified plain, sit Sir James Scott and his wife, Lady Fidelia Scott. He's a man of considerable stature, a retired British diplomat, officer of the Royal Order of Britain and a former chair of the London Economic Council. He came to Mexico thirty years ago as the British Consul in Guadalajara, and upon retiring stayed on, feeling, as he (often) puts it, more at home in a place that already is a third-world country than he could in a country that seems bent on becoming one. He is an aristocrat; to him democracy is something to be borne, not touted. Democracy was responsible for Brexit. His England exists now only in his memories. It is the Britain of Virginia Woolf, whose books he reads not so much as fiction but as a kind of fictionalized memoir: he would have been blissfully at home at one of Mrs. Dalloway's parties. He is shortish, stocky as a bulldog, hair like a white bristlebrush, with large, labourer's hands that he endeavours to keep in the side pockets of his very expensively cut blazer, which he wears, apparently unselfconsciously, with a monogrammed shirt and a cravat. His wife, whom he refers to among friends as Lady Scott, is two decades younger than he is, and was the consolation of many an aide of good family who'd been sent to fly the Union Jack in Guadalajara. She sits beside her husband, looking regal and demure, wrapped in expensive shawls, her large, sad eyes lamenting the necessity of travelling in a bus.

Their neighbours in the seat ahead are the Lethworths, Bob and Christine, from Sacramento, California. They seem young to be spending six months a year in Mexico.

At the age of nineteen or thereabouts, while living in San Francisco, Bob devised an algorithm that did something so essential that Apple bought it from him for seventy-two million dollars. That was all anyone in Colima knew about his past: nineteen, Silicon Valley, seventy-two million. He and Christine, now in their early forties, bought an entire block in Colima's Centro Historico and had it renovated into a single, ten-bedroom hacienda, with an interior courtyard filled with royal palms and jacaranda trees, an indoor Olympic-sized swimming pool, an intricately, overly designed garden, and a full-time staff of eight, three of whom lived in. Christine was the most popular hostess in the community; she held a salon every Friday evening when the couple were in residence, one of the few places left where the old values were still valued – good conversation, good food, excellent wine, and an appreciation of the fine arts. Only rarely was politics discussed, and never current American politics. Of course, they'd voted for Kamala, but it was not always safe to assume that their guests had. In her living room, surrounded by expensive Mexican folk art and some really exquisite pieces from New York, the wealthier expats mingled with visiting violinists, ballerinas, and Hollywood directors (and occasionally writers, for Christine also hosted a monthly book club), and an invitation to the salon was a prize always worth a subtle boast: "Sorry, can't come to dinner on Tuesday, we're going to the Lethworths."

These six, occupying the rear of the bus, represent the cream of Colima's expat community. Despite their present circumstances, they are serenely comfortable and secure, honest and highly principled; they genuinely like Mexico and Mexicans, at least those they've met, and understand that most of the country's current problems are the result of four centuries of colonial rule – that, for example, if there is rampant corruption in the country today, it's because the country's current rulers learned all there was to know about rampant corruption from their colonial masters. They saw how money talked, and now they want it to talk to them. These foreigners have no problem with that. They, too, have seen how money talks.

In the seat ahead of the Andersons, across the aisle from the Lethworths, are two missionaries from an obscure Protestant order located somewhere in Canada, the Church of the Living Christ. They are dressed like lay nuns, in simple, grey cotton dresses, with wide, white collars and gold crosses. One, Sister Ann, is getting on in years, and has a face so pitted by acne she looks as though someone fired at her point blank with birdshot. The other, Sister Debbie, is younger, with a gentle but pale face above a consumptive chest, and the air of one who has been crushed under the weight of a devouring fanaticism that turns otherwise unremarkable people into visionaries and martyrs.

Directly behind the driver, occupying a double seat by himself, is a man who is unknown to the others. During the head count before they boarded, the driver mentioned his name: it sounded like Klausman or Houseman. He didn't look German, so maybe it was Houseman. The man sits, or rather slouches, looking straight ahead, hardly moving, as though staring at the back of the driver's neck. It may be nerves, or he may be miles away, thinking of the life he is leaving behind or, perhaps, of the one he's moving towards. Neither vista appears to be giving him much pleasure. Christine Lethworth can see the muscles on the man's jaw working, he is clenching and unclenching his teeth as though trapped in a bad dream. Whatever it is, his unnatural stillness makes her uncomfortable. She has seen this kind of thing before, back in the States, lost men, no longer young, strung out on drugs for so long she could see the life force draining out of them. The vacant stares, the slurred speech, the emptiness. Is the man an addict? He's roughly dressed, faded denims, shirttail poking out under a frayed leather jacket. He wears his greying hair pulled back in a short ponytail held by a red elastic band. No hat. Maybe it's in the bin above his head, where she saw him stow an old canvas knapsack. And he needs a shave; who would go to an airport looking like that? Well, a lot of people these days, she thinks; no one dresses up to travel any more. Getting on an airplane, even in business class, is no more special now than stepping onto a subway car. But this man bears watching. She gently nudges her husband with her elbow, and when he looks at her, she nods in Houseman's direction. Lethworth follows her gaze; his eyes narrow slightly and he nods. Duly noted.

But it's the tenth passenger, the woman sitting in the other front seat, across from the drug addict, who holds everyone's attention. She's not an expat. She looks Mexican. Perhaps half Mexican and half American, from Texas or New Mexico, somewhere close to the border? Barry knows who she is, or at least has seen her before, she was a regular in one of his own favourite haunts. He leans towards his wife and whispers something; the word "hooker" is heard in the back. Heads turn. Christine Lethworth is sure she's never seen a hooker before. The woman is short, her feet barely reaching the floor, and certainly well-padded, with pudgy fingers pinched at the knuckles like strings of cocktail sausages. Her tight, dark skin glistens and her full breasts jiggle beneath her deeply cut blouse. But her face is sweet and attractive, if a little swollen, and Sir James catches himself thinking she'd be quite alluring if she lost three or four stone. She looks refreshingly simple, in his opinion, no doubt a pleasure to be with. She's like a ripe, red apple, or a plump peony bud ready to burst into flower, and she views the world through two magnificent black eyes shielded by slightly bulging lids that give her a sultry appearance; below them, her charmingly pursed mouth seems perpetually poised for a kiss, with, when she smiles, which is often, two neat rows of tiny, gleaming teeth.

"La Gordita," Barry Anderson whispers to his wife, again a little too loudly. "That's what they call her, La Gordita." The woman looks up but not around. Has she heard? But then she does turn, and bestows such a warm, unabashed smile on her fellow passengers that a general silence falls over them, and everyone lowers their eyes – everyone except Anderson, who seems intrigued by her. She certainly doesn't keep many of her talents hidden, he thinks.

But soon the conversation picks up again, as if La Gordita's presence has suddenly made the three other women fast friends, almost intimates. They seem determined to make a display of their status as legitimate wives, to blot out this outsider's obvious shamelessness. In matters of love, the legal kind always tries to lord it over its illicit sister.

"However did she find five hundred dollars for this trip?" says Christine Lethworth, keeping her voice low.

"I very much doubt she did," replies Lady Scott.

"What does *gordita* mean, anyway?"

"Something like 'tub of lard,' I think," whispers Lady Scott, who took Spanish lessons when the couple first moved to Guadalajara, but has since let them drop. "It's a kind of deep-fried tortilla stuffed with potatoes and carrots. I don't think it's meant to be pejorative."

"Of course it is," says Carol Anderson. "Look at her." They look. "How can it not?"

The three men are similarly united by the presence of Houseman, whose very existence seems to challenge every unexamined notion they have of themselves. They talk money, not bothering to keep their voices down, expressing a certain disdain masked as sympathy for those who don't have it. Sir James mentions the losses he suffered after the first Brexit vote, when the bottom fell out of the pound sterling, but speaks with the air of one for whom such a trivial concern hardly inconvenienced him for a year. Bob Lethworth counters by saying he always keeps "a few thousand" in bullion for just such emergencies, implying that he means ounces, not dollars. As for Anderson, he arranged to sell their house in Colima to the state, apparently it is a heritage building of some kind from the Revolution. "The rebels stored guns in the basement," he says. In any case, the state owes him a considerable sum of money, which he hopes to collect in Manzanillo before boarding the plane.

"Good luck with that," says Lethworth, shaking his head.

"I never liked that house," puts in Carol Anderson. "It always felt cold in the mornings."

They exchange warm, almost conspiratorial glances, more than the simple camaraderie of the road. Although they have little else in common, they have money, and that makes them brothers and sisters in the great Free Masonry to which those who can always jingle a few pesos in their pockets belong. They exude a certain confidence in the rightness of their own opinions, even in matters of which they have no knowledge, particularly in matters about which there can be no knowledge. They are rich, therefore they must be smart. They do not look at Houseman, and Houseman does not look at them. He is obviously different, not a Free Mason, more like a man who knows what it is like to have only enough money for either a good meal or a bottle of whiskey, and always chooses the whiskey. He does not look as though he receives letters from his children in university, or emails from his financial advisor, or invitations to fundraisers, as the others regularly do. Every now and then they see him glance across the aisle at La Gordita, who smiles back. But that means nothing; her type smiles at everyone.

The bus continues its crawl through the mud, the front end swerving and the windshield wipers banging away. Colima the city is in the lowlands, although the route they are taking will mean swinging high up into the mountains, almost up to Cerra el Péan. Here there are great ruts in the road, often filled with stones the size of bowling balls, which seem to have risen to the surface with all the rain. They travel so slowly that by ten o'clock in the morning they have not gone more than forty kilometres. The men have climbed out of the bus three times so it could fishtail up the steeper foothills, and climb back in cursing and scraping mud from their shoes with a stick. They are beginning to worry; they're supposed to be in Minatitlán for lunch, but it now appears they'll be lucky to get there before dark. They're watching for a roadside restaurant when the bus becomes stuck in a particularly large sinkhole, and it takes almost half an hour for the driver to work it free. Sir James looks calmly but pointedly at his watch.

Has anyone thought to bring food? Of course not. Has the driver packed sandwiches for them? No? As their hunger grows, so does their anxiety. And not a barbacoa or even a taqueria in sight. Gun battles between the army and the cartels have frightened off the innkeepers, who didn't want to be forced to feed and billet the victors. The driver stops for gas at a Pemex station at a lonely crossroads in the middle of nowhere, but there is no Oxxo store attached to it, as there would have been on one of the well-travelled routes. There is, however, an old woman, her head covered in a black beggar's shawl, cooking what look like empanadas on a brazier beside the Pemex office. They can see her wrinkled hands patting the dough and placing it in a pan with an inch of cooking oil. Would they be gorditas? they wonder, amused. Under a sagging lean-to are stacks of plastic bottles of water and Coca-Cola, in shrink-wrapped bundles of twenty-four, and a picnic table covered with a checked plastic tablecloth, with plastic utensils and jars of condiments in a plastic box at the centre. While Manuel is inside paying for the gas, the passengers remain in their seats without moving, watching the old woman perform her tasks. Who eats here? Not even La Gordita goes outside to buy food from her.

"So much plastic they use in this country," comments Christine Lethworth.

When, after what seems a lengthy absence, Manuel comes back to the bus, he pokes his head in first to ask if anyone needs to use the baños or wants to buy food from la señora. There's a general "No, thank you," from the passengers. "Agua? Water?" "No, we're fine."

"No bathroom on the bus," chuckles Barry Anderson.

"No doctor, either," adds Lethworth.

"All right, then," says Manuel, and he climbs into the driver's seat. Soon they are back on the road, which is marginally drier now that they are out of the rain. At least there is less slipping and sliding. And the heat of the day is settling in. They may make it to Minatitlán in time for dinner.

"My stomach feels like it has a hole in it," Anderson says when the Pemex station is safely behind them. "I missed breakfast this morning."

"So did I," says Lethworth. "I'd pay another five hundred for a Big Mac right about now."

Anderson snickers. "I wonder where that woman gets her beef from?"

Carol yawns, and almost immediately her husband yawns. Soon everyone is yawning, each according to their characters, manners, and social position. Anderson yawns loudly, stretching his jaws as wide as they will reach and exhaling with a rush of foul air. After a silent intake of breath, Lady Fidelia daintily covers her mouth with her hand. Houseman, although he yawns with the rest of them, keeps his jaws tightly clenched, as though they were wired shut, his entire body shaking from the strain.

Several times La Gordita stands as if to get something from the bin above her seat. She hesitates for a second, looks back at her neighbours, then quietly sits down again. The faces watching her are pale and pinched. It's past one o'clock. They have been travelling for eight hours without so much as a crust of bread in their stomachs.

"I'm feeling rather peckish myself," says Sir James, looking at his wife. "How can we not have thought to bring emergency provisions?"

Everyone except the two missionaries reproach themselves for the same thing. The older of the missionaries looks as though she discerns a deep purpose behind the day's ordeal. The younger one looks pained, as though she were trying to.

At this point, Houseman gives a jerk and, almost reluctantly, sighs and produces a pint bottle of tequila from his inside jacket pocket. To everyone's surprise, he turns around and offers it to the Lethworths. It is, of course, refused, but warmly. "Thanks, but a bit early in the day for me."

Houseman waves the flask to the others, and again it's refused by all except Anderson, who takes a gulp, makes a face, and, returning the flask, says: "It's not bad stuff. Warms the cockles and kills the appetite." The alcohol puts him in an expansive mood, and he says they should do what the sailors on the little boat did in the song. What song? What did they do? They ate the fattest passenger. The thinly veiled allusion to La Gordita shocks the others. No one replies to him, and only Houseman smiles. The missionaries hold themselves very still, determinedly lowering their eyes and no doubt giving thanks to their Living Lord for the torment he is putting them through.

At three o'clock they are still creeping along, the road becoming narrower and steeper as it climbs into the sierras. Surely they are out of the danger zone by now? Isn't this area controlled by the army? Wouldn't they have made better time on a paved highway? Lethworth stands and, lurching to the front of the bus, leans over and asks Manuel if they're getting close to Minatitlán, "or anywhere there might be a decent restaurant?"

"Soon, soon," Manuel says, nodding without taking his eyes off the road.

"You must be starving, too," says Anderson.

Manuel smiles. "No, graçias, I had my comida in the petrol station."

"Ah, good," Anderson says, and returns to his seat.

At that point, La Gordita stands and takes a large travel bag from her overhead bin. Then she sits down heavily and opens the bag. The first thing she removes from it is a ceramic plate, brown with bright yellow and blue flowers painted on it. Then she takes out a heavy glass; then, wrapped in newspaper, a large Mexican baking dish with two whole chickens in it, cut into pieces and cooked in their own juices. It's still warm, and the fragrance fills the bus. Other good things come from the basket: bolillos, tortillas, pâté de campo, fruit, sliced meats, enough food to feed a family of six for days. The tops of four Coca-Cola bottles poke up among the packages of food. She carefully breaks off a chicken leg and begins to eat, her eyes closed and her cheeks puffed out like those of a fat squirrel. On a bolillo, she spreads some of the pork pâté. She sits quietly in her front seat, keeping her back to the rest of the bus, but the smell of chicken and sauce wafting throughout the bus brings every eye upon her and produces a prodigious amount of saliva in everyone's mouth. Carol Anderson turns to look dreamily out the window. Never before, not even as an art student, has she been so hungry. She hates La Gordita at that moment. The other women must feel the same, because they eye her like birds of prey, as if they want to pounce on her, throw her off the bus — this prostitute, her precious plates, her stupid cheap carry-on, and all her damned food. Except maybe not the food.

Anderson, sitting behind La Gordita, peers over her shoulder, devouring the bowl of chicken with his eyes. "I guess," he says, "our little friend here had more foresight than any of us. Looks like she thought of everything."

La Gordita turns and looks at him. "Would you like some, señor? You are perhaps not used to going without food so long."

Anderson nods. "As a matter of fact," he says, "I don't mind if I do. I'm famished. All's fair in love and war, eh, Carol?" And, turning to the others, he adds: "There's always someone willing to help a guy out, isn't there." He takes a section of the *Los Angeles Times* – not the business section – from his briefcase and spreads it on his lap so as not to stain his trousers, and, reaching over the back of La Gordita's seat, selects a chicken thigh dripping with juice. He bites into it and chews with such evident enjoyment that his deep sigh is heard by everyone.

In a sweet, little-girl's voice, La Gordita asks the missionaries if they would like to share her meal. Her English is quite good: Well, thinks Lady Fidelia unkindly, it would have to be, wouldn't it, a woman of her profession? The missionaries accept and, without raising their eyes, say a quick grace and begin eating. Houseman doesn't refuse her offer, either; turning in his seat, he places his knees beside those of La Gordita and one of the missionaries to make a kind of table, using more newspaper. Mouths open and close and open again, chewing, swallowing, gobbling up more. Lethworth, in the back, works hard at resisting, and quietly urges his wife to follow suit. She succeeds for a while, then, with a shiver that seems to rise up from her entrails, she gives in and reaches for a bun and the dish of pâté. Then Sir James, adjusting his tone of voice, asks their "charming companion" if she might allow him to offer a small morsel to his lady-wife. "But of course, señor," says the charming companion, offering the chicken dish with a warm smile.

A slight hitch arises when the first bottle of Coke is opened, as there is only the one glass. It's filled and passed from passenger to passenger, and used only after being wiped each time with a handkerchief produced by Carol

Lethworth. Only Houseman, no doubt out of politeness, or perhaps he is drunk, raises the glass in a mock toast without wiping it, and drinks from the wet spot made by La Gordita's lips.

Houseman is not of the monied class, they can all see that. He's not even an expat, he's a drifter. He came to Mexico years ago as a steward on a hundred-and-twenty-eight-foot yacht owned by a retired rear admiral living in Seattle. His job was to wake the rear admiral every morning at ten o'clock sharp carrying a tray with a pot of coffee, a carafe of freshly squeezed orange juice, and a bottle of vodka. It was also his responsibility to see that the ship's pantry was well stocked with food and drink, especially drink, for the rear admiral was a formidable party-giver. Every weekend he'd arrive at the Seattle Yacht Club with a dozen friends, having first called Houseman to tell him to have the party room and guest bedrooms readied. The guests and the rear admiral would drink and dance until two or three in the morning, which meant that Houseman had to stay up late also, mixing drinks, clearing and washing glasses, serving canapes, and making sure the guests staggered safely to their designated staterooms without falling over the side. Despite his penchant for partying, the rear admiral was a stickler for order. Everything had to be ship-shape. Houseman's and the five other crew members' white uniforms had to be spotless and carefully pressed. The oranges had to be fresh and the vodka chilled and Russian. Houseman would often be up until dawn, polishing guests' shoes or preparing lavish breakfasts that few felt like eating. At noon precisely, the rear admiral would appear on the bridge and give the captain the chart he'd prepared for that day's cruise, even if it was just across the harbour to refuel. But one day the rear admiral took it into his head to sail to Puerto Vallarta, altogether a three-month voyage, since he had friends in most of the major ports down the coast. Houseman tried to jump ship in La Jolla, but the rear admiral caught him packing his bags and begged him not to leave. Houseman negotiated a pay raise and stayed. But as soon as they reached Puerto Vallarta, he went ashore and vanished into the bars and brothels in the city's north end, and didn't emerge until a month later, when he saw from the top of the Iglesia de Nuestre Virgen de la Mare the rear admiral's yacht raise the U.S. flag and leave the harbour for the open sea. He was in Mexico with little money and no visa, in fact no papers at all except his American passport, since he hadn't come ashore through the port authority. And so he rarely stayed in one place long, travelling from city to city, picking up odd jobs wherever he could: bartending in Barra de Navidad, managing a small hotel in Manzanillo, organizing beach weddings in Playa Azul, until he ended up in Colima two days before the cartels took over the city. At first, he was relieved because he thought the cartels would not be too particular about credentials. In fact, he approved of the cartels. They were outlaws, like him. Then a friend of his, an American he'd met on the bus and with whom he was sharing a room in a cheap hotel, vanished, and Houseman panicked. Setting up shop in the doorway of the hotel, he sold all his friend's clothing and most of his own, including his steward's uniform and his last good pair of shoes. Tucked into the pages of *Under the Volcano*, a book that had belonged to his disappeared friend, he found his friend's passport, exit visa and six hundred American dollars. The next day he purchased four bottles of tequila and a ticket to Manzanillo. He doesn't know what he is going to do in Manzanillo, but he's been there before and feels certain that his luck has finally turned.

He toasts La Gordita again, this time with his flask, and she blushes with embarrassment. "Madre de Dio," she stammers, looking back at the other passengers, all of whom are eating her food, "I didn't dare offer anything to such illustrious hidalgos . . ." Then she falls silent, fearing she has offended them. But Anderson takes her meaning. "Not to worry," he says, "in a case like this we're all in it together, right? We all need to help one another. Come on, everyone, dig in! Who knows if we'll even make Minatitlán by nightfall? At this rate we won't get to Manzanillo until this time tomorrow!"

"But our flight is at ten-thirty tomorrow morning!" says Lethworth.

"If there's cell coverage in Minatitlán, we can change our tickets."

They can hardly eat La Gordita's provisions and drink Houseman's tequila without including them in their festivities, and so they all chat generally together, cautiously at first, but, as their appetites are satisfied, more freely. Bob and Christine, who know just the tone to take with Latinos, are gracious and refined with La Gordita, if a little studied; Lady Scott, especially, exhibits the kind of guarded condescension that noblewomen usually manage with trusted servants, which ensures harmony without implying equality. Servants – and she senses the servant in Houseman – do not want to be their employers' equals; it makes them resent their servitude and renders them unhappy, and no one wants an unhappy, resentful servant. Look what happened in France. Lady Scott can be charming. She praises the chicken, saying she hasn't tasted the like since leaving London. "Don't you remember, James, that wonderful dinner party at the Vandermeers'? The coq-au-vin was divine, as is this!" Only Carol Anderson, who knows what tricks her husband gets up to when he senses an easy victory, holds herself back; she says little, but eats much.

They talk about the drug war, of course. The atrocities reportedly committed by the cartels, the frustrating incompetence of the Federales. "I blame the generals," says Sir James. "They're all on the take." Although they themselves are fleeing from the danger, they respect those who have had to stay behind. There are many valid reasons for staying put, they say. For example, if one has property to protect. Or can't afford a ticket. "Or family," adds La Gordita, shyly. "If they have family to protect. Fortunately, my family is in Guanajuato." Which settles one question about her: she isn't flying to Los Angeles. "She's not in good health, my sister, that's why I was taking this food to her."

"We're sorry to hear that, señorita," says Christine. Can they really call her La Gordita to her face? "We'll pay you for the food, of course."

"Of course," comes the general chorus. "And for your time, too. For cooking it for us. Yes, absolutely." No one suggests replacing Houseman's tequila.

"What does your sister do in Guanajuato?" Anderson asks, and his wife jabs him in the ribs with her elbow.

"Nothing," says La Gordita. "She's in a hospital there. A sanatorio."

"Ah, good," Anderson says, with what may have been sympathy. He is thinking about the museum of desiccated cadavers he's seen in Guanajuato.

Christine Lethworth, attempting to steer the conversation forward, says she has been to Guanajuato many times.

"That's where Diego Rivera grew up," she says. "His old house is now a wonderful museum, like yours, Mr. Anderson. Some of his early paintings are there."

"Please, call me Barry," says Anderson.

"The man was a damned Communist," says Sir James, accepting the glass from Anderson and wiping the rim with his handkerchief. "Ruined his art, wouldn't you say, madam? Have you seen those wretched murals in Detroit? Disgraceful. Well executed, I'll give him that. But hard to look at. Mocking the Lindbergs like that, sheer cheek. I won't say you can't mix art and politics, but it should be like a good martini, eh? Swirl the glass with politics if you must, but for God's sake fill it up with art."

"But isn't everything politics?" says Christine Lethworth. "Like, saying you're not political is a political statement. Not voting is a vote."

"No, I'm afraid it isn't, my dear," says Sir James, huffily, passing the glass to his wife. "Not committing suicide is not the same thing as committing suicide."

"Apples and oranges, Sir James," says Lethworth. "In the last election, not voting was in effect a vote for Trump. No two ways about it."

"Ah, good," says Anderson. "I guess we know how you voted."

"We're from California. How do you think we voted?"

"With the herd, I suppose."

Sir James chuckles. "It was the herd mentality that settled America in the first place, was it not? All those insufferable Puritans, emigrating en masse."

"They didn't emigrate, they were expelled."

"Same thing. That's what the colonies were for."

"I thought we were talking about art," says Christine.

"My point exactly," says Sir James.

"I thought it was mine," says Carol, and that, for a while, is that.

For the next quarter of an hour the bus jolts along a particularly unmaintained stretch of road, through forbidding countryside, in which nopale cactuses, pepper trees, and stunted mesquite prevail. Inches from the road, it seems, the terrain drops precipitously into deep canyons down which no one can bring themselves to look. Even making conversation is difficult. After a lengthy pause, La Gordita turns in her seat and says, "I am not emigrating from Colima, I am only going to look after my sister until she is well. I will go back then. I have my business there. I work from my house." Everyone's eyes seek the windows, of course she does, and she adds, "I am estética, peluquera. How to say? I make people's hair nice. And fingers. At first I think I stay," she goes on as if to herself. "I have everything I need in my house, the army is not so bad, I think is better to put up with a few soldiers, no, than to run off to God knows where." Why would a hairdresser have to put up with soldiers, Carol wonders. "But when cartels show up, I say no, this is too much. They make my blood to boil! They are animals, they kill people, they ruin lives. They make widows and orphans. And for what? For money!" She pinches her thick forefinger and thumb together and looks directly at the men who boasted earlier about their financial problems. "I weep with shame that they are mexicanos. I watched them from my bedroom window, those pigs with their machine rifles and their grenade throwers, I could barely stop myself from throwing furniture down on their heads. Two of them came to my house, and I flew at their throats: criminals are not harder to choke than honest people, eh? And I would have killed them, too, if my maid had not stopped me. They threw me down." I'll bet they did, thinks Carol. "I couldn't stay in Colima after that. When my sister became unwell, I decided to go to her, and here I am!"

The others congratulate her for her bravery. "Bravo! Bravo!" Christine Lethworth wonders if she would let La Gordita do her hair. Mexican hairdressers know nothing about curls. Maybe her nails, she thinks, looking down at them in her lap. Houseman gives La Gordita the kind of approving, benevolent smile a saint bestows on an acolyte, hinting at some unspecified act of bravery on his part that he is too modest to brag about. "Una verdad luchadora," he says, "a real fighter. Isn't she?" His flask is almost empty, and he asks Manuel how much longer to Minatitlán. "Soon, soon," is the reply, and Houseman shrugs. "Everything is soon," he says. "In Mexico, soon means later. Luego. And luego luego means never!" He speaks in a doctrinaire manner, perhaps he was a teacher in a former life, thinks Carol Anderson. His Spanish is good, though heavily accented. He proclaims the kind of things that have lately been seen pasted on café walls. "The army commits more atrocities than the cartels!" he says. "The army has no respect for human rights! The army cannot be relied on to settle civil matters like drug trafficking!" Houseman ends with a piece of eloquence in which he magisterially dismisses "that traitor Claudia Sheinbaum!"

"Sheinbaum a traitor?" says Lethworth. "How so?"

"She campaigned as a leftist, said she would clamp down on the cartels and corruption. But when she was elected, she showed she was as far right as AMLO. She's a banana-republic Donald Trump!"

This infuriates La Gordita. She turns redder than a chili pepper, stuttering with indignation: "I'd like to see what you would do in her place." The others picture her behind a salon chair, waving her scissors about. "The army is the only thing stopping the cartels from winning the whole country! And even the army is corrupt! No wonder so many of us are crossing the frontera when our country is ruled by such devils!"

Houseman keeps his disdainful, superior smile, and says, "The cartels are good for the country. They're national heroes!" He seems to be preparing to elaborate when Sir James interposes, not without some effort, by proclaiming with authority that all opinions, if sincerely held, are worthy of respect. Lady Scott and Christine Lethworth agree. Both secretly despise people who defend Republicans, and the kind of flashy, despotic rulers Republicans seem to favour, but would never say so. They smile consolingly at the indignant young hairdresser who is not afraid to speak her mind. They hope that, were they ever faced with her difficulties, their own sentiments would echo hers, and they would not hesitate to voice them as strongly as she has, even in front of their husbands.

But oh, dear, thinks Christine, her smile fading, are we falling for the hooker with a heart of gold?

The afternoon wears on. Little by little the plateau begins to darken. Distant lights from isolated buildings dot the landscape. "What the hell time is it?" demands Barry Anderson. "Going on six!" exclaims Sir James. Despite the altitude, the heat continues to make everyone perspire heavily, especially La Gordita, with her tight clothing and layers of fat. Christine stands up to check that the air-conditioner is working, and makes sure the fan is aimed at La Gordita.

La Gordita, fanning herself with a magazine, smiles gratefully up at her. Carol does the same on her side for the missionaries, who seem not to notice.

Indeed, the missionaries have paid almost no attention to any of their fellow passengers except La Gordita. Missionaries in general seldom bother trying to convert atheists. They focus their efforts on people who already have a religion, just the wrong one. It is easier to convert a devout Catholic or Muslim to another faith than it is to instil faith in someone who has none to begin with. Unless, of course, they are children.

The driver turns on the headlights and tail-lights. Ropes of red clouds raised by the bus's tires puff out behind them, and on each side of the road the shrubbery seems to unwind from a never-ending roll of dust-covered branches and leaves. No stars shine overhead. It's as though they are driving up a long, steeply inclined tunnel, with no light at the end of it. No one complains about going too slowly.

Except for the green and red dashboard lights, the inside of the bus is in darkness. There's a stealthy movement between Houseman's seat and La Gordita's: the dash lights go black for a second and then come back on. Anderson squints, his eye searching the shadows, and thinks he sees a man's shape sitting beside La Gordita. It sits up sharply, as if from a sharp, soundless slap, and the dash lights go off and on again.

Finally, they begin to pass rows of open concrete buildings with tables in them, like garages with no doors, lit by weak overhead bulbs: the outskirts of Minatitlán. They have been travelling for fifteen hours almost without stopping, and have gone barely a hundred and fifty kilometres. Still, it's better than being back in Colima. Fifteen hours is enough to cut that cord. They enter the town and stop before a white, stucco building with the words *Hotel Santa Ana* painted crudely in pink letters beside the archway leading to the hotel's interior courtyard. Manuel drives through the archway, stops and gets out, slides open the passenger door, and a familiar sound startles the travellers into immobility: the bolt of an assault rifle being drawn back. No one moves. It's as though they are afraid they'll be massacred if they so much as turn their heads. Manuel appears at the door and turns on the dome lights, revealing three rows of pale, frightened faces, mouths open and eyes wide with surprise and fear.

In the brighter light of the courtyard, beside a young man holding an automatic rifle, stands a chunky, dark-skinned man with black hair, fierce eyes under heavy brows, wearing baggy, cotton trousers and a white shirt. In his right hand he holds a wide, glittering sombrero with a row of large, silver medallions circling the dented crown. Under his large nose an enormous moustache crosses his face like a furry leech. He looks like a cartoon of a Mexican bandito. Someone inside the van laughs. It's a joke. They've been met at the hotel by someone going to a costume party. Where are his holster and pistol? Where are his bandoleras? Oh, look at those boots! What, no spurs?

In a Spanish dialect no one recognizes, although his meaning is clear, the costumed man invites the travellers to step down from the van: "Pero lente, por favor."

The missionaries obey first, with the resigned docility of martyrs arriving at their place of execution. Sir James and Lady Scott come next, followed by the Lethworths, then Carol Anderson, being shoved from behind by her husband. The latter, setting his foot on the ground, says, "Good day, señor" to the man dressed as a bandit, more from a sense of self-preservation than politeness. The Mexican, insolent as people are when they hold the upper hand, looks at him without responding.

Although La Gordita and Houseman are sitting closest to the door, they get out last, haughty and serious. La Gordita stops before the postcard of the Virgen de Guadalupe and makes the sign of the cross, struggling to remain calm; as he descends from the bus, Houseman strokes his chin with a trembling hand and nods amicably to the Mexican. They each want to preserve their dignity, knowing that in such encounters they represent something larger than themselves – stoicism, perhaps, forbearance, at least a worldly approach to life. They are revolted by the subservience of their companions, and want to distinguish themselves from them in the eyes of their captors. La Gordita holds herself proudly aloof from the other women, while Houseman, as if it were up to him to set an example, conveys in every aspect of his bearing the resistance he imagines he has always shown towards authority. The Mexican's grotesque costume is, as far as he's concerned, a uniform, and he knows what people become when they are given a uniform. Still, he is too wily to show overt aggression. This ridiculous figure, whoever he is, is definitely in control of the situation.

They are led into the hotel lobby, and the Mexican orders his lieutenant to collect everyone's passports. There is a feeble attempt at outrage, but eventually each of them hands over their documents. The costumed bandito takes his time looking over the group and comparing their faces with their photographs. He takes an especially long time with Houseman's, looking up at the man and then down at the passport, then up at Houseman again. Houseman is visibly unnerved.

"I have shaved my beard," he says feebly, "as you can see." When the Mexican is finished, he puts the passports in his pocket, says, "Bueno," and walks off towards a door behind the reception desk.

"Who the hell is that?" Barry demands of Manuel, when the door closes.

"He is José Hernandez Guitierez, subcomandante of the cartel that is occupying this town."

"What? I thought the army was in charge here."

"The Federales pulled out last night," says Manuel. "Los Caballeros Templarios are in charge now."

"The Knights Templar!" says Bob Lethworth. "We might as well have stayed in Colima!"

"No," says Manuel. "These people have no interest in you. They will let you go, as long as you don't make trouble for them."

"They don't want the States to get involved," says Barry Anderson, "that's what it is. They keep us hostage here, Trump's boys'll come down on 'em like a ton of bricks."

They are not noticeably reassured by this image of Donald Trump as a champion of liberty and justice. No one in Mexico has ever confiscated their passports before. That's something Nazis do in World War II films. But for the moment they are hungry, and Manuel tells them that a meal is being prepared for them even though the kitchen is closed. How does he know that? He seems particularly well informed. Everything is being taken care of by the shuttle company, he says, not to worry. It is just for one night. They should be in the dining room in half an hour; meanwhile they can go upstairs to view their rooms. He gives each of them a room number. They can leave their heavy luggage in the bus. Dragging their carry-ons behind them like refugees, they climb the stairs to the second floor and find themselves in a corridor that ends at a glass door marked with signs showing that behind the door is an ice machine and another stairwell. One of the signs says Ruta de Evacuación, with an arrow pointing down the stairs.

Forty minutes later they are in the dining room, where the hotel manager is standing beside a buffet table on which has been placed two coffee urns, pitchers of fruit water, and trays of vegetables and pastries. He is a former car dealer from Leon, a large, asthmatic man whose throat wheezes and whistles when he talks. His name tag says he is Octavio Tontavida Lopez.

"Señorita Consuela Dolorosa?" he asks the group.

La Gordita gives a start. "Yes?" she says.

"Señorita," says Tontavida, "the subcomandante would like to speak with you."

"With me?"

"Yes. If you are indeed Señorita Dolorosa."

She looks frightened. She thinks for a moment, then declares: "I am she. But I do not wish to speak to him."

This causes a stir around her; everyone speaks, trying to guess the reason for the request.

"I think, señorita . . ."

"I will not go."

Sir James goes up to her. "You're making a mistake, my dear," he says. "Your refusal may have considerable negative consequences, not only for yourself but for all of us. You must not resist those who are more powerful than yourself, and right now this Mexican bandito is in charge. Surely his request cannot present any danger to yourself, it's no doubt merely an overlooked formality. He saw your name on your passport, and . . ."

"He is a pig."

Everyone joins in, cajoling her, encouraging her, pleading with her. You don't know that. He seemed harmless. A mere formality. And in the end, they convince her; how can there possibly be anything wrong with just going to see what he wants?

"All right, I'll go," La Gordita says. "I'll do it for you."

"And we thank you for it," says Lady Scott, taking her hand and releasing it.

She leaves, and the others wait for her to come back before taking their places at the table. Each of them secretly wishes it was them instead of La Gordita who was called. She is so volatile, so unpredictable, who knows what she'll say if the Mexican asks her about the financial status of her fellow passengers? What would they themselves say? No, we're just tourists, no money, we came to Mexico because we couldn't afford to go to France. Something like that. But they must appear rich to La Gordita, and she might not hesitate to say so.

After ten minutes, La Gordita comes back to the dining room, breathing hard (maybe from the stairs?), her jowls quivering and her face livid with indignation.

"That pig!" she stammers.

"What happened?" the others ask her. "What did he want?"

"Don't ask!" she says. "It doesn't concern you. Trust me, the man is a pig."

They are too hungry to press the issue. They take their places around the table, at the centre of which is a large plate of thin arachera steaks and a bowl of boiled potatoes and broccoli. The matter of La Gordita's visit to the subcomandante is dropped for the moment, and the conversation becomes general. The six from the back of the bus order two bottles of wine, and Houseman orders a beer — Modena, he specifies, and pale, if they have it — and when it comes, he opens the bottle with a care he must have learned as a steward, holding his glass sideways and pouring slowly so as not to make too much foam. He licks his lips as he pours, remembering how hot it was in the bus, even with the air conditioning. He looks like a priest filling the chalice before Holy Communion. Funny, thinks Sir James, how fanatics always seem to prefer beer over wine. Revolutionaries have not the temperament of a connoisseur. They will not wait for changes to develop slowly but inevitably through well-established channels, but must have their revolution on the spot, cold and frothing, chug it back as fast as they can and order another before the first is down. *¡Viva la revolucion!* is their motto, and *¡Una mas!* is their cry.

The hotel manager and his wife join them for dinner, as they were too run off their feet to eat at the regular hour. That's the hotelier's life, says Señora Tontavida. Her husband's asthma makes him hiss like a leaky steam pipe and he cannot eat and breathe at the same time, but Señora Tontavida more than makes up for it by talking almost nonstop throughout the entire meal. Only Lady Scott seems to be listening to her — perhaps she is used to having tiresome dinner companions — and the hotelier's wife is no doubt flattered to be holding the attention of such a distinguished guest. The cartel fighters impressed her when they first arrived in Minatitlán, she says. They are men and women of the soil, after all, not the scrapings of the cities, as the army seems to be, and they are not as arrogant and demanding as the soldiers were. She has two sons in the army, and she knows how the army trains them to be disdainful of the people they're supposed to defend.

But after a while the cartelanos showed their true natures, she says, lowering her voice and looking nervously at the door to the dining room.

"Don't, Valencia," her husband wheezes, but she goes on.

"The subcomandante is staying here, his name is José Hernandez Guitierez, but he is better known as El Zopilote, the Vulture. His daughter had to flee to los Estados Unidos last month because she posted a photo of herself dressed as a nun." Everyone around the table looks confused, especially the missionaries, but no one asks her to explain. "He is all right, I suppose."

"He is a pig!" spits La Gordita.

"All the same," the manageress says quickly, "he is better than his subordinates. At least he bathes. And he works hard, so many people always coming to see him and get their orders from him. He is mostly polite to our staff. It was he who negotiated the takeover of the town without too much blood being shed. There was some, of course, there is always blood when there is a war. But it is sad to see so many young men intent on killing one another. With them, it isn't for money, it must be in their natures, don't you think? They are like children, strutting around with their machine guns and their smartphones, I don't know, I don't think I will ever be able to understand them."

"War is a barbarous business," Houseman declares loudly. Tontavida glances at the door. "It's bad enough when we attack a real enemy, but these phony wars the government gets us into are just bloody-mindedness. The war on drugs. The war on terrorism. How can you have a war on something as nebulous as poverty, for example?"

"Now it's the war on numbers," Bob Lethworth says gloomily.

"Maybe we should have a war on politicians," says the manageress. "They seem to make war just to amuse themselves, to have something to show for their time in office."

Houseman's eyes light up. "Now you're talking, señora!" he says, raising his beer glass to her, or perhaps to the waitress.

Sir James looks disgusted. First it was Communism, and now it's Anarchism. These Americans have no idea, they are political idiots. Anything for a sensation. He agrees with Virginia Woolf, who wrote that revolutions spring from laziness, fear and the love of affecting scenes. "Do you not know how much power these drug lords have over the people of this country, how looked up to they are?" he says to Houseman. "They are idolized. Like movie stars in your country. And why? Because, like movie stars, they are almost unimaginably rich, that's why. They have so much cash it's rotting in their vaults. They can't spend it fast enough, and when they do spend it, what do they buy? Every peasant's dream: exclusive casinos, luxurious mansions, cars, and women. Baubles!" No one looks at La Gordita. "If these narcos are so heroic, why don't they do something useful with their wealth, something the government can't afford to do? Build hospitals, for example, or endow universities. Ha! The government wouldn't dare send the army after them if they were using their money to, let us say, build a new airport in Mexico City!"

"Do you mean," says Lethworth, "that the internal affairs of an entire country should be financed by criminal activity?"

"Why not?" Sir James shrugs. "When a pharmaceutical company gives a hospital a million dollars, do we inquire into the ethics of its drug testing methods? Do we ask where the money came from? If a lumber company endows a school of forestry in a university, and builds a building to house it, do we mention clearcutting and habitat loss in our welcoming speeches? Why stick at cartel money?"

"If the Mexicans approve of the cartels," says Barry Anderson, "it's because they have made all their money off us Americans. Four tonnes of cocaine a month going into the U.S. of A., and all that money comes back into Mexican coffers. Mexicans love anyone who will poke a Yank in the eye."

"Stop it!" cries La Gordita. "You are both talking nonsense. No one in Mexico admires the cartels. They are extortionists and murderers. They corrupt our young men and steal our daughters. They give our country a bad name. They make it impossible for us to cross the border. In Afghanistan they have the Taliban; no one from that country can emigrate to the United States because everyone thinks they are terrorists. But not everyone in Afghanistan is a terrorist! In Mexico, we have the drug cartels. We can't go into the United States because they think we are all involved in drug trafficking."

Again, Houseman, who is on his third beer, raises his glass to salute La Gordita. "Brava, señorita," he says, slightly slurring the words. "Bravissima!"

Dinner is over. The women stand and say they're going upstairs to bed, and the men look at one another and then they, too, rise. They have spent the past eighteen hours in each other's company, and are anxious to put the long day behind them.

IN THEIR ROOM, halfway along the corridor, Barry Anderson stands with his eye at the peephole in the door. "What are you doing?" asks his wife, who is in bed. "Just looking," says Anderson.

"Come to bed," says his wife.

"In a minute. Someone's moving around out there."

It's La Gordita, looking enormous in a pink chiffon nightgown trimmed with white lace. She's carrying an ice bucket and heading for the glass door at the end of the hall, where the ice machine is. Aha, thinks Anderson, she must have her own supply of booze. Better not let Houseman get wind of it. No sooner has he had that thought than Houseman's door opens and the man steps into the corridor. When La Gordita comes back with her bucket of ice, Houseman stops her and whispers something. La Gordita shakes her head and continues towards her room, and Houseman follows her. The two speak in low tones outside La Gordita's door; she seems to be using her bulk to prevent him from opening it. Anderson can't hear what is said, at first, but as Houseman continues to insist, in his drunken manner, La Gordita raises her voice, and Anderson catches a few words.

"No, you can't!"

"Why the hell not?" Houseman says. "What's it matter to you anyway?"

La Gordita says something low and urgent.

"Fuck the subcomandante," Houseman replies. "He won't hear us. He's in another part of the hotel."

La Gordita holds him off. "You don't get it, do you," she says, shaking her head. "It isn't just the subcomandante. The enemy is here, in this hotel, watching us, listening to us. We are prisoners here. I'm frightened!"

Something of her urgency must have penetrated into Houseman's fogged brain, for he stops trying to get past her and seems to be attempting to focus on her face. "All right," he says, "just a drink, then, to settle our nerves. I'll protect you."

"Go to bed," she says, veering him gently towards his own room. And off he weaves. Anderson nods appreciatively. His estimation of La Gordita has gone up another notch. He expected as much from Houseman. This is the second time she has repelled his advances. Prisoners, are we? We'll find out tomorrow. Then he quickly undresses in the dark and joins his wife, who is already fast asleep.

THE PLAN WAS to leave Minatitlán at eight the next morning in order to make it to Manzanillo in time to catch their plane, and so at a quarter to eight everyone gathers in the lobby with their suitcases, expecting El Zopilote or his lieutenant to be there to return their passports. At eight, there is no one else in the lobby, not even the hotel manager or his wife, and no Manuel. Nor do there seem to be any other guests. The entire hotel is ominously quiet. There's no one behind the desk, and the manager's office is locked. Sir James rings the bell on the reception counter several times, but no one comes. Does anyone know what room the subcomandante is in? No. Lethworth tries phoning the shuttle company back in Colima, but there is no answer. Too early, probably, and now it doesn't look as though they will be able to catch their flight from Manzanillo. Phone calls are made, their flight is changed to the next day, but they are in a hurry to leave Minatitlán. They wait in the lobby, not knowing what else to do, and by nine-thirty there is still no one else about. Finally, the men decide to organize a search party. They don't think Manuel stayed in the hotel, because he wasn't present at breakfast. But Minatitlán is a small town, the brochure on the reception desk says the population is barely six thousand, there can't be that many hotels, and they will recognize the bus. The women, with the exception of the missionaries, are delegated to try the rooms upstairs to see if they can find the subcomandante. The older missionary says she and Sister Debbie will wait in the lobby in case the van arrives. It feels good to have a plan.

The men soon find the Plaza, with its crumbling bandstand and sculpted box trees surrounded by colonial mansions and fairly choked with little stalls selling everything from azaleas to zapatas. Wrought-iron park benches are arranged around the gazebo, in which, in simpler times, bands must have played concerts and, at Christmas, the town set up its life-size figures of Mary, Joseph, and the three Kings. How innocent it all seems now. There is little trade at the shops, and few people in the Plaza except for a half-dozen men in fluorescent yellow vests clearing the pavement of dirt and rocks washed down from the surrounding hills during the heavy rains; they are throwing the wet gravel into the back of a pick-up truck marked Ciudad de Minatitlán. Astonishingly, several cartelanos are helping them, their machine guns leaning against one of the Plaza benches. There are more cartel soldiers on the side streets, drinking in the cafés, often at the same tables as the locals, or lined up in the post office to buy stamps and mail letters. At the public lavandería, where women wash their sheets and towels in large, concrete basins, cartel soldiers carry the wet bundles to the cars. Elsewhere, a group of soldiers is digging a trench in front of the Basilica de Nuestra Señora de la Salud to repair a broken water main. Despite what La Gordita said the night before, life is going on. Well, it does, doesn't it? thinks Sir James. It must. He wonders aloud if this is what Vichy was like during the war. They enquire at two or three hotels, simple establishments hardly distinguishable from the houses around them, but find no sign of Manuel or the bus.

"He's probably driving the cartel army to the front," Houseman says indignantly. "If there is a front. I sensed some degree of collaboration between him and that subcomandante last night. Old buddies, I bet. He probably knew he was driving us into this hornet's nest. Maybe he was driving slowly on purpose, to give the narcos time to settle in."

"Well," says Anderson, "we can't go anywhere without him, so we'd better keep looking."

"Not me, I've had it," says Houseman. "I'm going back to the hotel to see if the women have found that murderer in the clown suit." He strides off towards the Hotel Santa Ana.

The others find Manuel in the next café, sharing a table with the subcomandante's lieutenant. They do, indeed, seem to be on friendly terms.

"Manuel!" says Sir James. "We were supposed to leave two hours ago! Why didn't you bring the bus?"

"Because I had orders not to."

"Orders? From whom?"

"From El Zopilote."

"I don't understand," says Lethworth. "Why would he want to keep us in Minatitlán? If he wanted money from us, he would have asked us last night."

"I don't know," says Manuel. "You'll have to ask him. I've been asking Juan-Carlos, here, but he doesn't know any more than we do."

"Where's the subcomandante now?" asks Anderson. "He still has our passports."

Manuel turns to the lieutenant, who shrugs. "No sé."

"Was it El Zopilote himself who told you we weren't leaving?" Sir James asks Manuel.

"No, it was the hotel manager who passed it on. Tontavida."

"When?"

"Last night, after dinner, as I was leaving to go to my hotel."

Perplexed, the three men return to the Santa Ana, where they find the women in the lobby; they had no luck finding the subcomandante. One of the chambermaids told them he never rises before noon, and no one is allowed to see him except the lieutenant and the hotel manager.

"Nothing to do but wait, I suppose," says Houseman, settling in one of the large, comfortable chairs beside the fireplace. From his jacket pocket he produces his flask, refilled from the supply in his backpack, and a package of cigarettes he must have purchased on his way back to the hotel. Chesterfields, Sir James notices, which he finds amusing, given the man's rabid defense of all things Mexican. What's wrong with Mexican cigarettes? The fellow should be smoking Delicados, should he not? And that morning in the breakfast room, Houseman filled his plate with waffles and raspberry jam, passing on the chilequiles and juevos rancheros in the warming pans. These paper revolutionaries, these so-called anarchists, they want to tear down the established political order, all right, but by no means deprive themselves of their old familiar comforts. And he certainly looked abject enough whilst the subcomandante was studying his passport. Look how his hand shakes when he lifts that blasted flask to his lips. It can't all be the drink.

At eleven o'clock the hotel manager appears in the lobby, and everyone but Houseman and La Gordita jump up and surround him, asking about their passports and the bus. But all the man says is that the subcomandante told him last night not to return their passports, which are locked in the hotel safe in his office, and not to let them leave until he, El Zopilote, gives the word. That's all he knows. He repeats his story three or four times, until he is overcome by a fit of coughing and retreats in the direction of the desk.

"When can we see the subcomandante?" Carol Anderson calls after him, and the manager turns, says, "Perhaps after his comida," and, unlocking his door, disappears into his office.

"Comida?" says Lethworth, "but that could be hours from now. Our flight leaves Manzanillo at ten-thirty tomorrow morning!"

"Ten-twenty!" corrects his wife, who is wringing her hands distractedly.

Just then the subcomandante's lieutenant comes down the stairs and tells them Subcomandante Hernandez will see them at one o'clock.

"If we leave here at two," says Anderson, "we could still be in Manzanillo tonight. We don't have to be at the airport until eight in the morning tomorrow. All is not lost."

"We won't be leaving at two," says Houseman sourly from his chair by the fire. The others remonstrate with him, all but La Gordita, who sits in her chair looking distraught. The sight of her reminds Anderson, who says: "Let's not forget to bring some food this time."

They eat a light lunch in the dining room. La Gordita barely touches her plate. They're finishing their coffee when the lieutenant comes back to say that the subcomandante will see the men now. Sir James, Lethworth, and Anderson stand up, but Houseman remains seated, saying proudly that he will never lower himself to beg for his human rights, nor does he recognize the subcomandante's authority over him. Sir James marvels at the man's chameleon-like ability to switch colours as the surroundings suit him. Earlier, the subcomandante was the people's hero; now he's a power-mad tyrant who must be defied. The others are relieved; they do not want this hothead at their meeting with El Zopilote. Getting permission to leave without too many unpleasant concessions is going to be tricky enough.

Upstairs, the three men are shown into the subcomandante's room – actually a suite, the finest in the hotel, with a living room that boasts a large fireplace, a glass table and six chairs, a long wooden bench with gaudy cushions at each end, and a well-stocked bar. Everything is heavy and ornate but somehow still manages to look comfortable. By the large window that looks out over an ash tree and a small square, a bamboo bird cage holds a spotted bird the size of a thrush, but with a long, downwardly curved bill. The bird flits back and forth continually as though unable to comprehend why it cannot simply fly over to the tree in the square. El Zopilote is sitting casually on an armchair beside the fireplace, smoking a cigar with his feet up on a low table. He wears a ridiculously flamboyant dressing gown, red satin with wide, black lapels and cinched at the waist with a twisted silken cord; the men suspect the gown belonged to some city official or other who has recently disappeared. What is it with these Mexicans and their dressing gowns, thinks Anderson. The subcomandante does not get up, or even look at them, but presents them with the indifferent, almost insolent profile of a military leader pleased with his victory over superior forces; in other words, he is enjoying himself while he still can.

The men stand silently for a few minutes, until El Zopilote turns to them and asks them what they want.

"Our passports, for starters," says Lethworth. "And then to continue our journey. We have to be—"

"Out of the question," says the subcomandante.

"You mean you aren't going to let us go?"

"Correct."

"Why not?"

"Because I don't want to."

"Do you mean to keep us here as hostages?" asks Sir James. "As bargaining chips? If so, I'm afraid you won't get much for us. Or from us. No one's going to pay you for our release, we're not in the least important to anyone. And we have no money ourselves."

The subcomandante gives him a long, slow look, exhaling a thin stream of cigar smoke in the men's direction. "Do you think I need your money, Sir James?" he says. "Do you think I need anything from you? Will the government withdraw its army if I keep you prisoners here? Or will los Estados Unidos send their big helicopters and their SEAL units to your rescue? Do you think you are living in some Hollywood blockbuster, señors? Is one of you Tom Cruise and another Bruce Willis? Eh?" He looks at Sir James. "Are you James Bond in disguise, señor? No, I think not. I am keeping you here because it pleases me to do so. You are like this bird," he says, indicating with his cigar the cage by the window. "A cuitlacoche. One of my men caught it this morning and brought it to me, because he knows I like birds. They have so much raw energy, do they not? That is all, gentlemen. You are dismissed."

The three men exchange glances, and leave the room.

The travellers pass a gloomy afternoon in the hotel lobby. Houseman finishes his flask and goes up to his room to replenish it. The others talk the situation over until they are bored with it. What does the subcomandante want? "Well, obviously," says Sir James, who has had some experience with diplomatic crises, "he wants to hold us hostage here to discourage the army from trying to take back this wretched town. At the first sign of hostilities he kills the captives, that sort of thing."

"Possibly," says Lethworth. "But why would the Mexican government care if he shoots a few Americans? I think he just wants our money."

That thought alarms the others almost as much as the prospect of being shot as hostages. The women, of course, have brought all their best jewelry with them, it's in their carry-ons, and in Lady Scott's case at least some of it is irreplaceable and quite valuable. Christine Lethworth's is insured, but still, there are some nice pieces. Carol Anderson's earrings were designed by artists she knows, or knew, in New York, they're one-of-a-kind works of art, plus she's wearing her grandmother's engagement ring and a brooch left to her by a favourite great-aunt. The men worry about their credit cards. Maybe they should cut them up, or better yet, burn them, along with their debit cards. They've heard of kidnappers torturing their victims for PIN numbers and then killing them. The thought of their accounts being drained dry after they are dead is somehow deeply disturbing.

"I think you're all insane," says Houseman, freshly installed in his chair by the fireplace. "You heard what the man said. He's keeping us here because we amuse him. He is keeping us as his pets."

DINNERTIME ARRIVES and there is still no news from the subcomandante. As they are being led into the dining room, Señor Tontavida appears to relay another message from Subcomandante Hernandez: he would like to know if Señorita Dolorosa has changed her mind yet, and if so would she join him in his quarters.

La Gordita stands beside her chair, pale and trembling. Everyone looks at her. Then she suddenly explodes with rage. "No! Tell that pig of a subcomandante that I have not, and will never, agree to his request. Never!" Her whole body quivers.

Tontavida looks aggrieved, as though he takes her rejection personally, and leaves the room. La Gordita is again surrounded by her companions, as she was the previous evening, who this time want to know what it was the subcomandante asked her, and why she has refused. At first La Gordita says nothing. But Barry Anderson settles the matter by saying: "Come on, people, let's not be naïve. We all know what the subcomandante wants. Am I not right, señorita?"

"He wants me to sleep with him, yes. But I said no."

At her words, Houseman bangs his palm down on the table, rattling the plates and cutlery for two place settings in each direction. "Goddamn! So that's it!"

In fact, everyone looks rattled, some more than others. "Of *course* you said no, you poor thing," says Carol Anderson, putting a soothing hand on La Gordita's round back. "What a terrible man. You did the right thing, of course you did. Didn't she?"

Of course she did the right thing, everyone agrees. Sir James sputters that Houseman's famous Mexican heroes are nothing but barbarians after all. "Rapists and thieves," quotes Anderson. Bob Lethworth won't go that far: "Clearly this man is a rat, but we can't judge an entire country by the behaviour of one man."

"Of course we can," says Sir James. "Obviously this subcomandante is just one man, but he exists in a milieu in which such a man can rise to the top of the rubbish heap. A great many people must approve of his behaviour."

The missionaries, who are making their first appearance since lunchtime, keep their eyes on their plates and speak only to each other. They have spent the afternoon out of the hotel, no one knows where.

When the women, including the manageress, have gone upstairs to bed, the men turn to the manager in hopes of learning more about this subcomandante, who is keeping them so whimsically in such an untenable position. They order drinks from the bar, and stand the manager to a large margarita. But Tontavida will say nothing about the subcomandante's intentions, although he speaks openly and amiably about everything else – his asthma, which he's had since childhood and is getting worse; his business, which is normally very good but is now suffering from this occupation (almost no tourists, since all the embassies have declared the entire state of Colima a red zone); his wife, who, he says, is the real businesswoman behind the hotel's success. It is she who manages the hotel's website, and emails regular reports to guests who have stayed here in the past, just to remind them of the wonderful time they had in Minatitlán. He himself understands nothing about websites or Facebook pages. It's all he can do to send emails to his daughter in Mexico City. He studied anthropology at the University of Guadalajara; there are some interesting archeological sites not too far from Minatitlán, and of course there is El Salto, the waterfall, if the gentlemen are interested in keeping themselves entertained during their stay. They are not. After a while, his asthma sets in, and he starts coughing and wheezing and can no longer talk. Saying that he left his inhaler upstairs, he leaves them without having made them any wiser about the subcomandante or his plans.

The next morning they are once again in the lobby at eight. For some reason, they still have eight o'clock in their heads as their leaving time. But once again there's no bus in the courtyard, and no sign of Manuel. They know by now not to expect the manager before ten, or the subcomandante before one, and so they're faced with the prospect of another long morning sitting in the lobby watching Houseman drink himself into a stupor and La Gordita tap her fingers nervously on the arms of her chair as she pretends to read her magazine, which appears to be about famous Mexican television stars no one else has heard of. But watch her they do, to see if she shows any signs of having given in to the subcomandante's request during the night. She doesn't.

Hardly anyone speaks to her. When, at about ten-thirty, she stands and announces she is going out to find a pharmacia, and asks if anyone wants to go with her, no one does. As soon as she leaves, however, the others convene a hasty conference to discuss their predicament. It's obvious now to everyone that their being kept in Minatitlán is directly linked to the subcomandante's determination to sleep with La Gordita. As long as she refuses to give in, they won't be allowed to leave. Anderson says he kept a vigil at his peephole until well past midnight last night, but did not see any movement in the corridor other than Houseman's several trips to the ice machine. He sounds disappointed. Who would know if she went to the subcomandante? And who would blame her? She must be as aware as they are of what's at stake. No one gives voice to their thoughts, but it's clear from the way they speak – with hushed voices, harsh faces, furtive glances towards the sliding glass doors through which the woman may at any moment reappear – that they are all of a mind. Something has to be done.

After lunch, La Gordita again says she's going out to shop – on her earlier foray she saw that many of the boutiques have reopened – and again no one offers to accompany her. But no sooner is she out of sight than Sir James says that a walk would do them all good, and so, after taking their suitcases back up to their rooms, they leave the hotel, being careful to turn in the opposite direction to the one taken by La Gordita. The afternoon sun is brutal in its intensity. The women are wearing long sleeves and straw hats with long, colourful scarves tied around the crowns and draped down their backs, like medieval maidens at a jousting match. The men, following behind them, are hatless. Bob Lethworth has a full head of hair, but Barry Anderson's fair hair is thinning, and his face and scalp are quite red. His wife urges him to buy one of the Panama hats they see stacked in the doorway of a tienda, but he says, "No, I'm all right. We'll be on the plane in the morning," and then no one wants to insist he buy a hat.

The women poke into the tiny shops while the men wait outside on the narrow sidewalks. There's more activity in the streets today, more people going about their business, with, it seems, fewer cartelanos standing about carrying weapons.

Suddenly, Anderson says what everyone else is thinking: "How much longer is that hooker going to keep us waiting in this bloody town? There, I've said it. But really!"

Sir James replies, reasonably, that they don't know she's a prostitute. She said she was a beautician, and well may she be. They can hardly suggest to her that she give in to the subcomandante's demands. It's unthinkable. "That notion," he says, "will have to come from her, not us."

Lethworth says that if the army launches a counterattack with the idea of retaking Colima, then the major battles will no doubt take place somewhere in the vicinity of Minatitlán. "And we'll be in the thick of it!"

"Thanks for that," says Anderson. "Something else to worry about."

"Suppose we just rent a couple of cars and drive ourselves out of here?" says Lethworth.

"We still don't have our passports."

"Oh, right."

"We could bribe Tontavida to give them to us. They're in his safe, after all."

"The subcomandante would have his head on a pikestaff. Probably literally."

"Then it looks like La Gordita is our only hope."

Just then the three women come out of the shop, La Gordita with them. "Look who we found," says Carol Anderson. "She bought the prettiest scarf."

"Tarting herself up for the subcomandante, do you think?" Anderson jokes to Lethworth under his breath.

"One can only hope."

"And speak of the devil," says Anderson. At the end of the street, the subcomandante himself appears, his stocky, costumed figure with its Pancho Villa sombrero outlined against a dark doorway that gives into an interior courtyard. El Zopilote bows to the women as they approach, and smirks at the men, who don't smile back – except for Anderson, who says a quick, "Buenos tardes." La Gordita blushes and hurries on, and the other women hesitate, not knowing whether by joining her they'd be declaring an allegiance with her that they do not in fact feel.

"He's not all that bad looking, is he?" says Christine Lethworth when they catch up with La Gordita. "I mean, I'm not suggesting."

"Maybe I should tell him you think so," says La Gordita, laughing.

"Don't you dare! I was just kidding."

"He isn't interested in us," puts in Carol Anderson, injecting a wistful note into her voice.

"What would you do if he were?" asks Lady Scott.

"Why, exactly what Señorita Dolorosa is doing, of course," Carol says. "Tell him to get stuffed. How can you even ask?"

But Lady Scott gives her a knowing look.

Dinner that evening is a silent affair. The Tontavidas don't join them, and everyone avoids looking at La Gordita. As soon as they finish eating, they go upstairs to bed. There's a faint stirring of anticipation, almost as on Christmas Eve, as they all wonder if, when they wake up in the morning, they'll find that La Gordita has done the right thing during the night, and they can all leave. They don't even care if they make their flight, they just want to be in the bus and on the road.

In the morning they are awakened by church bells, and La Gordita is not at breakfast. Hopeful eyebrows are raised, but the missionaries say they saw her leaving at six-thirty for early mass. Anderson wonders if they tried to stop her.

"I have an idea," he says. "Let's try to convince El Zopilote to keep her here and let the rest of us go. I mean, what's the point in detaining all of us?"

"Splendid idea," says Sir James, and he goes out to find Tontavida to persuade him to put the proposition to the subcomandante. The manager is in his office, having got up early to send a personal email to someone in New York who enquired about a room. He listens to Sir James's proposal, goes upstairs to relay it to El Zopilote, and comes back down to the breakfast room almost immediately, shaking his head. "Not a chance," he says. "The subcomandante thought you might suggest something like that, and he told me to say, Shame on you. He intends to keep you all here until La Gordita gives in to his wishes."

At this, Carol Anderson bursts into a fit of outrage. "What is this?" she cries. "Some kind of weird psychological experiment? Are we on a reality TV show or something? Why the hell *won't* she give in to him? I mean, it's not like she's used to turning down men, from what I gather. Why is she drawing the line at this one?"

"We don't know that, Carol," says her husband placatingly.

"I do know that. I know it for a fact. Chantal told me as much." She turned to the others. "Chantal Forster, our neighbour back in Colima. She told me her gardener was a regular visitor to her so-called beauty shop on Calle Tortadero, and he was hardly the only one. None of the women who work there trained as manicurists, I can assure you. I didn't want to say anything earlier, but I'm saying it now. That woman is no better than she should be. So why is she digging in her heels now, when it means we are kept prisoners in this rotten hotel? Sorry, Señor Tontavida, but I mean, really! It's her that's keeping us locked up here, not the subcomandante. He's actually behaving rather respectfully, if you ask me. He could have chosen any one of us, he probably would even prefer us, but he didn't. He settled for the one who, he must have thought, would put up the least resistance. He respects decent, married women. He's not a rapist. All he had to do was point at any one of us and say, You, and he could have taken us by force, with all his soldiers here to help him. But he didn't."

She pauses as the image of what she has said settles in the minds of everyone in the room. What would the women have done? What would the men have done? Lady Scott's eyes glisten. "That's what I was trying to say earlier, my dears. We might count ourselves lucky now, but we must be prepared for the worst. Who's to say that if the señorita persists in her opposition, the subcomandante won't lose patience and turn to one of us?"

"But prepare how?" asks Lethworth. "We can't just tie her up and hand her over." He looks around at the others. "Can we?"

"Certainly not," says Sir James. "We must try to persuade her."

"But how?"

They put their heads together.

They talk in allusions, at first. Nothing specific, nothing gross. The necessity for decisive action simply has to be impressed upon the woman. This is no time for scruples. No one will judge her, no one will blame her. It is agreed that, in her hearing, no one should allude to the difference between her situation and theirs. No one is to imply that there's a moral component to the deed, unless to say that morality consists in doing what is good for the largest number of people. Yes, that's a good line. They'll have to be more specific. They have a flight to catch, period – best not to mention that the flight will already have left by the time they get out of here. They'll change their tickets again tonight. Just say there is more urgency for them than there is for her; after all, she can fly to Guanajuato anytime, her exit visa isn't about to expire, her sister might be ill, but she isn't dying. Is she? And if she is, all the more reason for La Gordita to get away as soon as possible. Brilliant!

"My God," says Sir James, "to hear us, one would think we were trying to persuade her to accept a winning lottery ticket!"

Only Houseman remains aloof from these deliberations. He wants no part of them. He has as much interest in getting out of Minatitlán as the others, perhaps even more, given that he gave the subcomandante his friend's passport and exit visa. He doesn't think the others twigged, but Sir James probably has an eye for that kind of thing. But what they are planning to do is appalling. They are treating La Gordita as they would a prostitute, behaving like pimps. He says as much.

"We're not pimping!" says Anderson. "Think of us as a dating service!"

"You're procuring!"

"You're drunk!"

"Panderers!"

Just then the dining-room door opens and La Gordita comes in. "Is there any coffee left?" she says brightly. Everyone looks at the coffee urn as though at an ally they hadn't thought of. "I'm always hungry after praying."

THE ATTACK BEGINS at lunch. The women sit close to La Gordita and talk among themselves about the virtues of self-sacrifice. Apropos of nothing, Christine Lethworth mentions how much she misses her children. Bob bought their son and his wife a house in Sausilito. "There are so many things I did for my kids," Carol Anderson says, "which at the time I really resented, you know? I gave up my career for them, I put my whole life on hold, I thought I'd never get back into the work force. I had my own design business, nothing grand but it kept me busy. But you know what? I look back on those years and I wouldn't have had it any other way. I have such a great relationship with my kids now. It wasn't really a sacrifice at all."

"I know what you mean," says Christine. "It wasn't a sacrifice, it was more like an investment."

"Exactly! An investment in their happiness and in ours. I was reading just the other day, a feminist reinterpretation of history, how the women who historically have been scorned for their deeds – by men, usually – should really be hailed as heroines. I think they used Judith as an example, how when she seduced the tyrant Holofernes she saved an entire city. And look at Cleopatra. She saved Egypt from the Romans by taking Mark Antony as her lover. There were lots of other examples, I can't remember them all, but the point was that throughout the ages women have used their charms, their beautiful bodies, as weapons on the sexual battlefield. They exchanged virtue for victory and revenge. These women don't deserve our censure; they have earned our devotion." She takes a sip of tea. "It was an interesting book."

"As Shakespeare said, beauty hath charms to soothe the savage beast."

"Peace is always represented as a goddess," says Lady Scott, "never as a god. I find that interesting."

La Gordita looks at Lady Scott, for she is no fool and knows exactly what these women are doing. "And what about you, señora, what would you do if you were in my place?"

Lady Scott says, sincerely, "I would do the right thing."

FOR THE REST of the day, they leave La Gordita to her reflections. They speak to her from time to time, in the hotel lobby, in the dining room at dinner (the missionaries took their meal elsewhere, perhaps in their room), and when they do speak to her, they're not quite as warm as they were.

There are no more invitations to share details of their private lives; it's as though they are no longer interested in her other than as a travelling companion; her private life is her own business. They want her to make the right decision, of course, but they know she has to believe that she is making that decision herself, that they aren't making it for her.

After dinner, Tontavida comes into the lobby and asks once again, on behalf of the subcomandante, if Señorita Dolorosa has changed her mind. Breath is held. La Gordita answers briefly: "No, señor." Breath is slowly expelled.

That evening, a sense of failure quiets the coalition against La Gordita. Houseman even seems to encourage her determination to pretend to a virtue they are certain she doesn't possess. They wrack their brains for more examples from history of self-sacrificing women, but come up only with women whose sacrifices were a mistake. The writer Colette, for example, who for years wrote novels published under her husband's name and eventually had to take him to court to gain her rightful recognition. No, that wouldn't do. What about Joan of Arc? No, no, the poor woman was burned at the stake. But that was by religious fanatics; the subcomandante isn't a religious fanatic. At the mention of religious fanatics, Lady Scott turns to the eldest of the two missionaries and asks her if she knows of any examples from religion, perhaps from the lives of the saints, of women who committed some act that, at the time, was considered immoral or even criminal, but which the Church pardoned because it accomplished a greater good. Sister Ann considers the question, but her answer hardly seems encouraging, at least not at first. "Of course," she says, "the Catholic Church sanctified many women who committed brave acts, but only after those women had been tortured, raped, mutilated, or had otherwise died horrible deaths. It was their deaths, not their lives, that the Church exploited in order to edify, or perhaps pacify, its believers. Obviously," the missionary continues, "we are not Catholics, we do not glorify death. We look to make our lives useful while we are on earth, rather than after we have left it. We are not missionaries in the sense you seem to understand the term. We do not proselytize, we do not ring doorbells on Sunday mornings, or dance on street corners singing Hare Krishna. We work. If we convert others to our way of seeing the world, it is by example, not by trickery and coercion. These past two days, Sister Debbie and I have been volunteering at the hospital; we are both trained nurses and there has been much bloodshed here of late. We are not licensed to practise in Mexico, of course, but we can change bandages and bedclothes, administer antibiotics, comfort the victims' families. We can serve. We are on our way to Manzanillo to work in an orphanage, to prepare food and give aid to children who have no family to provide those comforts for them. We do not sit around in hotel lobbies bemoaning our fate and waiting for someone else to come along and fix things for us. We roll up our sleeves and try to fix as much as we can ourselves."

"Then, sister," says Lady Scott, trying to salvage something from the woman's words, "you think God rewards good deeds?"

"We do not presume to know what God thinks, Lady Scott. All we know about God is what Jesus tells us and shows us. He performed many good deeds during his brief life."

"In fact, in doing so he often broke the moral codes of his day, did he not?"

"He did. He defied the false authority of the occupying Romans, and of the political leaders of Judea, all of whom wanted him to stop whatever he was doing and just go away. But he was not trying to convert anyone, he was simply doing good. Healing the sick, feeding the hungry . . ."

"Freeing the imprisoned?"

"Freeing the wrongfully imprisoned, yes."

Why, are they not wrongfully imprisoned? What did the old woman mean by adding that caveat? Lady Scott lets the conversation drop for fear of spoiling the effect of the missionary's words. She thinks about saying something like, Render unto Caesar the things that are Caesar's, but does not want to risk the woman adding her damaging Parthian shot to the sentiment. La Gordita's is a simple soul, susceptible to such casuistry. But Lady Scott is not so naïve as to believe the two missionaries are not trolling for souls as they change bandages or stir thin soup in foreign-run orphanages. Is the Living Jesus never mentioned when the orphans are taught to say their nightly prayers? Are religious tracts never left on bedside tables? They are hoping to make converts one bedpan at a time. Lady Scott and the other women finish the meal in silence. They hope the seed of good deeds has fallen on fertile ground, and that during the night it will germinate and bring forth fruit.

That night, the three married women lie sleepless in their beds, pondering the question La Gordita put to Lady Scott. What would they do if the subcomandante comes for them? Carol Anderson looks at her husband in the dark, listening to his ragged breathing, remembering how she had dreamed of opening an art gallery in a small town on the coast of Maine. She can see the artwork she would have had on the walls, bright, joyous seascapes, gulls wheeling above bobbing fishing trawlers. Christine Lethworth tries to envision Bob springing at the subcomandante's throat, as La Gordita did with the cartel soldiers in Colima, to protect her honour. She can't quite see it. Sir James, too, is awake. He asks his wife outright, and she replies without hesitation that she would go. Then she turns to him and asks him what he would do. Challenge the subcomandante to a duel? Sir James chuckles. "No, my dear, you do enough duelling for both of us. But I would be very concerned for your safety. The subcomandante is not a Cambridge-educated cultural attaché or a career civil servant." In other words, he is not what Lady Scott is used to.

"And yet I do not see him as a violent man, do you?"

"My dear, he is not called El Zopilote for nothing. What do vultures do? They let others do their killing for them."

The following afternoon, Sir James proposes they all go for a walk. They might as well visit the famous waterfall. So far, all they have seen are a few tawdry tiendas and hole-in-the-wall cafés. On the street that leads to the falls, he takes La Gordita's arm, and they walk slowly together, falling slightly behind the others. He speaks to her in that familiar, patronizing way that older men assume with younger women, calling her "dear child" and "poor thing," reminding her in every phrase of his superiority in matters concerning the ways of the world. Lady Scott looks back anxiously, fearful that his well-intentioned directness will ruin whatever headway the women have made with La Gordita.

"So," says Sir James, "you'd have us all just remain here forever, I suppose. Except we won't, you know. I was listening to the news last night, as it happens, and the army even now is massing outside Minatitlán for an attack. We could all be caught in the crossfire, including yourself.

The cartels may even shove us in front of them as shields. Think of it. How simple it would be for you to save us from this predicament. Oh, I don't mean it would be easy, I don't wish to offend you in any way. I simply ask you to look at the two alternatives, and consider which one seems less traumatic for all concerned."

La Gordita says nothing for a few steps. She is wearing high heels and having some difficulty with the cobblestones.

"Have you ever seen what crack cocaine does to a human being, Sir James?" she asks. "I have, many times. And crystal meth? And now fentanyl? You may not think of this subcomandante as a violent man, but if killing tens of thousands of people every year for twenty years isn't violence, then I don't know what violence is. My sister —" but she does not finish the sentence.

Sir James walks on in silence. When Lady Scott turns to look at him again, he meets her eye and shakes his head sadly.

El Salto, too, is a disappointment. Perhaps if the sun weren't so merciless. Or if there weren't so many plastic bottles floating in the water. The curve of the river from the town is lined with trees and large houses – it is impossible to walk along it – and farther on the view is marred by a large water treatment plant. The water itself is murky with runoff from the recent rains. They stand on a stone pier for a while, watching desultory gulls and larger white birds that Sir James identifies as cattle egrets cruise aimlessly above the lake, then turn back to the hotel. Barry Anderson covers his head with a handkerchief. Carol mentions the Panama hats again, but he says no, he's fine.

In the dining room that evening, the others save a place for La Gordita between Lady Scott and Christine Lethworth, the two women with whom she seems to have the best rapport. But La Gordita does not come down. The others wait, but she does not show. There's much speculation as to what that may mean. Has she gone out? Is she avoiding them? After several uneasy minutes, Señor Tontavida enters the room and announces that Señorita Dolorosa sends her regrets, but she is indisposed, and would they please excuse her for the evening. Dinner will be brought in shortly. As the manager turns to leave, Anderson hurries to intercept him at the door.

"Is everything all right?" he asks.

"Yes."

Anderson searches the manager's face. "You mean . . . ?"

Tontavida nods curtly. "The subcomandante has ordered dinner for two in his quarters." As he leaves the room, Anderson turns to the others and performs a fist pump to the ceiling. "Yes!" he whispers hoarsely. "Dinner for two in the Vulture's room!"

A wave of relief shoots up from everyone, as though a pressure valve has been suddenly released. Hands clap, foolish grins are exchanged. Anderson calls the manager back and orders two bottles of champagne. "And to think," he says, "I almost cut up my Amex card!" Everyone laughs and talks at once, glad to be able to speak of trivial things now that the need to talk of serious matters is behind them. They are like children let out into a schoolyard after a rigorous exam. Bob Lethworth tells Carol Anderson he thinks her skirt is amazing, did she buy it in Mexico? Oh no, she ordered it from Italy, she's had it forever, but it wears so well it's perfect for travelling. Christine Lethworth tells Sir James that she loves a man with a British accent, everything he says sounds so clever. "Quite so," says Sir James. The jollity continues throughout the main course. More champagne is ordered. Anderson's eyes twinkle merrily as he tops up Lady Scott's glass. "I wonder what the subcomandante is having for dessert?" he says, to which Lady Scott replies without missing a beat: "A tart, I imagine!"

"No, plump pudding!" puts in someone else.

Roars of laughter greet both remarks, then fade after a moment as everyone pauses to envision what exactly *is* going on in the subcomandante's room at that moment. Then Anderson stands and raises his glass. "A toast!" he calls. Everyone thinks he's going to salute La Gordita, but, "To our very persuasive wives," he says, and everyone agrees that's much more appropriate. The three women blush charmingly and raise glasses to themselves. Even the two missionaries join in. Sister Debbie is on her third glass, and says she has never tasted champagne before in her life, and it is quite marvellous, and could she have another glass please. "What, more!" laughs Anderson, and pours.

Only Houseman seems out of sorts. He hasn't joined in the general jubilation, although he's had his share of the champagne. Anderson sees him sitting quietly by himself and goes over. He staggers a little, but no one notices. "What's the matter, Houseman?" he says, slapping the man on the back. "Not feeling celebratory? Just growing fond of this pissy little place, were you?"

Houseman sits back and scowls at the assemblage. The merriment subsides for a moment. "I can't believe you people are actually proud of what you've done!" he says. "That poor woman . . ." He stands abruptly and heads for the door. "That poor, decent woman!" he repeats, and slams out.

"His flask must need refilling," says Anderson.

But the fun does not immediately resume. "He's right, though, you know," says Bob Lethworth. "We have acted a bit selfishly."

"Oh, come on," says Anderson, "you're not falling for Houseman's little ethical act, are you?"

"How do you mean?"

Pressed for an explanation, Anderson relates "the curious incident of Houseman in the nighttime," when Houseman tried to force his way into La Gordita's bedroom and was physically repelled by her. He hasn't even told Carol about it.

"What!" says Lethworth. "You mean he —? The hypocritical bastard!"

"But she pushed him off?" says Carol. "Well, what on earth . . ."

The ladies laugh with renewed relief – it isn't they who behaved badly, it's Houseman! Houseman is a nasty fellow! He'll be back, don't worry, he'd rather drink our wine than his own tequila.

"No wonder he's furious. He must be wondering what the subcomandante has that he hasn't."

"You mean, other than vaults of money and an army?"

"And the key to this fair town, don't forget."

"Let's go to bed before he does come back," says Anderson. "I don't want to see his ugly mug any more tonight. We've had too much fun."

And so, the party breaks up. In their rooms, everyone begins re-packing the items they took out of their suitcases over the past three days. While brushing her teeth rather furiously, Carol Anderson remarks to her husband that she'd have thought Lady Scott would be better at hiding her disappointment that the subcomandante waited for his little prostitute rather than go for her.

"Who?" says Anderson. "You mean she would rather he . . . ?"

"Nothing sadder than seeing a woman of her stature running after anything in uniform, not that that clown suit he wears can be called a uniform, but you know what I mean. Anyone who exudes power. It doesn't matter where they got it. Obviously. Makes me sick to my stomach!"

"I'd never have guessed!"

"Hmmph. She was positively giddy with it."

AT EIGHT O'CLOCK the next morning the hotel lobby is buzzing with anticipation. The manager goes around and returns everyone's passports and Houseman's exit visa. He also hands each couple a bill for two nights' stay, telling them that the shuttle company paid for the first night, but not the second and third. This is met with some indignation, at first, but everyone is so delighted to be almost on the road again that they pay up without further protest. La Gordita is the only one who has not yet come down. Manuel arrives with the bus and starts loading the luggage. Sir James goes into the breakfast room, tips the servers, and comes back carrying a large bag of sandwiches for the journey. Barry Anderson looks at the souvenir kiosk as if he might, at the last minute, buy a T-shirt with a print of an avocado on it, or perhaps a little wooden burro with a tiny cask of mezcal on its back.

Finally, La Gordita comes downstairs. She looks a little sheepish, but she strides boldly into the lobby as if into a group of friends. She is no longer wearing the tight skirt and low-necked top she wore earlier, but has on a long skirt and a smart blouse with the nice-looking scarf she bought in the tienda on their first outing, the one Christine said looked so good on her. And no high heels this time, but comfortable sandals. She is, in fact, dressed much like the other women. She feels a bit like a gypsy.

No one speaks to her. No one even looks her way. Carol and Christine actually turn to the window to avoid her, pretending to be making sure Manuel doesn't miss any of their suitcases. Sir James takes his wife's arm and leads her to the reception desk to look at the postcards. Houseman sits in his habitual chair by the fireplace, looking disgustedly at everyone. La Gordita stands frozen in the middle of the lobby, stupefied with astonishment. She must be mistaken. She goes up to Carol and Christine and says, "Good morning, are they loading our luggage already? How exciting to be on our way at last!"

"Well, and about time, too," says Christine, almost under her breath.

La Gordita is practically in tears. She stands looking about the lobby; everyone is suddenly busy doing something that does not involve looking at her. When Manuel comes in and says, "All right, everyone, let's go," there's a rush to the bus. La Gordita follows slowly behind and is the last to board. She sits in her former seat at the front, across from Houseman, with her back to everyone. Her plump cheeks glisten with tears and ruined mascara. Carol Anderson, seeing them from the side, whispers, "She hasn't even washed!"

The bus pulls out of the courtyard. Sir James and Lady Scott lean back in their corner and go to sleep. The Andersons study their iPhones; Barry checks their route on Google Maps to see when they can expect to be in Manzanillo. Bob and Christine Lethworth talk quietly to each other; only the occasional word is audible to the others: "airport security," "presents," "limousine." The two missionaries study the prospectus for the orphanage they're going to work in in Manzanillo. The front page has an image of Christ with his arms spread wide, and children from a range of backgrounds and races standing safely in their shelter. Houseman crosses his feet and sticks them out into the aisle, folds his arms, and looks bored. He glances occasionally out his window but never at La Gordita. She had her chance.

This time the road is better. In some places it has actually been repaired after the flooding, possibly by army engineers in preparation for a renewed campaign to take back Minatitlán and then Colima. They're getting out just in time. The bus makes good time. At eleven o'clock, Carol Anderson stands up, takes a bag down from the overhead bin, and removes from it a package of sliced ham, a rope of cheese, a small loaf of bread, and two bottles of mineral water.

"Jolly good idea," says Lady Scott, and from her own bag she takes the lunch that Sir James had prepared by the kitchen. There are several plastic containers of chicken sandwiches, sliced carrots and jicama, and curried potato salad. Sir James produces a bottle of red wine and asks the Andersons if they would care for a glass. They all begin eating and drinking. Even Houseman reaches into his jacket pocket and takes out a Ziploc bag containing four hard-boiled eggs and, from his other pocket, two bolillos, already sliced and buttered.

No one offers La Gordita food, it's as though she were not there, and she has forgotten to pack any. She did not have time, in any case, as the subcomandante kept her occupied until minutes before the bus was scheduled to depart. He seemed to have enjoyed her company, and did not want her to leave at all. Stay here with me, he said, though teasingly.

He behaved like a proper gentleman, a real hidalgo. They had a lavish dinner, several bottles of very good wine, a fancy dessert with lots of cream and chocolate. She would like to tell these hypocrites how well the subcomandante treated her. And what he said when she asked him, before she left that morning, why he chose her. Why her? Why not one of the American women, who are more beautiful than she, more sophisticated? "Because you are the real Mexico," he said. "In your veins run the rivers of my country. Your breasts are my Sierra Madres. Your skin has been darkened by the same sun that warms me in the morning. What would I want with those skinny, dried-up gringas? Why would I lower myself to elevate them? No, my little Adelita, it is you I want, you of whom I dream, you for whom I fight."

But she will never tell them that.

Beside her, Houseman brushes crumbs from his lap and begins to hum a tune. It takes her a second to recognize it. It's the American anthem, "The Star-Spangled Banner." He is laughing and humming so loudly the others stop talking and eating to listen. His humming grows more and more insistent, becomes almost aggressive, and he even sings a few words under his breath. "The land of the free, and the home of the brave." Except he sings: and the home of the slave. She realizes he is sending a message to the others, that he is as disgusted with them as she is, he is mocking them, insulting them by turning their sacred hymn into a more accurate, less self-congratulatory song. The land of the free and the home of the slave; how can it be both? He's telling them what he thinks of them. She almost smiles over at him, but then she remembers he didn't share his meal with her, either. He isn't defending her; his is a private vengeance. It has nothing to do with her.

He can tell them what he thinks of them, but she will not. She will not give them that satisfaction. She will not remind them that it is because of her that the subcomandante allowed them to leave. They'll remember that he held them captive; they will forget that it was she who let them go.

Neither will she tell them how, that morning, after she and the subcomandante made love for the last time, and had breakfast in his room, such a fine room, such a delicious breakfast, he went over to the window, where the cuitlacoche was still frantically fluttering back and forth in its cage, and he took the cage to the window and opened it, and let the bird fly off into the sky. They watched until it disappeared behind the monastery beside the Plaza. Then he turned to her and said, Go, Adelita, you must not keep them waiting.

ABOUT "LA GORDITA"

"La Gordita" is a cover of "Boulle de Suif," Guy de Maupassant's first short story, published in 1880. There's a story about de Maupassant that I like. Along with many Parisian intellectuals of his day, de Maupassant hated the Eiffel Tower, "this giant ugly skeleton" that pierced the heart of Paris. Yet most days he ate his midday meal in a restaurant at its base. When asked why, he replied that it was the only place in Paris from which he could not see the Eiffel Tower. This, to me, reflects the kind of ironic stance vis-à-vis reality that exists in much of de Maupassant's writing.

Maupassant (1850–1893), the first writer of the modern short story and (as a protégé of Gustave Flaubert) an early adherent of realism in literature, affected a sardonic detachment from his subjects that infuriated Leo Tolstoy. Taken together, Tolstoy and de Maupassant present a Janus-like figure, with Tolstoy facing implacably towards the past, and de Maupassant looking bemusedly into the future (with Turgenev, who introduced de Maupassant to Tolstoy, caught somewhere in the middle). As in the restaurant at the base of the Eiffel Tower, de Maupassant immersed himself in a reality that he despised, and described it in such uncompromising terms that what he felt about it became clear without his having to beat readers over the head with expository explanations. It is in this ironic detachment that Maupassant's modernist realism lies.

"Boule de suif" translates literally as "ball of suet" or, more colloquially, "tub of lard" – the schoolyard taunt that overweight children have had to endure for decades. In Mexican Spanish, "una gordita" is both a double tortilla stuffed with meat, potatoes, green peppers, and carrots, and also a term of endearment, the feminine form of "gorda," which means chubby. In de Maupassant's story, a coach-full of middle-class burgers are fleeing Rouen in response to the Prussian occupation of the city in 1871, during the Franco-Prussian War. The group includes members of the Rouen bourgeoisie, two nuns, a coarse man who sees himself as a revolutionary, and a somewhat rotund woman who is referred to as a prostitute and is known as Boule de Suif. One day out of Rouen, Prussian soldiers stop the carriage and the passengers are held hostage in a small inn until Boule de Suif agrees to sleep with the Prussian officer in charge; at first, she refuses to debase herself, and the others, too, are shocked by the officer's vulgar demand. But as the hours drag on, each of the other passengers in turn, including the nuns, try to convince Boule de Suif that it is her duty to sacrifice her honour for the good of her betters. Boule de Suif reluctantly gives in to their wishes, sleeps with the officer, and the passengers are allowed to proceed to their destination. But once on their way, rather than show Boule de Suif their gratitude, the passengers revert to treating her like vermin. In their eyes, she has behaved like the prostitute she is. And there the story ends.

"Boule de Suif" was an overnight sensation, catapulting its author to immediate success. By the time the Eiffel Tower opened in 1887, what de Maupassant said about it mattered, although not enough to change the course of history. Maupassant went on to publish three hundred short stories and seven novels in the next thirteen years. Whether early tremendous success is good for a sensitive writer is debatable; Tolstoy thought it was not. In Tolstoy's view, de Maupassant wrote too much, and too little of what he wrote reflected a clear, moral relationship with his subjects. He had talent, Tolstoy said, inasmuch as he "possessed that gift of seeing something that others do not see." But he was weak, in varying degrees, in the three principle requirements Tolstoy considered essential in a great artist – a strong moral stance; clearness of exposition (or beauty of form); and sincerity, by which Tolstoy meant "an undisguised love or hatred for what the writer is describing."

It's true that de Maupassant never actually tells the reader what his strong moral stance is. He disguises what he thinks of his subject, and therefore, according to Tolstoy, the reader does not know what to think of it. When reading *Anna Karenina*, for example, we know what Tolstoy thinks of adultery – it leads inevitably to tragedy; in "Boule de Suif," we don't know what de Maupassant thinks about infidelity; we don't even know what the characters think of it: the men eye Boule de Suif speculatively, and the women are put out that the Prussian officer has chosen Boule de Suif instead of them. Moral ambiguity is as present in de Maupassant's stories as it is in life. Boule de Suif doesn't throw herself under a train, or take poison; she gets back in the carriage and continues on with her journey.

We are, it seems, returning to a Tolstoyan attitude towards morality: ambiguity is out. Editors say readers want a strong, clear, moral stance. They tell us that we have entered a new age of romanticism, in which readers want to be told what to think about what they are reading, and also who it is who is telling them what to think, so they can decide whether or not they will continue reading. Realism is not as attractive as it once was. Perhaps that's why there are more recent translations of Tolstoy and Flaubert than there are of de Maupassant.

But is it not clear, in "Boule de Suif," what de Maupassant thinks of the characters who board the coach? He doesn't step to the side of the stage, like a character in a play by Molière or Brecht, and say, "In my view, these people are self-important, hypocritical buffoons, and their treatment of Boule de Suif is an abomination that should not go unpunished." But do we not know exactly what de Maupassant's view of contemporary reality is from the very fact that their treatment of Boule de Suif *does* go unpunished? That in fact it is rewarded? Maupassant is not so much interested in telling us what he thinks as he is in urging us to examine our own responses to the story. Nonetheless, his own moral stance is unambiguous. Sitting with him at his corner table in that restaurant, we may not be able to see the Eiffel Tower, but we are certainly aware that it is there, and by watching de Maupassant refuse to look up at it, we know exactly what he thinks of it.

THE WOMAN WITH THE DOG

I

AT BREAKFAST EVERYONE was talking about the new student; she'd brought her dog with her. Her dog? Her dog. What kind of dog? Pomeranian, I think, or maybe Shih Tzu, one of those little yappy things, anyway. Jesus, how'd she manage that? Will Esterhaze, whose fourth summer residency this was, and who was by now used to the kinds of craziness students got up to, thought that bringing a dog, even a small one, was unusual enough to warrant further investigation. Whose course was she taking? He glimpsed her during the orientation session later that morning; a thirty-ish, darkish-blonde woman of medium height with, yes, a small, off-white dog in the crook of her arm. She wore a beret the same colour as the dog, which made Esterhaze wonder if she'd knitted it herself from the dog's actual hair; he'd seen Inuit women make sweaters with hair combed from their dogs. But this dog was no Husky; it would have taken her years to get enough hair from this glorified rat to make a beret. Who wore a beret in July, anyway?

He saw her several times that day. She wasn't in his creative nonfiction class, she was taking fiction with Brenda Stokes. Of course. Students always thought they could get away with writing about people they knew by calling it fiction. The woman was invariably alone, except for the dog. He found himself looking for the off-white beret bobbing through the crush of students during the breaks, and being curiously perturbed when he didn't see it. No one seemed to know anything about her. She was from out of town, otherwise she wouldn't be staying at the college; she kept pretty much to herself, and she'd brought her dog with her. It was small enough to fit in one of those carry-on dog things that would fit under the seat in front of her. Everyone referred to her as the woman with the dog.

He didn't know why, but he felt sorry for her. She looked lonely, clutching the dog as a kind of talisman of familiarity. The way his seven-year-old daughter took her koala-bear stuffy to school every day. Anyone who talked to their dog must be lonely, and he could see her clucking away at it, ostensibly to keep it from barking, but more likely to calm herself. Pomeranians, if that was what it was, were a highly excitable breed. When she wasn't carrying it in her arm, she kept it in a cloth shoulder bag, and during meals he could see her passing bits of food to it and saying encouraging things. Who's a good boy, what a handsome boy you are, what silky curly hair you have, or whatever nonsense pet-owners say to their pets. He wished, though, that she were in his creative nonfiction class so he could get to know her a little, or a lot, depending on the kind of things she wrote. He suspected she didn't have much to write about, which would be why she'd gone into fiction.

Esterhaze was forty-five, but he thought of himself as a young forty-something who hadn't changed significantly since he was a young thirty-something. He therefore considered himself and his older students as vaguely contemporary, not the same age, maybe, but the same generation. He was in his second marriage; the first had been when he was a student himself—his degree was in English Literature, but he'd always written — and had ended dramatically after he'd graduated. He and his current wife had two children, Jason, twelve, and Kristal, who was seven. His wife was the same age he was but seemed older. She was tall and thin, not slender as in physically fit but frail, as in neurotically self-controlled. She read books not, he suspected, because she was interested in literature, but so that he could not lay claim to an area of expertise from which she was excluded. She read competitively, mostly books that he would never read, so that her views of them were definitive. She called him William, even though he preferred Will. Will sounded younger. He was of the unvoiced opinion that she was not all that bright. His mind was quick, hers was narrow, not to say obsessive, which he associated with dullness, and her taste in home décor, things like rugs and throw cushions, with which their small house abounded, he found tacky and embarrassing. She followed trends too much for his liking. When the trend was for Provençal, their house became a kaleidoscope of yellows and vibrant blues, as though they were living in one of van Gogh's unmedicated nightmares. During her Mexican phase all the dishware suddenly became glazed pottery painted with unlikely looking blue and white birds and flowers. It got to the point where he disliked being home. It wasn't his home, really, or even theirs, it was hers, and he felt she tolerated him in it only to the extent that he played along with her fantasies. And play along with them he did, when he was there, buying Côte-du-Rhône reds when she was in her Provençal phase, and putting on mariachi music and pouring mezcal when she invited guests over "for a real Mexican comida." But he managed to take himself away from home as often as he could. When he wasn't off researching his books – he wrote about natural history, environmental issues, travel stories – he went to conferences, attended literary festivals, taught summer workshops like this one, and maintained a totally unnecessary office downtown. He had begun having affairs long ago. They came easily, and it was simpler for him to have them than to justify not having them. He saved his mental gymnastics for his work. Perhaps as a consequence, he did not have a high opinion of women. He kept this to himself, obviously, since eighty percent of his students and all his editors were women, and women predominated in his department – the chair was a woman novelist with whom he got on after a fashion, although he hadn't liked, no, hadn't quite grasped the point of, her most recent book. It would be worth his career to be caught speaking disparagingly of women, and he liked teaching, even apart from the money. But he couldn't deny a certain satisfaction when he heard even women talking about the different ways in which men and women thought and wrote. Women might do anything a man could do, but for different reasons. Women are from Heaven, he once quipped at a party, men are from Hell. What he didn't add was that, like Samuel Clemens, he preferred Hell.

Despite – or perhaps because of – his opinion of women,

he felt he needed to have women around him, not all the time, mind you, but at least half the time. Six months on and six months off would be ideal. He thought of women as muses – sometimes they created their own works, but more often they inspired creativity in others – and he considered them his audience. He often found himself bored in all-male company. During late-night drinking sessions in the pub after evening classes, his male colleagues' conversations, no matter how promisingly they began, almost always veered off into the mundane or the maudlin. After a while he would find himself scanning the room for that particular sheen of hair, that slender, sleeveless arm, those unmistakable contours under the table that drew the eye like a moonlit path through a dark forest. He felt he knew how to talk to women, how to hold their interest, when to speak and when to say nothing. He never indulged in empty flirtation or flattery, he spoke as though to people who were as carelessly brilliant as himself. He dripped sarcasm, excoriated false reputations or pretentious poseurs. He betrayed confidences and hinted at the true story behind such-and-such a book or this-or-that celebrated author. He was handsome, he was witty, and he was published – well published, by one of the top houses. And he was never quite serious, never entirely honest. Women found him intriguing. He found women irresistible. Because he thought of them as so unlike men, they were mysterious to him, even dangerous. They were forces to be conquered. Territory to be occupied. Resources to be mined.

All of which, of course, made for a series of short, exhilarating relationships with no suggestion of long-term, complicated entanglements. That was always understood from the start, at least by him. If one of his conquests began making the kinds of demands that someone wanting a longer commitment would make – planning a future together, for example, farther ahead than their next rendezvous – he would feel the relationship becoming an enormous, complex problem, like a short story whose ending was proving trickier than he had anticipated and was threatening to turn into a novella or, worse, a novel. He put such work aside. He didn't write novels. He didn't even read novels; his wife read novels. He wrote shortish works of creative nonfiction. Short, prose pieces, the endings of which were implied in their opening lines. In his writing, as with women, he was good at openings.

ON THE SECOND DAY of the residency, he decided to have lunch in a restaurant in the small town in which the college was located. He knew of a French-style bistro on the main street, where the food was markedly better than that served in the college dining hall. He'd conducted his workshop that morning and all had gone well. He had two student interviews lined up for later in the afternoon. Lunch would be a pleasant interregnum, with a quiet book and a glass or two of wine. He was seated at a table in an interior courtyard with a large tree at the centre and raised garden beds scattered about. Small birds – sparrows? – hopped under the tables, picking up bits of bread crumb. He was looking at the wine list when the woman with the beret walked in and was shown to the table next to his. The dog was in its cloth sling over the woman's shoulder. By holding the wine list at a slight angle he could examine her without seeming to. She was well dressed, carefully made up, nice hands, and she looked intelligent. She might almost have been on holiday, perhaps feeling at loose ends and adventuresome, as one did when one lived with someone but was travelling alone. He waited to see if she would take a phone from her purse and start texting, but she did not. Instead, she picked up the wine list and gave it a vague sort of attention.

Before he joined the department, stories had circulated about the college's creative writing program being a kind of sexual free-for-all, in which faculty and students regularly paired up, formed partnerships, separated, reformed, changed partners, and generally dwelt in a world of their own making. He didn't know if the stories were true, he suspected they were exaggerated, but the days in which they could be true were over. Now a faculty member could be dismissed for looking sideways at a student. Memoranda were regularly sent reminding one to leave one's office door open when meeting with students, male or female; warnings were also issued against seeing students off-campus, particularly alone, and most especially in establishments where alcohol was served. Such as this restaurant. Esterhaze generally adhered to these admonitions – few of his affairs had been with students – but when he looked at the woman sitting so innocently next to him, so calmly spreading butter on a slice of baguette, seemingly so mature, the stories of teacher-student liaisons, of late-night parties in the faculty lounge, or midnight bacchanals on the lakeshore below the college, came back to him as echoes of a less inhibited time, a more creative time, a time when the division between mentor and acolyte was not a wall but a door through which the acolyte was invited to pass. Was, in fact, being groomed to pass. Why else were they there, if not to become part of the literary community to which the faculty presumably already belonged? He remembered the first time he'd had a beer with one of his profs, the author of six or seven well-thought-of books. He'd felt as though he had passed a kind of initiation test, that not just his career but his entire life was undergoing a process of change. He looked at this woman and thought of those days, and his pulse quickened.

The dog, now curled up on the woman's lap, stared at him with its small, beady, black eyes. Esterhaze stared back. She had a nice lap. Her skirt rode halfway up her thigh. When she crossed her legs it would ride higher. The dog gave a sharp, warning bark. Heads turned. The woman looked down at it, said something soothing, crossed her legs, then looked over at Esterhaze, apparently without recognizing him.

"He doesn't bite," she said.

"Would he like some bread, do you think?" he asked.

"I only give him gluten-free," she said.

"Did you have a good workshop this morning?"

She looked up quickly and he saw recognition dawning. "You were at breakfast," she said. "Are you a student, too?"

"Thank you, but no," he said, although he'd had students in his classes who were older than him. "I teach. Creative nonfiction."

"But you're staying at the college?"

"Yes," he said. "I don't live here. They trot me out for summer residencies. I've survived four, so far. This is your first, I take it?"

"Yes," she said. "I thought I'd be terrified, but it's all kind of, I don't know, ordinary."

He shrugged. "Writers are ordinary people when they're not writing," he said. "But it's early yet, I'm sure things will liven up. Brenda's a good teacher." He paused as his steak frites arrived. "My name's Will, by the way," he said, offering his hand. "Will Esterhaze."

She reached across the dog and, placing her hand in his, gave it a small shake. "Jessica Morrow," she said. "And this is J.C." The waiter who had brought his plate had stayed to take her order, and she asked for the salade niçoise.

"Do you take him everywhere?" Esterhaze asked.

She laughed. "Oh, no," she said. "But my boyfriend, he's a marine biologist, is going to be at sea while I'm here, so I had to bring J.C. Didn't I, Poopsie?" she said, lowering her mouth to one of the dog's hairy ears. "Sometimes I call him Poopsie. It's my boyfriend who calls him J.C."

"For Jesus Christ?" he asked. Please don't make her a born-again Christian.

"No, for Jacques Cousteau."

"Ah, marine biology," he said. "Cool."

Her salad arrived and they ate in silence for a while. He signalled for a second glass of wine, and she ordered a glass of pinot grigio. So she knew something about wine, good. He wasn't a wine snob, but he thought people revealed something about themselves by the kind of wine they ordered. There was a big difference between a pinot grigio and a sauvignon blanc, for instance. She had a sense of adventure, a willingness to explore. She had a boyfriend, but a boyfriend who went to sea was less of a problem than a husband. He read his book, hoping he didn't seem like one of those airline passengers who didn't want to speak to his seatmate. Sunlight, filtered through the leaves of the large tree above them, danced on the pages, making the words difficult to read. She took some pages from her bag and set them on the table beside her salade niçoise, but spent more time fussing with the dog than reading them.

They finished lunch at the same time, and he suggested they walk back to the campus together. It wasn't a long distance, but the college was up a steep hill and the day was hot and humid enough to make walking burdensome, and so they walked slowly. They fell into one of those free-ranging conversations about nothing in particular, as if they had no ties, no calls on their freedom, and were happy to talk about whatever came up. So, her boyfriend was a marine biologist, what was his specialty? Marine mammals. Whales? Well, seals, actually, grey seals. Apparently they're declining, which has implications for the cod fishery.

He knew something about the cod fishery. He'd written an article about it for *Canadian Geographic* a few years before. In fact, he'd become something of an expert on the decline of the cod stocks on the Grand Banks. He didn't mention this to Jessica, not wanting to put himself on in the same camp as the boyfriend.

"So you live on the east coast?"

"Yes, you?"

"No, I'm a city boy, for my sins. During the winter term I teach online."

"I grew up in Toronto," she said. "I moved down east when my boyfriend got a job as a post-doc at the oceanography institute." The path took them along a leafy ridge overlooking the lake. "The light off the lake is different than at home. Lighter, somehow."

"Is it? I read somewhere that humans might at one time have been marine mammals. *Homo aquarius* or something like that."

"*Aquaticus*," she corrected him, "but I think that theory's been debunked.

"Ah."

"Well, so Kevin says."

"Kevin?"

"My boyfriend. He's going to meet me in Toronto after the residency, we're thinking of going to Niagara Falls."

"Sounds like a plan. Look, we're back on campus already."

"Just in time," she said, "poor little Jacksy-Wacksy needs some water, don't you Jacksy-Wacksy-Poopsy-Woopsy?"

"See you around, then."

But he felt that a relationship of sorts had been established. That evening, after dinner, alone in his room in the college, he opened a bottle of wine and thought about her as he read his students' papers. They hadn't made any specific plans to meet again, but of course they could hardly not. In the dining hall, if nowhere else. Perhaps he'd sit with her — God, listen to me, it's like I'm back in high school. Can I carry your books, Jessica? Jessie? Jess? Whatever it was, he would call her Jessica. It made her seem older.

It was past midnight when he went to bed. After turning out the light he looked through his window at the circle of rooms around the college's quadrangle. Lights were on in many of the rooms as students revised their poems or essays or short stories for the next day's workshops, or else sat up chatting and drinking, or who knew what else? Which curtained window, he wondered, was hers? Perhaps she felt like a teenager again, too, back in school, not knowing anyone, with strange men eyeing her, cozying up to her, obviously or not so obviously (which was he?) trying to establish a closer relationship with her, their hormones racing. He remembered her slim forearm as she picked up the wine glass, her soft, grey eyes as she looked out over the lake. And he thought about her dog, little Jacksy-Wacksy, and stepped away from the curtains.

"There's something sad about her," he thought. "I must ask Brenda what her fiction is like."

II

THE NEXT DAY it was so stuffy in the un-airconditioned seminar room that he took his students outside, on the quad, where they sat at a picnic table in the shade of a spreading maple. The sky was hazier than usual; over the lake, the sun appeared as a yellow smudge on an expanse of grey canvas. The students sipped from water bottles, but Esterhaze stuck to coffee from a thermos with the college crest on it, partly because he preferred coffee, partly to suggest a degree of seniority over his students, and partly because he could add scotch to it in the afternoons.

He and Jessica met after class in the same restaurant – whether by chance who could tell? – and this time shared a table, again in the leafy courtyard, amid the fluttering of birds. The heat pursued them even there; the waiter brought a small bowl of water for the dog. Esterhaze had no student interviews that afternoon, and Jessica decided to skip the panel on How to Find an Agent. "I can tell you in four words how to find an agent," he said. "Write a good book." After lunch they walked about the town, which consisted of two principal streets and a limited variety of local shops and chain stores, and eventually found themselves in a small park on the shore of the lake. They sat in a belvedere, looking out across the water, as two frustrated lovers might have in the 1890s. J.C. chased and barked at the gulls, sending them into whirling disarray, while Esterhaze and Jessica talked about writing; he warned her of the precarious life of a writer, which she countered with the even more precarious life of a post-doc. Was she implying that an affair with him would be a step up? A holiday from home?

Great: that was how he would view it. After a while they went into a pub called the Barley Corn, took a corner table and ordered a half litre of wine. He was aware, he thought they both were, that they had crossed the boundary of the proscribed professor-student relationship, that if they were seen cozying up they'd both be in trouble, but she seemed not to find anything amiss and he didn't draw the obvious to her attention. They weren't cozying up anyway, they were simply two adults relaxing in one another's company. They were being writers together; a fellowship, not a courtship.

On the way back to the college, they stopped at a deli and he bought a few things to eat in his room, because, as he explained, he liked to get up early and do some writing before the dining hall opened for breakfast. "What are you working on?" she asked, and he answered her vaguely: "A couple of short pieces." He bought a pound of coffee, some cheese, slices of Virginia ham, a small loaf of gluten-free bread, and six bananas. She stood by the door looking away as he paid for his purchases.

"Tell me about your work," he said to her as they resumed walking. "Have they workshopped your story yet?"

"Oh," she said. "It's nothing, really." She shook her head. "I've been working on something, a long thing, I don't know what it is, maybe a novella? It's partly fiction, I suppose, but there's a lot in it that isn't."

He realized that her appearance of being bored was an act, a façade hiding her inner suspicion that she wasn't good enough to be in the program, to be talking about writing with a real writer.

"I'd like to see it, if you'll let me," he said.

"Really?" she said. "Seriously?"

"Seriously. Don't tell Brenda."

"That would be awesome."

They were halfway up the hill to the college, at a point where the path cut through a grove of cedars before opening onto a playing field. Had there been a building here at one time, he wondered? Before the college, it would have been an idyllic setting for a small cottage. He felt a sudden, cool breeze coming up from the lake.

"'Where'er you walk, cool gales shall fan the glade,'" he said; "'Trees, where you sit, shall crowd into a shade.'"

She made no reply, but stopped and looked at him. He took her in his arms and kissed her. She tried to back away, but then kissed him back as avidly as he, and he was carried away by her fragrance, the taste of her lip balm, how small her waist was under his hand, and how, when she'd tried to back away, she in fact pressed her pelvis against his. They stepped apart and looked around quickly to see if anyone was watching. There was no one, and they kissed again.

"Let's go somewhere," he said, taking her hand and hardly daring to breathe.

"But where?" she said. "Not to the college, surely?"

"It'll be all right. You can't see my door from the office, and everyone else will be at the panel."

"What about, you know, protection?"

"Not a problem. I've had a vasectomy."

Her eyes glistened with a mournful desire. He let go of her hand as they crossed the field. His room was airless, and he opened a window, keeping the Venetian blind closed. They undressed quickly, their mouths touching; he pulled back the coverlet on his bed and they were under it, furiously entwining, while the little dog ran around the room sniffing at chair legs, shoes, her clothes on the floor. He thought of all the other women with whom he had been in similar circumstances, the lovely, lighthearted eagerness of the first time, the amazement of mutual discovery, the happiness, and the gratitude for that happiness. So unlike his wife, for whom lovemaking seemed a denial of her rights as a woman, an unfortunate compulsion of his, and a concession granted by her for future considerations. Some of his lovers had been like that, too, beautiful and cold, calculating exactly how much they were willing to give and what they were going to get in return. He'd got so he could tell just how long an affair was going to last by the amount of lace on their matching underwear.

But he sensed none of that with Jessica. She was as eager and open as he was. After the climax, the dénouement. She lay quietly in his arms, her eyes wide with surprise. She was so fragile, so vulnerable. Of course she was thinking about her boyfriend, of course she was sad that she was hurting him. That was what he liked about her, her instinctual understanding that pain was an unavoidable part of life, and therefore essential, that what was important was that we worked through our pain to reach the ecstasy that beckoned from the other side. And oh, that the ecstasy was worth it. It outweighed the pain and the heartache and the disappointment. And that pain and heartache and disappointment diminished each time they were experienced, whereas the ecstasy never faded, was as intense each time it was achieved, if anything it increased in intensity.

She propped herself on an elbow to face him, pulling a strand of damp hair from her mouth with a painted fingernail. It was a familiar, almost iconic pose: show a woman in a film in such a position and you know at once she's an adulteress.

"This is so wrong," she said.

"This is exactly right," he countered.

"I shouldn't have let you kiss me."

"But you did."

"I tried not to."

"So did I," he lied.

"Now your opinion of my writing is worthless," she said.

"All opinions are worthless," he said. "I don't give opinions."

She smiled. "What do you give, then?"

"Assessments. I give the truth, honest and unvarnished."

"Oh dear, I don't know if I want that, either."

"I do it all up in a nice package."

"I'm hungry," she said. "Do you know what I was thinking when you were buying that ham? I was thinking, Good, I really like ham. Isn't that shameful of me?"

"Not shameful. Shameless."

He got up and, still naked and semi-erect, made two ham sandwiches and opened a bottle of wine. They ate sitting cross-legged on the bed. Each time he lowered his head to bite into the sandwich or drink his wine he let his eyes settle on her breasts. They were, of course, perfect, her nipples, still slightly swollen from their recent exuberances, pointed at precisely the right angle from her sternum to allow him to imagine resting his head between them. He felt himself stirred anew. She noticed and, after giving a small piece of ham to the dog, set their picnic aside, lay back and reached for him. But there was such sadness in her eyes that he hesitated. "What is it?" he asked, stretching himself on top of her. "Whatever you say," she said, "this is wrong. You have no idea how wrong this is." "And yet we're doing it," he said. "Yes, we are," and nothing more was said for quite a while.

Still later, with the lights in his room out, they opened the curtains and looked down onto the darkened quadrangle.

Tall maples and poplars ballooned above the rooftops; at their bases, soft lights illuminated shrubs and flowerbeds in cedar-chip mulch and separated by grassy paths. It looked to Esterhaze as though they were presiding over a well-tended fairyland, like Oberon and Titania. He opened a second bottle.

"You do this a lot, don't you," she said, still looking down onto the quad.

"What? This? No, not for a long time."

"So you would know if you had anything I might get?"

"I would. And I don't."

She didn't turn away from the window. He put the bottle on the desk, went over to the window with the duvet and put it around her like a cape. Her shoulders felt cold.

"Are you thinking of your boyfriend?" he asked her. "What's his name? Kevin?" Was it tactless to mention him now? Or was it a measure of how honest they could be with each other?

"No, I'm not worried about Kevin. It's not him I've betrayed, it's myself. I thought I was different from so many other women I know, who cheat on their boyfriends all the time, it's like, why even have a boyfriend at all except to help pay the bills and shovel the snow off the car? I think it's disgusting. They're such hypocrites. I'm not like that. Or at least I didn't think I was. But this is different, isn't it? It's not like I'm hooking up with someone I just met at a party. I really like you. You've been really sweet with me. And Kevin, he's, well, he's *Kevin*, he's a scientist, a nerd, he spends all his time in his lab looking through a microscope at seal sperm. It's all he ever talks about. I try to tell him it's as boring as a sack of mud, but he says, Boring? Sperm is the stuff of life! How can it be boring? I never thought sex could be boring, but you know what? I'm standing here beside you, and I know pretty much exactly how many millions of your tiny little sperm cells are right this minute swimming from my vagina to my uterus!"

"Really? How many?"

"Well, I guess zero in your case, but normally about two hundred and fifty million. But who cares! It's boring! Still, I swore I'd never be unfaithful to him. And here I am, and it was great, don't get me wrong, but I hate that I did it. Is that schizo or what?"

"It isn't schizo. And you aren't betraying yourself by sleeping with me, you're betraying yourself by feeling guilty about it. You're not hurting Kevin by doing this. This is normal, it's healthy. It's listening to your body instead of that little Puritanical voice in your head that was put there by who the hell knows who, society, your parents, somebody who isn't you." God, how many times had he made this argument in just this situation? Why do women insist on beating themselves up over having a bit of a fling? Were they all raised to think that if you enjoyed something, it must be wrong, or bad for you, that desire for a man was a sin? Hadn't they noticed that they only start crying mea culpa *after* they've had the good time? Sure, he'd thought of his wife while he was making love with Jessica, but that was to help him *justify* his actions, not turn them into an occasion for self-flagellation. He put his arm around her and pulled her closer. She rocked away and then back, and looked at him with a mixture of happiness and dread. "Nothing bad is going to happen," he said. "This is just between us." He kissed her eyes, her cheeks, her ears. They sat on the bed and he pulled the duvet over their heads to make a tent. "No one gets in here but us," he said. She kissed him. There was a sharp little bark from beside the bed. "Well, no one but us and Jacques Cousteau," he said, and they laughed.

Towards midnight, he suggested they get dressed and go down to see the lake under the full moon. There wasn't a soul on the quad, and they passed through the college gates unseen. The college was situated at the top of a bluff, not a cliff exactly but steep enough that the path down to the lake switched back and forth through the trees. He had taken it many times over the years, and always counted the curves. Eleven. He'd brought a blanket and the rest of the second bottle of wine. They sat with the blanket over their shoulders, looking out over the lake's whispering blackness, at the shimmering wavelets and the brightened sky above the water. They remained silent for most of the rest of the night. The lake's gentle rhythm promised peace, continuance, reminding them that nothing that happened to mere humans made an iota of difference to the universe. Life was permanent, and therefore salvation must be possible, because where there is permanence there is the certainty of continuance. Kevin might find them out, Esterhaze's wife might suspect something (she always did), Esterhaze might be fired and Jessica sent home in disgrace, and still the lake would break quietly over these glistening rocks and the moon would watch it doing so. He looked at her and wondered if she, like him, was marvelling at the thought that two days ago she was unblemished and innocent, blithely looking forward to the workshop, as aflutter as a ninth-grader on Labour Day, and now here she was sitting beside her lover watching the pre-dawn light play its roseate fingers softly over the distant tree tops. Nothing, he thought, was inherently good or evil until thinking made it so.

Okay, not original, but he felt the truth of it. He could feel himself feeling it. God, he thought, I could write with this woman.

"It's getting early," she said.

"Yes, we'd better go back." He looked up at the path nervously, imagining his class emerging from the shrubbery and discovering them. "You go first, I'll come up in a few minutes."

She scooped up J.C., who was sleeping in his carry bag, and disappeared up the path.

After that, although they never sat together in the dining hall, they met every day for lunch, always in the same bistro. The waiter got to know them and could attest to the innocence of their meetings, if it came to that. After lunch they went back to Esterhaze's room and frolicked in bed for two hours before his interviews and the panel discussions. In the evenings, they walked together to the student readings, to student film night, to the gatherings in the Barley Corn, and sometimes on a sudden impulse he would pull her into the bushes and kiss her as he had that first day in the cedar grove. Her loveliness, the strong, pungent scent of the cedars and the nearness of the lake made him giddy. She told him one day she was having a hard time sleeping, that she longed to be with him, they didn't have much time, couldn't she spend the night in his room? Although the prospect terrified him – in previous affairs, this was when he would begin to plan his escape – he joyfully agreed. He left the pub early and she stayed for another drink with her fiction class, then said she was going to work on revising her story. But once in his room she was struck again by the guilt she had felt earlier, and told him she was afraid he would think her a faithless tart. He laughed and hugged her, and they made love like a married couple, their clothes neatly hung in his wardrobe, her toothbrush in the plastic glass beside his sink, her little dog curled up on the rug near the bed. Esterhaze lay awake for a long time. He usually read before falling asleep, but he didn't want to disturb her. She slept with her mouth partly open, like a child, or a portrait of purity in a children's book.

The boyfriend, Kevin, who was supposed to join her after the course, emailed to say his ship was delayed and he wouldn't be able to make it. Esterhaze had mixed feelings about the change in plans. Would she want to stay on anyway, and spend time with him in Toronto? That would be nice, but complicated. But she changed her ticket and prepared to go home early. She always met Kevin's ship when it arrived in port, she said, like a besotted sailor's girl. He was relieved.

"I'll miss you," he said on their last evening together. They had gone back to his room after the final panel discussion, but she decided not to spend the night. He was to catch an early train to the city; her shuttle to the airport wasn't until noon. Everyone would be dashing about packing, handing in their keys, saying goodbye, someone would surely notice that she wasn't in her room. She didn't cry. She looked at him sadly, as though having already distanced herself from him; he thought he saw a tinge of relief in her eyes, too, a sense that life was soon to return to the normal and the known. Or perhaps he was projecting. His wife said he often did that.

"No, you won't," she said, smiling. "But I'll write to remind you. Not emails, real letters, on paper."

"That will be marvellous." He gave her his office address.

"I love you," she said. "This has been the most fantastic thing that has ever happened to me. But I'm afraid it will end here."

"Of course it won't," he said. "I'll keep you right here with me," and he touched his heart. "You and your little dog." Where was the little bugger? Oh, there, she mustn't forget it.

When she was gone, he walked about his room, consumed by a strange restlessness. Should he pack tonight? No, plenty of time in the morning. He'd be able to read in bed before going to sleep, and work in the morning before breakfast. He hardly remembered what book he'd started. He sat in the leather easy chair and tapped his fingers on the arms. He wanted a drink. He poured himself the last of the scotch. He wondered what he was feeling, and realized with a start that it was loneliness. He really *would* miss her, damn it. He hadn't been lying, and that made him feel virtuous. If she'd doubted him, perhaps sensing in him an impatience of which he himself had been unaware, it would have been shrewd of her, but she would have been wrong. Each of his women had been different, of course, but the overall effect had always been one of sameness, and it was possible he had been unable to hide his assumption that she, in the end, though lovely and gentle and really quite beautiful, and passionately abandoned in bed, would be not that different from the others. They all said they loved him, they all swore they would never forget him, that they would write, and some of them did, for a time, and he wrote back, for a time. But then their real lives resumed, like a forest filling a gap in the canopy made by a lightning-struck tree. Had something in his manner, in his voice or his eyes, betrayed that maturer, but in this case erroneous, view? He hoped not. They'd made each other happy. She was happy now, tonight, humming to herself as she packed her things, remembering how he had unhooked this bra, pulled down these panties, undid these buttons. But tomorrow, on the plane, or later in her apartment, her mind would slowly pull itself away from the past and become occupied with the near at hand. As would his. His missed her now, at this moment, and he enjoyed missing her. But the moment would pass.

His dreamy eye lighted on his desk. There, in the middle of it, beside his computer, was a stack of papers he didn't recognize. He jumped up. It was a manuscript. The top page read: "Small Fish, by Jessica Morrow." Oh Jesus, her story. He'd forgotten all about it. Shit, this business was a long way from being over.

III

THE STORY WASN'T BAD. He wasn't good with fiction, but he had an ear for elements in any writing that rang true, and he thought that some sections of her story sounded more genuine than others. He assumed that those sections were fictionalized versions of her own life. The east coast setting, the nerdy partner, the recurring arguments about having children when they weren't married (he for, she against), all felt to him as though they came from somewhere deeper than she had reached with the fictional overlay, which had to do with a snowstorm and a power outage. He wrote her a careful email telling her he thought the story was very good, very compelling, but had she considered writing it as nonfiction? It seemed to him the nonfictional elements were stronger.

"Do you really think I should be writing nonfiction?" she emailed back. "I mean, really?"

"I do," he wrote.

In the city, as predicted, he slid easily into his old routines. He walked his daughter to school every weekday, continued on to his office, had lunch with friends, started teaching online, easing a new crop of students into realizing the possibilities of creative nonfiction. In the evenings at home he read, or watched television, or worked with his wife in the garden. He thought often about Jessica, wondering what she was doing at that moment. What *would* she be doing? He hadn't the foggiest, he knew almost nothing about her. How did she pass her days? He imagined her doing whatever she did with the same ardour and sweetness she had shown in his bed – noodling in the afternoons with her insensitive scientist boyfriend, for example – which fired in him a jealousy he hadn't experienced before. He preferred to imagine her looking up from a book (perhaps one of his?) at the light slanting in from the Atlantic, thinking of their nights together, the vigil beside the lake. He'd expected that after a month or two as the steady, reliable homebody, his memories of her would become cloudy, that eventually she would fade into the faceless oblivion his former lovers occupied. Instead, he found himself remembering odd bits: her smile, the way she nibbled at her dog's ear, how she forgot to stop talking when she took a sip of wine, her passion for the short stories of Alistair MacLeod. This time, his memories didn't dissipate. If anything, they became more vivid. He'd be sitting in his study and a dog would bark on the street, and he'd be assailed by the clearest picture of little J.C.'s ridiculous head poking out from under his duvet, and the breath would leave his lungs. His wife preparing fish for dinner produced in him an almost uncontrollable longing to get into his car and drive somewhere, to be in a hotel room, alone, and to call Jessica and beg her to join him.

And she would. These irrational urges, these fantasies, he told himself, and never mind what he'd told Jessica, were unhealthy, they were splitting him apart. He'd always been able to compartmentalize, to keep his home life with wife and kids separate from life with his dalliances, but this time the affair with Jessica kept bleeding into his marriage, and he would bounce dangerously back and forth between frenzied happiness and depthless despair, neither of which states were like him. One day in a shopping mall with his wife and children, he saw a woman ahead of them wearing an off-white beret, and his heart nearly burst through his ribcage. He had to get a grip. His wife remarked on it that evening at dinner — ah, those dinners in college with Jessica and his students around the table, all yammering away about first-person narrative and pathetic fallacies. How exhilarating it had been.

"What is it with you?" his wife said. "Some kind of late-onset bipolar affective disorder or something?"

"Can't a fellow be happy sometimes and other times not?"

Later, when the children were in bed, she looked at him witheringly. "Give her up, William. I don't know who she is this time, and I don't care. But give her up or I'll expose you to the college."

But he couldn't give her up. He thought if he could talk to someone, even in general terms, it might relieve the pressure on his brain. But all his women friends were also friends of his wife, and would undoubtedly sister up against him. And his male friends, well, his male friends were either happily married or wished they were, and would not sympathize with the way he was risking the settled life he had achieved. Or they would rib him about being a rake, which this time he didn't feel he was. He attempted to bring the subject up at lunch one day with a fellow writer he knew. "I met this fantastic woman last summer when I was teaching at Dorset," he said.

But his friend affected not to hear, and changed the subject. Later, as he was getting into a taxi, the friend said, "You mentioned Dorset College. That sounds like a good gig. Who would I call to apply for something like that?"

To make matters worse, it began to look more and more as though Jessica had dumped him. The letters she'd promised to send him never came. It saddened him, but perhaps it was just as well. A month later, she did send him an innocuous email – he imagined her writing it late at night, after Kevin had gone to bed, or when he was at sea, grappling with seals – saying she'd taken his advice about the story and was writing it as nonfiction. She'd have to change a few names, though, what did he think? What did he think? He'd have to think about what he thought. Changing the names would make it fiction, he wrote back. And you're okay with that? she asked. Okay with what? Had he missed something? What was she writing about, anyway? But he was happy she was still thinking about him, caring what he thought.

In October, when the trees in the park where he took his children had turned such bright shades of red and yellow that playing under them was like lingering under a raging fire, an editor at *Canadian Geographic* called and asked if he'd be interested in doing a follow-up article about the apparent resurgence of the Grand Banks cod fishery. He was about to pass on it when he remembered Jessica saying something about her boyfriend studying grey seals and their impact on the cod population. Would the magazine send him east to interview a few experts and, you know, get a better feel for the lay of the land? It would. The sudden prospect of seeing Jessica again almost made him drop the phone.

A week later he was on the east coast. He'd called the oceanographic institute and arranged to meet Kevin in his lab in the morning, after which he would take Kevin out for lunch and then maybe Kevin could show him some of the more salient features of the town he lived in. If Kevin had a wife or a girlfriend, Esterhaze wrote, she'd be welcome to join them. Kevin had a better idea. Why didn't they go to Kevin's apartment for lunch, after which the three of them, "me and you and Jessie, my girlfriend," could head out to see the sights. An excellent plan, he replied. Jessie. His room at the Lord Nelson Hotel looked over a cemetery. The trees among the gravestones were just beginning to turn. Things happened more slowly here than in the city, and yes, indeed, the light was different.

He'd expected Kevin's biology lab to be less advanced, too. He imagined wooden benches and Bunsen burners and maybe a wall of smelly cages with seals in them. Instead, the lab was more like an iStore: bright LED lights, white tables and chairs in grey cubicles, with desktop computers, huge monitors, banks of blinking hard drives. Kevin was tall and lanky with oversized glasses that kept his hair out of his eyes. He wore a white lab coat and had very large feet and hands. He stood up when Esterhaze entered and noisily dragged a chair from another cubicle. They talked for over an hour, Kevin bringing up screen after screen of indecipherable data: rows of numbers, mysterious acronyms with Greek letters, and lots and lots of charts and diagrams. Almost no words. He kept trying to get Kevin to describe something, but it was as though his entire universe had been reduced to numbers and vectors. Kevin showed him only one thing he thought he could use: a chart with two data sets plotted on it, one showing the decline in the grey seal population, and the other showing the gradual increase in the cod population. "See, the cod stocks start to increase about a year after the seal population starts to crash." "Why do you think that is, Kevin?" "Well, it could be because when there are fewer seals, they eat fewer fish. And it *would* take a year or so for that to show in the data." "Why are there fewer seals?" Kevin favoured him with a seraphic smile. "'Why' is a religious question, Will," he said. "Okay, sorry," said Esterhaze, trying not to show impatience, "what do you think is driving down the seal population?" "Well, for the past eight years we've been looking at declining sperm counts in adult grey seals. See here," and he brought up another series of charts and diagrams. But Esterhaze had what he wanted. He wrote "declining sperm counts" and closed his notebook. "Can you send me that chart, the one that shows the seal and cod populations going up and down?" "Sure." Kevin clicked a few keys on his computer and it was done. "One more question, Kev," he said. "What do you think might be causing lower sperm counts?" Not that it mattered to his story. "We don't know, Will, could be a lot of things: an aging seal population, pollution, something lacking in the diet." "Like cod, maybe?" "Maybe." And that was it. He could leave.

They drove to Kevin's apartment for lunch. "You're going to like Jessie," Kevin said. "She's a writer, too."

"Really?" he said. "I'm sure I will."

Jessica's reaction when he walked into the apartment was everything a drama coach could have asked for. She was taking a kettle off the gas stove, and when she looked up and saw Esterhaze she dropped the kettle. Water sloshed from the spout and put out the flame. She backed away from the stove and Kevin dove for it, turning off the gas and wiping water from the burner with a tea towel. Above his back, Jessica stared at Esterhaze with wide, panic-stricken eyes. She looked, he thought adoringly, as she had just before having an orgasm, a mixture of puzzlement and fear and wonder, as though she were passing through the pain and was about to throw herself into the ecstasy. She said nothing. Kevin noticed nothing. Lunch, lentil soup and some kind of meat-paste sandwiches, was on the kitchen table, and they sat. Since there were three of them it was difficult for her not to sit beside him, but she managed to keep her chair closer to Kevin's, so that he had almost half the table. She didn't look at him. At one point Kevin got up to go to the bathroom, and she finally met his eyes.

"What the fuck?" she hissed at him. "Are you insane?"

He had his story ready. "I have to do this article, and I remembered you telling me—"

"Why didn't you warn me?"

"I thought you would tell me not to come."

"You're fucking right I would have told you not to come." Tears brightened her eyes; with a practised hand she wiped them away. Kevin returned and they continued the meal in silence, until Kevin broke it with a renewed stream of seal data.

"Sperm count in adult males over five years old has dropped by fifteen percent over the past—"

"Kevin," Jessica said, "can we please not talk about seal sperm while we're eating?"

"What? Really? Does it bother you, Will?"

"It bothers *me*," she said. "Very much."

"It can wait," said Esterhaze. "I have all I need for the article, anyway."

"It's just numbers," said Kevin, sulkily. He was a large adolescent, he had no idea what a treasure he had in Jessica. She was entirely wasted on him. His forehead was still marked by acne, and Esterhaze guessed that on warm summer days he rode a skateboard to the university. Esterhaze suddenly remembered the little dog, and almost blurted out, Where's Jacques Cousteau?, but stopped himself just in time. They finished lunch and were sitting around the table with their tea. Kevin asked Jessica politely if he could talk about seals again. She sighed.

"As I was saying, male potency in adult seals has dropped," and he cited some figures that meant nothing to Esterhaze.

"How do you get the seal sperm?" Esterhaze asked him, feeling Jessica's eyes on him.

"Pardon?" Kevin said, blinking.

"Seal sperm. How do you actually acquire it?"

"We extract it from the females' vaginas after copulation. Why?"

"You *what?*" spurted Jessica.

"What's wrong?"

"You never told me that!"

"How did you think we got it?"

"I don't *know*, Kevin, I guess I thought the usual way."

Kevin laughed a little nervously. "Is that what you thought I was doing out there on the ice floes? Jerking off male seals?"

Jessica clapped her hands over her ears. "Jesus Christ! No, I guess you wouldn't want to disturb the fucking males, would you. Far better to traumatize the poor females. Holy shit!" And she stood up and stomped out of the kitchen. Esterhaze heard her footsteps go down a hall and a door slam.

"She'll be all right," Kevin said. "She's been acting really weird lately."

"Maybe I should go," he said. "We can paint the town another time."

"What time's your flight?"

"Six-thirty-five." He wasn't exactly lying. He was flying to St. John's at six-thirty-five, but the next day.

"I'll drive you to your hotel."

Jessica didn't come out to say goodbye. At the car, he told Kevin he'd left his notebook in the kitchen, and went back upstairs and knocked on the door. She opened it and he went in. "I'm sorry," he said. "I had to see you. I've been going crazy."

"Me, too," she said. "I was just getting over it."

"Please understand, Jessica. Please!"

She paled and looked at him fearfully. "I do understand. But it's been hell for me. I can't go through it all again."

"I thought in July that that was the end of it," he said, "but I haven't stopped thinking about you. I haven't been able to think of anything else."

"I know, me too. The whole time. Thinking of you was the only way I *could* stand it. But this is crazy, showing up here like this."

He tried to kiss her but she put a hand on his chest and held him off. "What are you doing? We're both crazy. You have to go . . . Go now! Please, Will!"

"I'm staying at the Lord Nelson," he said. "Room five-fourteen. I'll be there until late tomorrow afternoon."

"No. No fucking way. No!"

"Five-fourteen."

"Will, I . . . I can't!"

He went back downstairs, all his hopes poured into that ellipsis, the desperate look she'd given him as she closed the door.

Of course, she wouldn't join him at the Lord Nelson. And of course, she did. Not that night, but the next morning, after Kevin had gone to the lab. He opened the door and she flew into his arms. They spent the whole morning in bed. She didn't dare go out for lunch, it was such a small town, so they dressed and ordered room service: chicken Caesar salads and a bottle of pinot grigio – he'd remembered. They ate at a small table set by one of the windows looking out over the cemetery, happy as two otters, the midday sun pouring over them through the thin, musty curtains. The Atlantic reflected a different quality of light than the lake, didn't it, she said, and he agreed, not that they could see the ocean from there, but there was a cooler tone, a brooding greyness in the air above the headstones. Of course it was nearly winter. They talked about her writing, how her story was coming along.

"Oh, I've put 'Small Fish' aside for now. I'm working on something else."

"Well, don't throw it out. It's good."

"I'm taking your advice. Writing creative nonfiction and keeping everything just the way it happened, warts and names and all. It's really exhilarating. I'm loving it."

"Good. What's it about?"

"Us."

"Us! You mean—?" His stomach gave a lurch. The wine sloshed tempestuously in his glass.

"Don't worry," she said. "I'm not going to publish it." She smiled at him. "You're safe."

"You could go back to fiction," he said, his heart pounding.

"Will," she said after a pause, "what am I to you?"

"What?" he said. "What do you mean?"

"I mean, what am I? Where am I on your list of priorities?"

"There's no list, Jessica. That isn't how it works. Lists are for people like Kevin. Life isn't organized into neat little rows of lines and figures. It's a mess. It's like my desktop in my office, everything jumbled up and chaotic. Nothing's in a prescribed place, everything just is. I know where everything is, but it isn't in any kind of order. It's just there."

"So I'm just here?"

"Yes. Exactly. We're both just here."

"And tomorrow or the next day someone else will be here?"

"No, I told you, you'll always be here."

"That's bullshit, Will," she burst out. "It's just plain-ass laziness. You do that so when something new comes along you don't have to think about it. You just toss it on the pile and assume it'll still be there when you need it."

"No, I think about everything all the time."

"Do you want my advice? Will you take some advice from me?"

"Of course."

"Clear your desk. Make a list."

"Jessica."

"And then let me know where I am on it. Because if we're going to keep doing this, I need to know."

IV

They continued seeing each other over the winter. Jessica's mother still lived in Toronto, in the same house Jessica had grown up in, and every month or two she would have a health crisis, she'd be diagnosed with breast cancer, or she'd fall down the porch steps, or slip on some ice and sprain an ankle, and Jessica would have to fly to Toronto to look after her. Just for a few days. She didn't know if Kevin believed her or not, but she knew he wouldn't phone her mother to check. Her mother had never liked Kevin, and he hadn't spoken to her in the four years they'd been together. That was largely why she didn't want children. She called Kevin, usually from her mother's house, when Kevin could hear her mother talking in the background. Esterhaze rented the top floor of a quaint little Airbnb he knew, and they would spend long winter days together huddled under a madly striped duvet and, between bouts of lovemaking, eat delicacies from his favourite bakery. No one knew or even wondered where they were.

One morning, as he walked his daughter to her school, which was on the way to the Airbnb, he was thinking of the day ahead, how much he was looking forward to seeing Jessica again, realizing for the hundredth time that he'd never felt this way about an affair before. This thing with Jessica, whatever it was, was more permanent than an affair, more stable even than his marriage. The thought staggered him. It would be easier to give up his marriage than to give up Jessica. But of course, he couldn't leave his wife. She would expose him to the college. He looked at his daughter. And of course, he could never leave his children.

"Daddy," said Kristal, "why is there thunder in winter?"

He smiled down at her. He almost said, 'Why' is a religious question, but he thought better of it. "Thunder is the sound that lightning makes," he said. "You know how when you pull on a wool sweater and there's a spark of electricity you hear little clicks?" She nodded. "Well, lightning is a huge, huge, gigantic spark of electricity, and thunder is the loud, loud noise it makes."

"Oh." She looked confused and a little disappointed. "Mommy said it was God rolling bowling balls down his hallway."

"Really?" he said. A religious answer to a religious question. "I guess there are two ways of looking at everything."

"I like Mommy's way better."

The exchange made him realize he was living a double life. One was plain, ordinary, undisguised, out in the open, following all the conventions of society. To anyone watching, he had a wife and two children, a modest but adequate house, a serviceable car, a job of sorts, friends that he and his wife saw regularly, others they saw less often. His wife's father was a retired naval officer and considered Esterhaze unseaworthy. His own parents were dead, but he had an aunt whom he saw at Christmas and weddings. This was who he was. But it was the other, secret life with Jessica that, to him, was his real life. His constant life. It was his undisguised, public life that was the false one, insufferably false: nothing he did in that life mattered to him. His wife could leave him, his children grow up and move away, his friends could drift off, and still he would be the same person inside – precisely because he had this other, secret life to turn to. It seemed to him that everyone had a secret life that was more real to them than their public lives. No wonder, he thought, there was such a furor over the invasion of privacy by so much digital surveillance, cell phones reporting our whereabouts to someone, our texts and Instagram and Facebook posts going into some advertiser's database. It wasn't because we're afraid that our bad habits would be exposed; it's because we are being deprived of our real selves, the selves that no one else, not even our most intimate companions, are supposed to know about. And we need both lives, the public and the private, in order to be whole.

He dropped his daughter off at school and continued walking thoughtfully. Jessica had arrived the night before and stayed with her mother, but by now she was waiting for him at the Airbnb. The moment he got there she flung herself on his chest, looking pale and distraught. He kissed her and asked her what was wrong. Had something happened? Had her boyfriend discovered them? She shook her head and began crying. Thinking it best to let her cry for a while, he went into the kitchen and put the kettle on to make coffee.

"Don't you find this all so sad?" she said, coming into the kitchen after him. "Isn't this the most sordid thing you've ever done? I mean, lying to everyone, hiding, cheating on people who love us, terrified of being discovered? All the subterfuge, the falseness. This isn't who we are. This morning I told my mother I was going to the library to write! So now my writing, which is so important to me, the most important thing in my life, is just a pretext for meeting with my lover! What do you tell your wife?"

He shrugged. "She doesn't ask anymore."

"I hate this. Don't you?"

"You mustn't see it like that, my darling! You're dwelling on the bad side, the public side. Just now, on the way here, I was thinking that this *is* my real life, this is the self I want to be, and I'm happy that it's concealed from all those vulgar people who would only judge us and condemn us. Don't you see? Without our public lives, there wouldn't be this wonderful private life!"

But he understood now that, because this was no brief affair, he could not reassure himself that everything would be better when the affair was over. They would go on loving each other, and there would be no time when it would be better. He went to her and held her. Over her shoulder, in a full-length mirror hanging on the door of the hall closet, he saw for the first time that he was aging. He was no longer the handsome young man, the promising young writer, the carefree man about town. What had happened to him? Had love done this? He saw his hands on Jessica's trembling back, and thought that she, too, would age, that this clandestine love of theirs was going to take its toll on her, as it had on him, was already taking its toll. Look at us, crying and patting each other on the back like cousins at a funeral. He could not leave his wife. She would instantly tell the college he was having an affair with a student, and his life would be ruined. No other program would hire him, probably no publisher would want to publish his work. He would lose access to his children. Why did Jessica love him? Why did she still love him? Other women had loved him; even when he said or did something cruel or callous, they had gone on loving him. It hadn't made sense to him then, but now he realized it hadn't made sense because he hadn't loved them. Not once, not even his wife. Never in his life had he been in love. Not until now, now that his looks were fading, his hair was turning at the temples, and no doubt Kevin would say his sperm count was in decline. She went on loving him because that was what love did. That was love's cruel reality.

Look at him. Look at her. Love was transforming them both, and they were powerless to stop it.

"Don't cry, my sweet," he said, patting her back. "We'll think of something."

"But what?" she said, leaning away from him. "As long as you stay with her we'll be living in chains. This isn't freedom, Will, this is the worst kind of prison. I beg you to leave her, Will. Leave her! It's the only way we'll ever be happy."

"I need to think about it," he said. "This is all so new. I need time."

He saw how the morning would go. With endless, circular talk. Oh, God. He couldn't leave his wife, and he couldn't leave Jessica. Things would go on as they were, forever. Their secret lives and their public lives were not in harmony, they were clashing. They were in a terrible imbalance. They would go on being writers, they would write great things, but there was one great thing they could never write about, and that was the one thing that mattered.

But for now their love was in its infancy; they could go on as though they had all the time in the world to let it mature.

"About your story," he said. She was still sobbing in his arms. "The one about us."

She sniffed. "What about it?"

"How does it end?"

Over his shoulder, she could see through the front window. He saw it too, in the hall mirror. There was a low rumble of thunder, and now it was beginning to snow.

ABOUT "THE WOMAN WITH THE DOG"

This story is my cover of Chekhov's "The Lady with the Dog," published in 1899, when he was thirty-nine, after having moved from St. Petersburg to his dasha in Yalta, a resort town on the south coast of the Crimean Peninsula (now Ukraine). He hoped to find relief from his tuberculosis, but he did not recover; he stayed on in Yalta and only occasionally returned to Moscow to escape the boredom of living in what he called "hot Siberia." He was unmarried and indulged in occasional affairs and visits to prostitutes until, in 1901, he married the actress Olga Knipper, a former mistress of a friend of his. Olga continued to live and work in Moscow for six months of the year, then joined Chekhov in Yalta for the other six months. He seemed content with this arrangement. He had once written to another friend, Aleksey Suvorin: "Give me a wife who, like the moon, won't appear in my sky every day."

But who can say how he imagined Olga to be behaving in Moscow? Two years after their marriage, she had a miscarriage, and there has been speculation among scholars as to who the father was. It must have occurred to Chekhov to wonder, too. "By poeticizing love," he had written in 1895, "we imagine virtues in those we love that they often do not possess; this is the source of constant mistakes and constant distress." The mistakes and distresses are ten times worse when, instead of virtues, we imagine flaws. He also wrote: "If you are afraid of loneliness, don't marry."

"The Lady with the Dog" is not only a story about infidelity, although it is certainly that; it is also about the surprising awfulness of living apart from the person one loves, or rather the impossibility of living together. Dmitri Gurov, who is forty, works in a bank and has been married long enough to have three children. He is no stranger to adultery. He looks for amorous opportunities around every corner. While vacationing alone in Yalta, his senses alert, he meets Anna Sergeyevna, who is also married and vacationing alone. The inevitable occurs. When the vacation is over, they both assume the affair will end with it. And they are both surprised when it doesn't: Gurov finds himself obsessed with the idea of continuing his relationship with Anna, and travels to St. Petersburg to reignite their passion for one another. He succeeds, and he and Anna continue to meet occasionally in Moscow. Against all odds, they have remained in love. After following their intermittent affair, which goes on for years, the story ends with them trying desperately to think of a way to end the infernal secrecy and deceit without ending the affair. They cannot; they realize they must resign themselves to the double lives they have created for themselves.

There is no judgement in the story — Chekhov is usually quite generous with his weaker characters, recognizing that weakness in the face of the world's implacable awfulness is completely understandable. It is the strongly malevolent bastards who take advantage of the powerless who draw Chekhov's loathing: landowners who mistreat peasants, drunkards who abuse women. Gurov is not a bad man, he loves his wife and children; Anna is not a naturally deceitful wife, and is tormented by her infidelity. Chekhov presents the circumstances as realistically as possible. "It is not our job to judge," he wrote to the writer Lydia Avilova while he was writing "The Lady with the Dog." "Policemen judge, bureaucrats judge; our job is to write, only to write." There is no clear lesson to be drawn from the story; we do not even know what Chekhov thought about the affair, except that it weakens both

Gurov and Anna and so they elicit our sympathy. His story is a reflection of how life, in its sublime and infinite complexity, sometimes sends us on what looks at first like a short hike and ends up being a long, repetitive, painful forced march.

There is, however, a coda. In 1939, in Lydia Avilova's memoir, *The Love Affair of My Life*, she writes that she and Chekhov were secret lovers from the year they met, in 1889, until his death in 1904. In other words, that Chekhov was behaving very much like his character Gurov all the time he was writing about unfaithful husbands, even after he married Olga Knipper. According to Avilova, Chekhov's story "About Love," which appeared in 1898, the year before "The Lady with the Dog," was essentially about their clandestine relationship. Like Gurov, she wrote, Chekhov was "a busy bee who flies about and is happy to collect honey from anything that comes along."

There is reason to believe that Avilova greatly exaggerated the nature of her relationship with Chekhov. "About Love" is a story about a man and a married woman who fall in love with each other, but do not have an affair. It seems more likely that "The Lady with the Dog" is about Chekhov's affair with Lydia Avilova, if there was one, and that Anna is thus a fictional version of Lydia Avilova. I can understand that Avilova, in her memoir, would rather be identified with the virtuous woman in "About Love" than with the adulterous woman in "The Lady with the Dog," but why she would confess to her affair with Chekhov and then identify with a character who refused to have an affair is a conundrum that would greatly have intrigued Chekhov.

In my version, I replace the bank clerk Gurov with Will Esterhaze, an unhappily married university professor, and the gentle Anna with Jessica Morrow, one of his department's (though not his) graduate students. I am interested not only in how a modern couple arrives at the impasse in which Gurov and Anna find themselves, but also in the consequences of their decision, the way in which they fear their affair would be viewed by those around them, their friends, families, and colleagues. For although the business of the writer may not be to judge, judgement and subsequent sentencing has become a job eagerly taken up by others, with cancel culture and relentless flaming on social media destroying relationships and even careers. Both Jessica and Esterhaze's wife, the former subtly and the latter not so subtly, threaten to expose the affair and ruin Esterhaze's idyll. Esterhaze is therefore at a double impasse; he can go neither forward nor back. The question facing him is, can he remain stationary?

At the end of Chekhov's story, as at the end of, say, Yann Martel's *Life of Pi*, the reader is invited to imagine where the story might go from there, and how the reader imagines the ending of the story says as much about the reader as it does about the story. In other words, the story's meaning depends on what the reader brings to it. Again, Chekhov does not impose his view on the events, he merely sets the events down for us to ponder. For my part, I assume Gurov will do the honourable but cowardly thing by ending the affair and going back to his colourless life, as he has always done before. Esterhaze does not have that luxury; his old way of life is over no matter what he does. In Chekhov's story, Gurov has all the power, whether or not he has the courage or moral fibre to wield it. In my story, although power has become more equally distributed, the situation of the two lovers remains disturbingly familiar.

IT HAPPENS EVERY DAY

COBDEN, A SMALL TOWN in central Ontario, is located between the cities of Pembroke and Ottawa. Beside Highway 17 at Pembroke a sign reads: Ottawa 147 kilometres. On the highway outside Ottawa, a similar sign reads: Pembroke 135 kilometres. Consequently, no one in Cobden is able to say exactly where they are in relation to either Pembroke or Ottawa, except that Cobden is closer to Pembroke.

Last week, A, who lives in Cobden, had a job interview with a potential employer, let us call him B, in Ottawa. He took the 8:15 bus from Cobden to Ottawa and arrived at B's office at exactly 9:00 a.m. His interview ended at eleven, and he was back in Cobden, also travelling by bus, in time for lunch. He told his wife that the interview had gone well, and that he had to return to Ottawa two days later to discuss the details of the position. The next day, however, the bus company announced that, in the interest of saving time, the Pembroke-to-Ottawa bus would no longer stop in Cobden. Therefore, on the appointed day, A had to travel to

Pembroke to catch the bus to Ottawa. He expected the business of being shown around by B would take several hours, and because he did not want to leave his wife in Cobden without a car, he asked his wife to drive him to Pembroke so he could catch the 6:45 a.m. bus, which was the bus that would have stopped in Cobden if the bus company had not changed its schedule. Although everything else was exactly as it had been on the previous day, or so A thought, this time the bus took three hours to reach Ottawa, arriving at 9:45. And then he had to take a city bus to B's office. When, frantic and exhausted, A arrived at the office at 10:00 a.m., he was informed that B, annoyed by A's failure to appear at 9:00, had set out by car to speak with A in Cobden. A was advised to wait in B's office for B to return, but so anxious was he to apologize for being late that he decided to take the 12:20 bus from Ottawa in the hope of getting home while B was still there. He forgot, however, that the bus no longer stopped in Cobden, and he had to go all the way through to Pembroke. He left the bus station in a rush and called his wife to come and get him, but she informed him that B was still at their house, and she didn't want to leave him there alone. In desperation, A called a taxi. The driver informed him that he couldn't drive all the way to Cobden because that day was his daughter's birthday and he'd planned to knock off early so he could take her to Ottawa to spend the afternoon at Funhaven. A said he wouldn't mind if the driver's daughter came with them in the taxi; that way the driver could drop A off in Cobden and continue on to Ottawa with his daughter. The driver agreed, but when they stopped to pick up the daughter she was still in pajamas, and A and the driver waited until 3:30 while the daughter changed into clothing she considered appropriate for a trip to Funhaven.

It was therefore 4:45 by the time A arrived at his home in Cobden.

When A entered his house, his wife told him that B had arrived that morning, and in fact A had passed him on his way into B's office building and, without recognizing him, had hurried upstairs to his appointment. Despite the oddity of A's behaviour, B had stayed in A's house to await A's return. A's wife had made him comfortable, had given him lunch and tried to keep him entertained, and B had asked her several times when A might be expected back. When A finally arrived home and learned that B was still waiting for him in the living room, he was in such a hurry to see him that he tripped on a rug in the hallway, twisting his ankle, and, almost fainting with pain, hobbled into the bathroom to apply a tensor bandage. While there, he heard B – whether in the living room or already in the hall, A couldn't tell – curse loudly and stomp out the door in a rage. A never saw him again.

ABOUT "IT HAPPENS EVERY DAY"

This story is a cover of "A Common Confusion," one of Franz Kafka's later stories, not published during his lifetime. In his will, Kafka instructed Max Brod, his friend and literary executor, to destroy all his unpublished writings "to the last page," but Brod ignored these instructions and arranged for the publication of "A Common Confusion" in a posthumous collection of stories called *Beim Bau der Chinesichen Mauer* (*The Great Wall of China*), which was the title of one of the other stories that Kafka had asked Brod to destroy. In a stroke of irony Kafka would have appreciated, W.H. Auden called *The Great Wall of China* Kafka's "finest work, and . . . certainly the best introduction to him."

At the time of his death in 1924, at the age of forty, Kafka was being treated for laryngeal tuberculosis in the Kierling Sanatorium, outside Vienna, but from 1908 until his retirement in 1922, he was employed in Prague by the Workers' Accident Insurance Institute. At first, he investigated industrial accidents and assessed claims by workers who had been injured on the job. But he was eventually placed in charge of the division studying ways to prevent workplace accidents. Which gives us the delicious image of the author of "In the Penal Colony" thinking up ways to improve the working conditions of industrial employees.

The Workers' Accident Insurance Institute was part of what another Kafka biographer, Ernst Pawel, called "the pullulating Austro-Hungarian bureaucracy," a Byzantine warren of corruption, inefficiency, senseless and contradictory regulations, and self-serving pigheadedness that somehow, like bureaucracies everywhere, managed to avoid collapsing only by virtue of its own inertia. Max Brod, in his biography, says Kafka hated working in the Insurance Institute, but there is little evidence for that: Brod might have assumed Kafka hated working in a bureaucracy because Brod himself hated working in a bureaucracy. In fact, a great deal of Brod's Kafka biography is autobiographical. Kafka appears rather to have enjoyed the anonymity of his day job. The bureaucracy itself was mind-numbing, but Kafka was happy to preserve his mental energy for his writing: the job let him off work at two o'clock in the afternoon, and Kafka wrote far into the night. As well, he must, in the course of his investigations into the causes of industrial accidents, have encountered such a wide variety of injuries, of things going wrong, of machines flying apart and killing their workers, that no mishap would seem to him to be impossible, or even all that bizarre. He would have dealt with absurdities every day. Having been educated as a lawyer before becoming an insurance man, he would also have been familiar with the many intricate pathways by which industries tried to avoid paying out the claims of their injured workers. For Kafka, the events he depicted in such stories as "In the Penal Colony," *The Castle* and *The Trial* might have seemed surreal and absurd to their readers, but to Kafka they would not necessarily have been unrealistic.

In "A Common Occurrence," Kafka presents us with a world that makes no sense. In the story, a man, A, travels twice to town H to conduct business with B. The first time the trip takes ten minutes one way and ten minutes coming back. The next day, under precisely the same circumstances, it takes him ten hours to get to H and one second to return. The only way to keep one's sanity in such a world is to stop insisting that it make sense. Kafka recounts these strange circumstances in a deadpan manner, much as, in "The Metamorphosis," he describes Gregor Samsa's transformation into an *ungerheuse ungerfietesar*, a species of enormous vermin, as if it were no very surprising thing at all. Samsa can't find it surprising that he has metamorphosed into an insect precisely because he is now an insect, and an insect cannot be surprised that it is an insect. His altered condition simply makes it difficult for him to get out of bed and go to work. Samsa never once wonders what had happened to him or even why it should have happened. He is not an existential insect. Similarly, in "A Common Confusion," A does not marvel that a trip to the next town should take ten minutes one day and ten hours the next. It just does.

As J.M. Coetzee has pointed out, Kafka's writing style is not flowery – like Kafka himself at the Insurance Institute, his prose keeps its head down and does its job, careful not to call undue attention to itself. "Kafka's German," writes Coetzee, "tends to be restrained, even neutral." His intention is not to point out the absurdity of the world around him, but simply to describe the world around him. "I think what Kafka does [in 'In The Penal Colony']," Haruki Murakami's character says in the novel *Kafka on the Shore*, "is give a purely technical explanation of that complex machine . . . as sort of a substitute for explaining the situation we're in." Murakami does the same thing, both in *1Q84* and *Kafka on the Shore*, in which the inexplicable isn't a metaphor or an allegory for the way things are; it is the way things are.

Kafka doesn't tell us where the story takes place: it could be anywhere. Nor does he say how far A's village is from H, or by what means of transport A gets there and back. It doesn't matter. In my version, I imagine the story taking place in Ontario, and I preface A's dilemma with the information that Ottawa is either one hundred and forty-seven or one hundred and thirty-five kilometres from Pembroke, depending on which road sign one reads: anyone who travels in Ontario knows how eerily unreliable roadside signs are. I suggest that the source of A's predicament, presaged by the signs put up by the department of highways (where I worked for two summers while going to university), is the result of a bus company's decision to cancel its service to Cobden: in reality, there are no longer regular buses running between small Ontario towns. Ottawa itself, the country's capital city, does not have a bus station. We live in an age when occurrences that, in former times, would have been seen as absurd and outrageous, are now received with a shrug. We live every day in Kafka's world and, like Gregor Samsa, don't seem to find it odd.

Philip Rahv, in his introduction to the Everyman edition of Kafka's stories, suggests that Kafka's uniqueness lies in the "complete freedom with which he suspends certain conventions of storytelling." He goes on to say that

> . . . when we read in the first sentence of *The Metamorphosis* that the clerk Gregor Samsa awoke one morning to find himself changed into a gigantic insect, it is a mistake to think that by means of this bold stroke Kafka intends to call into question the laws of nature. What he calls into question, rather, is the convention that the laws of nature are at all times to be observed in fiction . . .

Since the 1920s, the usual conventions of storytelling have been called into question so often, by authors of diverse cultural backgrounds, that we might ask which conventions Kafka was flouting? German? Czech? English? Western?

In fact, so far have Western literature and Western society in general come from those early conventions that we no longer consider their suspension to be shocking or even particularly innovative.

And yet, Kafka continues to intrigue, not for his thwarting of literary convention, but for the tremendous scope of his imagination. In his belief in the absurdity of life he is the direct descendant of Nicolai Gogol and the precursor of Murakami. After Kafka's death, a former colleague of his who had worked with him at the Workers' Accident Insurance Institute told Max Brod that "Kafka attacked every question from the opposite end from which everyone else generally did." This is the key to his art. We don't admire Kafka for calling into question the notion that the laws of nature are to be present in fiction; we admire him for his prediction that a time will come, has come, when the laws of nature are no longer observed in nature.

DIARY OF A CONSPIRACY THEORIST

OCTOBER 3. This morning I slept late. I don't know why. Winter seems to be closing in early this year, maybe that's it. It stays dark longer. Anyway, when I woke up I checked my cell and saw it was after ten. Without stopping to shower or have breakfast, I threw on some clothes and rushed to the office. I never shave. If you have to change your appearance in a hurry, it's a lot faster to shave off a beard than it is to grow one.

When I got to work, everyone looked up from their desks. I thought maybe the Deputy Minister had been asking for me, as he often does, but in fact the opposite was true: yesterday I told the office manager I wasn't coming in today, said I was feeling stuffed up and needed a sick day. I'd forgotten all about it! The manager had been telling me all week how bad I looked, thanks very much, and saying I shouldn't come in if I was going to spread a horrible virus around the office. He always talks to me like I'm some kind of contagious liability, but it's true, I was coughing a lot and there was the kind of tickle in my throat that's usually followed by a headache and fever. I hate going into those large pharmacies full of coughing people looking for instant remedies, so I ordered some Tylenol online, but of course it hasn't arrived yet. And anyway, today I felt fine. I didn't tell him that, though, because they owe me a few sick days. That's what they call them, sick days, even though it's not the days that are sick, it's us. It's like calling unemployment insurance "E.I.," which means Employment Insurance, when it's really insurance you get for being *un*employed. It drives me crazy, but that's the way people think. So yesterday I told the manager I'd take a sick day today, and left early.

So today was a kind of non-day. Everyone kept away from me, told me I shouldn't have come in, wouldn't sit beside me at lunch. I felt like a pariah. On my way home I stopped at a Johnny Cash, one of those store-front loan shops that lend you money between paydays, so long, that is, as you have paydays. This Johnny Cash is located in a huge downtown mall, so customers don't have to go very far to throw away money they don't have. I'm fairly well known there, since most months I seem to run out of cash a week before I get paid. But if I pay back the loan on time, the interest isn't too bad. Like, if I borrow five hundred bucks and pay it back in two weeks, it only costs me eighty dollars, which doesn't seem unreasonable to me. Of course, if I take longer to pay it back, the interest shoots up to over three thousand percent. That's happened a couple of times, due to circumstances beyond my control, like the time my game box broke down a week after the warranty ran out. Today there were a lot of people in the shop, I had to wait in line. The guy who works there is slow and a real ass. He seems to think that only losers need to borrow money. Even though he knows me and knows I have a job and knows I usually pay back my loans on time and don't use the money to buy drugs or booze, well he doesn't know that but he should be able to tell by looking at me, he still makes me answer all the questions and fill out all the forms as if he doesn't know me from Adam and I'm trying to rob him, personally.

"Where do you work?" he asks me.

"Same place I worked last time I was in here," I say.

"Which is where? How do I know you still work there? People change jobs, you know."

So I tell him I work at the Mint. He looks up at me and says, "You work at the Mint and you need to borrow money? That's rich." I give him my employee number and show him my ID card and tell him my home address, even though I hate doing that, and he writes it all down with a plastic ballpoint pen. Where do people learn how to hold a pen these days? This guy grips it between his index and third fingers with the nib somehow twisted over towards his baby finger, and I have no idea how he can write anything like that, especially in those little boxes, but he does. No wonder he's slow. He hates me for making him write down all those letters and numbers. And for needing money. Why do people whose job it is to hand out money behave as though you're a beggar and he's dropping his own gold nuggets in your hat? I mean, they're making a fortune from people like me. Somebody is, anyway. Probably not him. Whoever it is should be down on their knees thanking me for giving them the opportunity to lend me money. But no, it's like I have some weird social disease and he's paying me to go away and infect someone else. Just like my office manager, come to think of it. Well, I do have a weird social disease. It's called having to work for a living. He has it, too, but he didn't get it from me.

I took the loan because I need to buy a new overcoat. The one I have is all right, it's warm enough, but the collar's too narrow. I want a collar that covers my ears when I pull it up, so I can wrap a scarf around my neck outside the collar, thus creating a filter between myself and the outside air, and keeping myself incognito at the same time. Fortunately, scarves are back in style, and you can bet that if scarves are back, then wide collars are coming back, too. They do this to keep us buying new coats and scarves; otherwise, the economy would stagnate and the government would topple. When they realize that high collars allow us to hide our faces from security cameras, they'll start making collarless coats and maybe ban the sale of hats with brims.

They're calling for a cold winter again this year, of course, because the weather stations are all run by the government and the government wants everyone to buy new coats. I should get some new gloves, too, come to think of it. Brown gloves. Brown gloves are warmer than black gloves, have you noticed that? I mean, if you go up north and look at the Inuit, you never see them wearing black gloves. Only brown. Actually, they don't wear gloves at all, they wear mitts. I had a pair of moose-hide mitts once, they were the warmest mitts I ever owned, and they were light brown, almost yellow, and fleece-lined. I should get a pair of those, except you can't wear mitts in the city if you're an adult. There's no rule, but if you look at people's hands you won't see anyone over ten wearing mitts. Maybe women.

After leaving Johnny Cash I was mulling this over outside one of the big department stores. It had started to rain and in my hurry this morning I'd forgotten my umbrella, so I was pressed up so close to the store that my breath was fogging up the huge plate-glass window. While I looked at the window display (humanoid aliens wearing designer clothing), a car stopped behind me and I turned and recognized it as the Deputy Minister's car. I thought it was probably his wife or daughter, so I pressed myself closer to the window and waited to see who was getting out. The driver opened the back door and, sure enough, out hopped the Deputy Minister's daughter, Belinda, like a bird being let out of its cage. She stretched her neck and peered up and down the street, drew her eyebrows together and glared up into the rain. I was instantly smitten, I mean, like, totally, hopelessly smitten. So smitten that, standing there pressed up against the glass window, I thought that if she really were a bird, say a goldfinch or a sparrow, and if she died, I would bury her under a strawberry plant, and every day after that I would go out and eat a strawberry from that plant.

She walked into the department store without looking at me. If I'd had my umbrella, I might have fallen in beside her and raised it over both of us, but as I was in my old coat and my hair was wet I probably looked like someone she would never notice or accept as a suitor. And besides, I'd just been to the Johnny Cash and thought maybe she would intuit that and reject me out of hand.

Before going into the store, though, she handed her dog to the driver, who, after she'd gone in, put the dog on the sidewalk and stood in the rain holding its leash and smoking a cigarette. The dog was tiny, with long white hair bracketing its face, and a little pink tongue always hanging out. Just as I was about to move off, I heard a voice say, "Hello, there, Meggy." I looked around and didn't see anyone except two women hurrying by under a single umbrella, one quite old and the other about my age, which is forty-six. After they passed I heard the voice again. "Shame on you, Meggy!"

And then I saw Belinda's dog straining at its leash to sniff the rear end of a second dog that was walking between the two women. "No, Fidel," Meggy said to this second dog, "you're wrong. I really was sick."

I know what you're thinking, because I was thinking the same thing. Fever. Whatever was making me sick was also making me hear things, like talking dogs. I know there are no such things as talking dogs. And yet I also know what I heard. I began to wonder if Meggy and Fidel were in fact real dogs. I mean, they might have been spy dogs, you know, robots or drone dogs. If they can make drones that look like insects, and robotic sex dolls that you'd swear were real women, they can easily make robots that look like dogs. It would be a simple matter to make a robotic dog that was so lifelike it could be switched for Belinda's pet, and that would make a lot of sense, because who has better access to the Deputy Minister's private residence than his daughter's dog?

It so happens that my apartment is in the same direction in which the two women and Fidel were walking, so I ended up following them. They led me down Lefèvre Avenue, then turned right on Citoyen, right again onto Carpentier and finally to a tony high-rise condo building on Union Street that had a plaque on the corner saying the building belonged to a company called Sverkoff and Associates. Serge Sverkoff is a former magistrate who went into real estate and became a big commercial developer. A lot of senior civil servants live in his buildings. The women entered the foyer and took the elevator up to the fifteenth floor. How do I know that? Because I followed them in and watched the numbers above the elevator door climb to fifteen and then stop. I don't know why I did this. I didn't really have a plan. But something strange was happening with those dogs, and

I thought I might as well keep track of it, because, well, you never know.

Tonight there is no moon, but earlier there was the most remarkable sunset: the entire western sky was lit a brilliant red. I walked all the way home staring up at it, my face exposed to the night air. That's probably why I slept in this morning.

OCTOBER 11. Wednesday morning, seven a.m.. After taking the week off I feel like a new man, and I've started coming back to work. I always arrive early, because the first thing I do after checking my mail is go into the Deputy Minister's office to turn on his computer. The DM likes to come in late and go straight to work, without having to wait for his computer to boot up. He just wants to sit down, enter his Department-Wide Log-in password, which I can't enter for him because I don't know it, and start to work.

I have been listening to him enter his password. All I can make out is that it has thirteen characters and he enters it using all his fingers.

The Deputy Minister is an intellectual. His office is full of books, many of which I can't read because they're in German. Some are even in Russian. They look serious, not the kind of books I would read anyway. I spend a lot of time on the Internet. I think you can learn more on the internet than you can from books, because it's so much faster and people don't worry too much about fancy writing. But the DM is an educated man, and he doesn't mind big words and always comes straight to the point. I've never heard him say a single thing that wasn't to some purpose. Whenever he passes me in the hall, or sees me in the cafeteria, he stops and asks me, "How's it going?" At first I thought he was just being vapidly polite, but every time it was the same question, expressed in exactly the same words: “How’s it going?” As though it was some kind of code. For a long time I could not figure out what he was really asking me. How is *what* going? But now I think I know.

When I told the moron in the Johnny Cash that I worked at the Mint, I was joking, of course. In fact I work in the Department of Supply and Services. You might think the Department of Supply and Services isn’t one of the more important departments in the government, not like the Department of Defense or the Department of Foreign Affairs, but there you would be wrong. Everything any government department needs, from pencils to helicopters, has to be procured from tenders submitted to the Department of Supply and Services by civilian suppliers. If, say, the Department of Culture and Recreation needs five hundred new office chairs, we put a Call for Tender out to every company we know of that makes office chairs. When we receive tenders from those companies, we select the company that will supply the best quality office chairs at the best unit price per chair. We are thus a very powerful and influential department. I used the example of office chairs just now, but when you think of all the things a government needs to carry out its national and international responsibilities – nuclear-waste storage containers; computer code descramblers; missile guidance systems – you get an idea of what an important government department we are. Without the Department of Supply and Services, the entire government would grind to a halt.

For some reason, the Deputy Minister has taken a shine to me. He doesn’t use the code-words *How’s it going?* with anyone else in my section. And he wouldn’t allow just anyone into his office to turn on his computer. And now fate has crossed his daughter's path and mine. I realize now that "it" is my relationship with Belinda. When he asks me "How's it going?" what he really wants to know is how Belinda and I are getting along.

It's almost noon, and the DM hasn't come in yet. Everyone else has gone for lunch, but I'm still at my desk, looking a few things up online, when the door opens and she – Belinda herself – comes in. I take note of how beautifully she is dressed. A white cashmere sweater and lovely, black, form-fitting slacks. She fills the room with light. She looks my way and asks, "Is my father in yet?"

"Belinda," I want to say, "kill me now, but for the love of God, do it with your own sweet hands!" But of course, I don't. All I can bring myself to say is, "No, I haven't seen him."

She pouts, a lovely little pursing of her lips. "He's supposed to be taking me out for lunch," she says. "It's my birthday and everything."

"No kidding," I say. "Congratulations. May I ask how old you are?"

She looks at me petulantly. What a stupid question to ask. But then she smiles and shrugs, as if giving in to an uncontrollable urge. "I'm twenty-two today," she says.

Emboldened by this unexpected pardon, I venture another question after glancing at her ring finger.

"And still unmarried?" I say.

"Yes," she replies, "still single. But I hope not for long."

She smiles again and leaves the office. I sit back in my chair, stunned, unable to move, and for several minutes, maybe half an hour, I analyze that parting smile. Was it conspiratorial? Intimate? Knowing? Superior? I am convinced she was telling me that she hopes I will soon find the courage to ask for her hand in marriage. I should have asked to take her out to celebrate her birthday in her father's absence. There is no longer any doubt. She loves me! And her father knows and approves! That was why he stayed away. What a dunce I am! Next time!

The office manager comes in. "You may as well go to lunch, Brown," he says. "The DM isn't coming in today."

"I know," I say. I hate people who toady their way up by kissing the backside of everyone higher than they, and then look down on the rest of us because we're trying to do the same thing. "He's taking Belinda to lunch," I say, just to rub it in. "It's her birthday."

I get up and put on my new overcoat, a nice wool with a faux-fur collar, that I bought online. Instead of going down to the cafeteria, I take the elevator up to the executive dining room on the top floor, in case the DM is having lunch there with Belinda. I only want to catch a glimpse of her, you know how it is when you're in love and you know you are loved in return, but the flunky at the door wouldn't even let me in to have a quick look.

When Belinda and I are married, I'll have him replaced.

NOVEMBER 6. So, here's what I've been working on in my spare time, and it has expanded my understanding immeasurable. Remember that unusually brilliant sunset I mentioned earlier, the night I saw Belinda in front of the department store? Well, I looked it up when I got home; as I suspected, that vermillion colour that spreads like fresh blood across the horizon wasn't natural. It was actually caused by billions of particles of chemicals suspended in the atmosphere. I watched dozens of YouTube videos showing that those weren't clouds refracting rays from the setting sun, they were contrails left by jet aircraft. For years, airplanes have been dumping tons of toxic chemicals into the sky. You can see them if you look up, but you think they're just contrails – harmless water vapour from jet engines, condensed in the cold air of the stratosphere. That's what you're supposed to think. But it isn't water vapour. They're called chem trails. They contain barium, or aluminum oxide, or polymer fibres (microscopic bits of plastic, like what they're filling the Pacific Ocean with), or silicon carbide. You can tell chem trails from ordinary contrails by how long they take to dissipate. Chem trails take much longer; in fact, they don't dissipate at all, they turn into cumulocirrus clouds, which is why the sunsets have been so spectacular lately. It's like the old saying: Red sky in the morning, sailors take warning. Only it isn't just sailors who should be frightened: the chemicals in those clouds are up there for a reason.

All very subreddit, of course, and the government is frantically denying everything, because it's mostly military planes that are dumping the stuff. Commercial airlines are in on it, too, but not as much. I don't know what they have to gain by killing people, maybe they make more money moving freight. But look it up. Check out c/Anon. Almost every time you look up at the sky you'll see at least two or three chem trails criss-crossing from horizon to horizon, filling the air like defoliants from crop dusters, polluting the atmosphere with chemical shit that we then have to breathe in when it settles. Why are they doing this? Well, that's what I've been finding out, and the answer isn't going to let you sleep soundly at night, let me tell you. I've barely slept a wink since I figured it out. Plus, there's a cricket in my room that makes its scratchy noise all night, keeping me awake. I read somewhere that there's a kind of drone that makes a cricket sound. I've looked everywhere for it. It must be in a crack in one of the walls. I've ordered some insecticide, in case it's a real cricket.

Today, when I came into work, the office manager took me aside before I reached my desk. I didn't even have time to take off my overcoat.

"What the hell's got into you lately?" he said.

"What?" I answered. "What do you mean? Nothing. Why?"

I thought he was referring to my work on chem trails. There's no privacy, we know that. Most of my YouTube line-ups are about chem trails, and lately I've been looking up robotic dogs and cricket drones, which I know has set off a few alarms somewhere, because I keep getting ads for sex dolls. My department could easily be tracking my internet searches. They do routine checks on all government personnel, well, on everyone, really, but especially on those of us with access to highly sensitive data. I never look stuff up on my work computer, of course, I always have my laptop with me. And I keep a fifty-two-cent postage stamp pasted over the camera eye — fifty-two is my lucky number. Even at that, I don't use the DWL. Still, they can get into a laptop if they want to badly enough; it's as easy as sending me an email with a malware attachment. I wouldn't even have to open it. How do you think the Russians got into the Pentagon's systems?

But that wasn't what the office manager wanted me for.

"Get a grip, man," he said. "You're pushing fifty."

"No, I'm not."

"It's time you started acting your age. What are you thinking? You're going nowhere but down. You're in debt up to your eyeballs — do you think I don't know how many times Johnny Cash has called us for a security check?" So, the dumb-ass clerk has known all along that I don't work at the Mint. What's his game? "Take a good look at yourself in the mirror, my friend. What makes you think a junior file clerk with a mug like yours has a chance, eh?"

I still didn't know what he was talking about. A mug like mine?

"The DM's daughter, numbnuts. Do you honestly think you have a chance with her? Do you imagine she even knows you exist?"

The Deputy Minister's daughter? Belinda? As far as I know, I haven't mentioned her for weeks. Have I mentioned her in any of my emails? I don't think so. I've been too wrapped up in my research. But I wasn't going to let this fat-head know that.

"You have no business talking to me like that," I said. "I don't understand you at all."

Of course she knows I exist. I spoke to her on her birthday. She practically begged me to take her out to lunch. No wonder the DM says hello every time he sees me, makes a point of coming over to shake my hand, asks my opinion on important matters, as though I'm already part of the family. But unlike the office manager, I don't take advantage of every friendly gesture that comes my way. I don't try to slither my way up the social ladder. I don't have to. I'm already up there. This chem-trail business, for example, runs very deep. It's bigger than this putz of an office manager can even comprehend. It's mind control. The chemicals the government is pumping into the atmosphere are intended to make us all docile, all good little online shoppers. Some even contend they're meant to make us all sterile, but I'm not so sure about that. Why would any government or corporation, especially an airline, want to wipe humanity off the face of the earth? It doesn't make sense. But keeping us docile, accepting, complacent? That I can see. All good little consumers/voters. Keep buying government bonds and flying to Florida every winter. All I need is proof that those chemicals are up there in unnatural quantities. If I can show that, and post my findings, I'll be famous. I'll be on every talk show in the country. I can write a book and sell it online. I can marry Belinda. My name will be known far and wide, while you, my sycophantic friend, will still be taking tenders for toilet paper so the Deputy Minister can wipe his ass.

NOVEMBER 8. Tonight, I went to the opera. I'd received an email from the National Arts Centre telling me that I must go, so I went. I was surprised to see so many people in the audience, all dressed in their finery. My new overcoat stood up well, I think. I didn't check it, but wore it to my seat, took it off when the lights dimmed, and kept it draped over my lap. Coat-check staff are known to go through coats looking for valuables, and I keep copies of my research on a thumb drive sewn into the lining of my hood. The opera was a new one, from China. The stage was well lit and draped with broad swaths of richly coloured cloth that billowed in the breeze that must have been created by huge fans off-stage, and the singers performed by climbing up silk ropes and singing as they dangled halfway up. So this is modern opera, I thought. It looked more like gymnastics. The rippling bands of cloth, especially the red ones, made me think of cumulocirrus clouds, which made me think of chem trails. The wind brings such frightening thoughts. Even though the opera was in Chinese, I understood perfectly what the singers were saying. They were telling me to climb halfway to the sky, look around carefully, and then sing out what I see. Which I fully intend to do.

One of the singers had a beautifully high, lyrical voice. She made me think of Belinda. My coat was over my lap — but let's not go there!

NOVEMBER 9. Barium. I'm pretty sure now that's what is making our sunsets so brilliant. It's funny, we look up and admire a beautiful sunset, little suspecting that it presents a deadly danger to humanity. It's like smiling into the teeth of a hungry wolf! Barium is a heavy metal that's normally insoluble in water, so it doesn't harm us if we swallow it, unless it's radioactive barium, which it very easily could be. Pierre Curie taped a patch of barium to his arm to see what it would do, and it burned a hole right through his skin. Furthermore, one of the compounds of barium, barium sulfate, *is* soluble in water, and if you get enough of it inside you it can kill you. Even in concentrations only slightly higher than one part per million, it has serious side effects, such as stomach pain, diarrhea or constipation, tinnitus, excessive sweatiness, confusion, heart palpitations. Which I get a lot of. And it can make your skin look as pale as skim milk. Which suggests leukemia to me. When barium is heated, it emits a phosphorescent red glow — exactly like these glorious sunsets we find so romantic. Clouds of barium scattered by jet aircraft and heated by the setting sun will glow red. It's as simple as that. And when barium sulfate settles to the earth, it gets into our water and causes serious damage to untold millions of humans. Increased drowsiness, lack of appetite, brain fog.

Why? Why is the government doing this to us? And how can I stop it?

NOVEMBER 11. Remembrance Day. I arrived at the office this morning at seven, as usual, and went directly into the DM's office, powered on his computer, and watched the screen slowly come to life. The department's mainframe is a beast that lives in the basement and is slow to awaken. When the prompt for the DM's password finally appeared, I typed in thirteen characters: belinda111003. As I said, the DM is an intellectual, and in my experience intellectuals are pretty dumb when it comes to dealing with cryptotechnology. When they have to come up with a password, they almost always choose something they think they'll remember without having to write it down or look it up, as if they're going to be asked for it on their death bed or when they're stuck on a desert island. They choose something like their wedding anniversary, or their daughter's name and birth date. Like: Belinda, 11 October 2003. Bingo! The screen went dark for a split-second, then came back on at the DM's personal page. I was in!

I typed "barium" in the search bar, and in three seconds I was looking at a requisition from the Department of Defense for six tonnes of the stuff, dated a week ago. Six tonnes! According to my research, a single gram of barium will kill a human being. Six tonnes is enough to kill six million people. With six tonnes of barium, the government could wipe out a large city or a small country. The military must be stockpiling it for future chemical warfare against its own citizens. I checked the Call for Tenders page and found that the request hadn't been processed and a call for tenders hadn't been issued yet. Saved by good old government inefficiency. I returned to the requisitions page, reselected the DoD request, forwarded a copy to myself, and then deleted the original. I heaved a huge sigh of relief.

I'd just saved six million lives.

Now I'm sitting at my desk, imagining what the DM's house is like. I'll be living there in a short time, and I want to be prepared. It's a big house, of course, circular drive, Greek columns. I imagine him going about in slippers and a smoking, as they say in French. Here at the office he's always so formal, so restrained; he is, after all, a career civil servant, impartial, unallied to any particular political party. But I would like to know what goes on in his head. In fact, I'd like to know how all such gentleman comport themselves when not in the public eye, because as the DM's son-in-law, I'm going to have to blend in with them. Do they play cards? Watch YouTube? Go to hockey games? And what do they talk about amongst themselves? Not chem trails, you can bet on that. Every time the DM asks me how it's going, I think of making a personal comment. "What are your plans for the weekend, Deputy?" I might ask. But something – my poverty, my low social position, my natural shyness – holds me back, and all I ever come out with is some bland comment about the weather. "Fine, sir," I say, "maybe a bit warm." He could take that to mean Belinda and I are getting on pretty well, but not exactly like a house on fire. The barium clouds must be working.

I wonder what Belinda's bedroom is like. I try to picture it in my mind's eye. There's a row of perfume bottles and lipsticks lined up on her dresser, and in front of them little velvet boxes for her jewelry. Her necklaces and earrings hang from the branches of a little jewelry tree. And there are vases of flowers on little tables in all the corners and beside her bed. Does she smell their delicate fragrance every time she breathes in? Does she leave her clothes lying about, that beautiful swan's-down sweater, her more intimate garments, too ethereal to be called clothes, purchased online from Victoria's Secret? But again, enough of that.

I also wonder about that dog of hers. Does she allow Meggy in her room while she's changing? Or when she comes out of the shower? Does it sleep with her at night? It probably has a camera in it, perhaps one in each eye for binocular vision. Who is watching? Whoever it is, is he ever tempted to speak to her? To tell her how beautiful she is. To say how much he adores her? I imagine I'd be less tongue-tied if I could speak to her through the medium of her dog.

NOVEMBER 12. Saturday. Today I will prove that there are unusually high levels of toxic chemicals in our air. If the military is planning to stage a coup by killing everyone in the capital with clouds of poison gas, they've probably already tested their ability to carry out such a threat. I have a friend who works in the city's health lab, and I can send an air sample to him. I have a Mason jar. I can't take the sample at street level, because there will of course be barium in it from all the car exhaust. That's what the opera singers were telling me. I must climb higher. The condo building I followed those two women to, with their robot-dog Fidel, would be perfect. Would the fifteenth floor be high enough? It's about halfway up. It would be better if I could get all the way up to the penthouse, or better yet out on to the roof.

In the lobby are three elevators, two on one side and a third across from them. This third elevator goes straight up to the penthouse, where Serge Sverkoff and his family live. The elevator door is wide open, who knows why, maybe one of the children dashed out for a pizza and left the door open. Anyway, I go in and press the button that says PH.

If anyone challenges me, I'll just say I got in the wrong elevator and didn't know how to stop it. But no one is waiting at the top. I step out of the elevator into a marble foyer furnished with two heavy chairs and a low, marble table. No security guards, which is strange. Neither do I see any cameras. A silver garden spade leans against one wall, between a large gilt mirror and a ghastly painting of a city skyline reflected in a black, oily harbour. There are two doors. One to my left, and another beside the elevator. I sense that the second door leads up to the roof. I'm right. In a flash I am standing on top of one of the highest buildings in the capital. From here I can see the Parliament buildings, the Senate chambers, and the Supreme Court. I feel dizzy and begin to sweat. My knees shake and there's a high-pitched whine in my left ear. Possibly a drone, but I don't see anything. The concentration of barium up here must be off the charts. I must hurry.

Quickly, I unscrew the lid of the Mason jar, swish the empty jar around a bit, then screw the lid back on. Everything is going smoothly. I tiptoe down the stairs to the marble foyer, which is still empty, and move cautiously towards the elevator, cradling the Mason jar in the crook of my arm. Just before reaching the door, I see that the second door is slightly ajar, and hear voices coming from inside the penthouse. I can't make out what the voices are saying, but one of them sounds familiar. I angle myself so that I can peer through the narrow opening, and see a man I assume to be Serge Sverkoff sitting at a polished dining table talking to another man, whom I immediately recognize as the Deputy Minister, my future father-in-law.

I retreat to the elevator and push the ground-floor button. By the time I reach the lobby, my breathing has returned to normal. Not a soul has seen me. I'm about to leave the building when I see the younger of the two women I followed last month coming in, with Fidel on a leash. Filled with curiosity, I say hello to the woman as she waits for one of the other two elevators.

"Do you mind if I speak to your dog?" I say to her.

She looks at me in some alarm, but eventually smiles and says, "Of course not."

So I kneel down and run my hand over the robot's head and back, as though petting it. Actually, I'm feeling for its infrastructure, for the wires and electronic components concealed under its "skin." The thing feels alarmingly lifelike. It sits on its haunches with its tongue hanging out, for all the world like a real dog, and stares at me. A mistake: have you ever seen a dog stare directly into your eyes? "Hello, there, Fidel," I say. "Have you had any more letters from Meggy lately?" The thing doesn't budge. I try to touch its tongue, but it snaps its mouth shut and growls at me. Incredible. I lean closer to hear any mechanical sounds, any whirrs or clicks, coming from its mouth, and the damn thing bites my nose, drawing blood. I jump back, almost dropping the Mason jar. Very well, I've been warned. I take a handkerchief from my pocket and hold it to my nose. The woman says nothing, which I think is strange, under the circumstances. Then the elevator door opens and the woman pulls the thing into it without looking back at me.

Well, now they know I'm on to them.

NOVEMBER 14. Monday. There has been a light, overnight snowfall. Now that I know what is mixed in with that snow, I am careful to protect my feet. I pull two plastic bags over my shoes and also a pair of heavy rubber galoshes.

As I trudge to the office, I think about the results of my research for the past few days. Here's what I've found so far: Ethylene dibromide (EDB). High levels were found in chem trails analyzed by Richard L. Finke, the Ohio journalist who, more than twenty years ago, first alerted the world to the dangers of "lethal contrails" (they weren't called chem trails until later). Finke thought we were being sprayed with EDB in order to weaken our immune systems and cause sterility, but EDB also causes depression and systemic collapse, which of course we now find all around us. Ingesting just forty millilitres of the stuff can kill you. Experiments with rats show that the offspring of male rats exposed to EDB are born with birth defects, behavioural changes, and brain abnormalities. EDB, originally synthesized as an anti-knock additive in leaded gasoline, was banned at the same time that leaded gasoline was banned. But it's still used as a pesticide against termites and beetles in the lumber industry and, according to Finke, continues to be added to military jet fuel.

Why?

And what was the Deputy Minister doing in Serge Sverkoff's condominium? Is he one of the associates in Sverkoff and Associates? Is it even legal for a senior civil servant, responsible for hundreds of contracts with goods and services providers, to be an associate of a developer? Isn't that collusion? Conflict of interest? Influence peddling? Insider trading? Think of all the kickbacks he could be getting. This bears looking into. It will entail no small amount of danger.

I'll have to keep all this from Belinda, at least for the time being. But I need to know what I'll be getting into.

The problem is, people think their thoughts are formed in their brains, but they aren't. Our thoughts are carried to us by wind from the Caspian Sea and in dust from the Aral Sea and sometimes from the Sea of China. That's why controlling airborne contaminants is so important. What we think is determined by what is in the wind. Bob Dylan, right? He tried to warn us. Then he had that motorcycle accident. We now know that the government is conducting large-scale thought-control experiments on us by manipulating the chemical composition of those very winds. They have been doing this since at least 1996. They can only get away with it if we remain complacent, numb, docile consumers, if we literally continue to shop until we drop.

First it was barium, then ethylene dibromide, and now aluminum. We know what aluminum cookware does to us (or we used to know, until the thought police shut down the campaign against aluminum; that was before we learned to ask where the research funding was coming from). It's well known that long-term exposure to aluminum oxide causes dissociative behaviour, cognitive dissonance and, eventually, full-on dementia. How have we forgotten that? And now the government is spraying huge amounts of aluminum into the atmosphere, using military and commercial aircraft, ostensibly to deflect solar radiation from the Earth's surface. They call it "albedo modification," look it up, they're quite open about it. They've convinced us that they're simply testing ways to offset global warming, in this case by deflecting solar radiation in the atmosphere before it hits the Earth's surface. That would be a great idea if it worked, but guess what — the temperature isn't going down, folks, it's going up. So why are they still pumping aluminum into the sky? I've seen the photographs. Boeing 737s and Airbus A380s with giant containers of chemicals where passenger seats should have been. Each container has a large, red hose running from it to the wings, where the spray nozzles are concealed under the ailerons. Contrails my Aunt Mabel.

Come on, people, wake up! What they're doing has nothing to do with global warming; most of them don't even believe global warming exists. It has to do with world domination.

Belinda, by the way, means "beautiful" in two languages: French (*belle*) and Spanish (*linda*). If you write the word "Spain" on a sheet of paper, and compare it to the word "France" written by the same hand on the same paper, you will see that they are actually the same country.

Now ask yourself this: What do Spain and France have in common? They both have unoccupied thrones, and their governments are in turmoil. Coincidence?

DECEMBER 3. Tuesday or Wednesday. The report from my friend in the health lab was in my inbox when I came to work this morning: disappointingly low levels of barium, average amounts of EDB, but extraordinarily high levels of aluminum. So they don't want to kill us just yet, they only want us to remain docile. And forgetful. At least in Ottawa. Early onset senility, selective dementia, we've all seen it. Today one of my older colleagues, a man in his sixties but still fit, rides his bicycle to work every day, told me he took a bus home last night, leaving his bicycle in the carpark. He forgot he'd ridden it to work! After twenty-five years of riding a bicycle to work, he suddenly forgets and takes a bus home. He laughed it off, but I could see he was shaken. Next week he'll have forgotten the entire incident, until it happens again.

A note attached to the report said the high aluminum reading probably came from the lid of the Mason jar. Right.

Everything is so neatly explainable once you've swallowed the Kool-Aid.

I must resist! I will not be complacent! I will act! I will remember things!

Slipping into a trance, I revisit the meeting I overheard in the penthouse foyer between Sverkoff and the DM. I can't make out entire sentences, but I can recall isolated words. I think I heard "the children." Then one of them, I think it was Sverkoff, said something like "meat" or "eat." And then I heard the DM say "fresh," or maybe it was "flesh."

I am on the verge of an important discovery when my concentration is broken by that idiot of an office manager.

"Have you heard the news?" he says, looking at me with gleeful malice. What, am I being let go? Arrested? No: "The DM's daughter is getting married," he says. "Her father has announced her engagement. Too bad, eh, Brownnose?"

Impossible! The office manager is making it up to torment me. Belinda and I are betrothed. I ignore him and go about my work. Someone in the office meekly asks who the DM's daughter is going to marry.

"No one we know," he gloats, looking straight at me. "Some developer's son. Anton Sverkoff."

Developers think they are kings. They act as though they own the earth. They tear down everything that gets in their way and build colossal monuments to themselves in its place. They destabilize the universe by replacing the known past with the unknowable future. We must concentrate! Focus! They are not kings, they are normal people. To be a developer requires no special genius or talent for anything but making money. A moral conscience is actually a deterrent. Name one philosopher/developer! They feed on the talents of others. Of course, Sverkoff and the Deputy Minister are in cahoots. There is no mystery in that.

In a flash the true significance of the conversation I overheard in the penthouse comes to me. Children, fresh meat. Oh, God! Sverkoff and the DM were discussing the consumption of human flesh!

There are two ways toxic chemicals enter our bloodstream. One is through the thin layer of skin on the top of the head, and the other is by being breathed into the lungs. Ethylene dibromide settles out of the air onto the top of our heads (and if they're adding it to jet fuel, why wouldn't they add it to normal gasoline?). Aluminum oxide has to be breathed in. Today, on my way home from work, I went into a Home Hardware and purchased a good, sturdy hat, with ear flaps. Appropriately enough, it's called a Hunter's Cap. I also purchased a package of military-strength face masks of the kind that hospital workers and health professionals wore to protect themselves from Covid-19. I looked at the N95s, but chose the R99, because it also filters out airborne particulates attached to oil. When I got home I carefully lined the hat with six-millimetre polyethylene plastic (for a minute I considered using aluminum foil! Idiot!). I will wear it and the mask and the boots whenever I am outside. And my new coat with the collar up. I must protect myself. I must not succumb.

At home tonight, I open an email account under the name Ferdinand Yen, and email the requisition form for barium by the Department of Defense, and the report from the health lab about high levels of aluminum in the air, to seventeen radio stations and two national newspapers. I also post it on several subreddit sites that continue to document the chem-trail conspiracy. Ferdinand Yen, Whistle-Blower!

How many cases are there in history of simple persons, shopkeepers or humble civil servants, rising to become people of true influence and noble integrity? An overnight rock star, for example, or a film sensation. One day you're walking down the street on your way to work, a film director sees you and boom! You're the next Matt Damon. Or you spend your weekends in the basement recording your music on GarageBand, and one of your songs goes viral. What will Belinda say when she sees me on *60 Minutes* or *The Fifth Estate*? What will her father say? We knew him when, that's what they'll say. We recognized his potential right away, I made him my right-hand man. I wanted him to marry my daughter. I prayed that he would ask me to marry him. That's what they'll say.

DECEMBER 8. I'm not going to the office today, even though it's Thursday (I think). How can I go on working for a government that I know is plotting to murder its own citizens? On the other hand, I need to stay close to the centre in order to expose more of its nefarious purposes. A quandary. I need time to think it through clearly. How can I be both compliant and non-complicit?

I could go to work and do nothing. But that's what most of my colleagues do, anyway, so it would hardly be a form of protest. Showing up on time and doing nothing are the only two things expected of a civil servant. So tomorrow I will get to work late and work like a dog when I'm there. Only not on the things they think I'm working on. I'll hide in plain sight.

No response as yet from the media. Since sending out the emails I've been keeping track of the newspapers and radio stations, and I've been googling "barium" every hour or so.

Nothing keeps coming up. I'll send out follow-ups tomorrow from the office.

This morning I googled "cannibalism." This is what I learned: Every year, dozens of people are arrested and convicted of eating their fellow human beings. This has existed throughout the ages, in every country, and is no less prevalent now than it was five hundred years ago. All the werewolf and vampire legends, and not a few fairy tales, such as "Little Red Riding Hood" and "Hansel and Gretel," derive from our basic natural urge to eat one another, especially children. How often have you heard someone say to a baby, "You're so cute I could gobble you right up!" There is a Chinese expression that says when things have come to a dire pass, we "exchange children and eat them." Kissing is a barely sublimated form of the desire to chew, which is why it often progresses to nibbling and sucking. Think twice the next time you see someone wearing a T-shirt that says "Eat me!" There are now and always have been special "clubs" in which "bush meat" or "mountain pork" is regularly served. Cookbooks have been written. Secret banquets held in hidden hostelries. And wedding feasts! In this subculture, weddings are viewed as celebrations of the devouring of the female by the male. The bride is willingly "served" to the groom, after which she is literally "consumed" by his passion.

For some reason, I receive a memory of that silver garden spade leaning against the wall in Sverkoff's foyer. Why would someone who lives in a penthouse condominium have a garden spade? And a silver one, at that?

Belinda! My darling! Your cheeks are as soft and smooth as a peach!

I feel sick to my stomach!

DECEMBER 20. It's frightening the things you can purchase online. For $200 I was able to buy a 3500-megawatt laser pistol capable of firing a killer beam twenty-five miles into the air (airplanes typically fly at altitudes of between five and eight miles). It's called "Inspyred." Its beam can be calibrated to be blue, red, green, or clear, and be set to steady, pulse, or strobe mode. It can blind anything with eyes, including pilots. This afternoon I took it to the airport, which accommodates both military and commercial jets, and hiding in some trees outside the fence at the end of the main runway, I aimed the laser into the cockpits of incoming aircraft as they were landing. Someone has to do something. A few commercial planes went wonky, but none crashed. And none of the military planes were affected; they were probably drones, or maybe the military has developed some kind of deflecting mechanism. I left when I heard sirens and security vehicles. I stood outside the Arrivals area, as though waiting to meet a friend, and every time a pilot came by dragging his carry-on full of duty-free swag I accosted him (it was always a him). "Stop spraying chem trails!" I shouted. "Stop poisoning our air!" Most of the pilots, buffered by their female flight attendants, scurried guiltily away – flight attendants, indeed! – while others told me to "Fuck off!" and brushed rudely past me. One actually took a swing at me. Security forces were alerted, and I beat a hasty retreat. I hid in a cubicle in a men's washroom, changed my jacket and put on my Hunter's Cap and mask, and left the airport undetected. I had made my point.

Dear Belinda. No, Dearest Belinda. No, Our dearest darling Belinda. It is with deep, no, profound, dismay no regret no sadness that we write are writing this email to tell inform you that we must break off no end our engagement. By the time you read this, we expect we will either have been killed no assassinated or granted asylum in an embassy in one of the world's more enlightened countries, possibly Kazajistan. We have not been honest with you, our dearest love. You know us as Brown, a lowly cipher clerk in your father's department, but in fact our name is Ferdinand Yen. Yes, *that* Ferdinand Yen. Our official designation, of course, is Ferdinand the Eighth of Spain and France (Yen is the name of our house). For weeks now we have been hacking into your father's computer and sending top-secret files to news agencies and websites, exposing the government's abysmal no nefarious no perfidious plan to destroy no obliterate civilization as it now exists (CAINE) and replace it with the New-Order World (NOW). You have no doubt been following our campaign in the newspapers, without realizing it has been your own dear Brown, as you know him, who has brought all this to light no out into the open no to the world's attention. We are reliably informed that they are coming for us. We expect the fatal knock on our door at any hour, and have taken the necessary precautions. We needn't tell you what they are. You probably won't read about it in the media, but we will have done our duty. It remains only for us to warn you, my darling, of the terrible danger you are in. Do not go through with your father's plan to marry you to Anton. Anton's father is a cannibal. He intends to kill you with a silver garden spade and serve you to the guests at your own wedding. We overheard him discussing this with your father. As a magistrate, Sverkoff has sent hundreds of no countless innocent defendants no souls no victims to the electric chair no gallows no lethal injection to cover his own crimes, but it is blood, the sight and taste of blood, that he craves. Also, your dog Meggy is a robot. If you don't believe us, ask it. You can disable it by attaching a powerful magnet to its head.

If they ask why we did it, tell them it was for the children. The children we once were, the children we are now, and the children yet to be born.

Your beloved Ferdinand VIII.

DECEMBER 23. I have shut down the government! They are calling it a budgetary impasse, but that is fake news. My exposing their conspiracy has thrown them into a blind panic. They are firing off memos and orders-in-council in all directions. Troops have been deployed, surveillance ramped up, computer codes changed, borders shut down. No one knows where the threat is coming from, except that it is internal. From the enemy within. There are more soldiers in the streets than I've ever seen before. Robot dogs roam the alleys and the parks teem with robotic squirrels. Bird-like drones fly continuously over the city. Fidel was no doubt equipped with a superior sense of smell, and now they have my scent. I have donned my rubber galoshes and my Hunter's Cap, and strapped on my vest, which I will hide under my new overcoat. The mall will be crowded with Christmas shoppers. The money-lender's shop in the temple will be full.

Save the children!

ABOUT "DIARY OF A CONSPIRACY THEORIST"

Nikolai Gogol's story "Diary of a Madman," written during the reign of Nicholas I, recounts the descent of its main character, a minor clerk named Aksenty Ivanovich Poprishchin, into a state of paranoia and madness in which he believes he is the King of Spain. The story is told from Poprishchin's point of view, in the form of Poprishchin's diary, and since Poprishchin does not consider himself to be insane, his madness is to be inferred by the reader. Gogol's story was covered in 1885 by Guy de Maupassant, in "The Diary of a Madman," in which a homicidal magistrate's diary is found after the magistrate's death, and read by a colleague: again, we get only the magistrate's point of view. Gogol's story was covered again by the Chinese writer Lu Xun, in 1918, in "A Madman's Diary," which is considered to be the first modern short story to be published in China.

When, in *Hamlet*, Claudius tells Polonius that "madness in great ones must not unwatched go," he meant that insanity at high levels can cause a lot of trickle-down damage – which is no doubt why A.J. Rowling tweeted that line on May 28, 2017, the day the White House announced that it was considering "advance vetting" of then-president Donald Trump's incendiary tweets. (This was shortly after Trump tweeted that an investigation into possible ties between his presidential campaign and Russia was "the greatest single witch hunt of a politician in American history.") Eventually, Twitter (now X) shut down Trump's account, evidently believing that madness in great ones should go not only unwatched, but also unread. Things have changed since then; Trump is back on X, and his long, middle-of-the-night ravings on Truth Social have become increasingly disturbing. It is now believed (at least by Trump) that madness in great ones must be read on a daily basis.

But madness in the not-so-great shouldn't be ignored, either. Mad public servants tend to delude themselves into believing they are loud and powerful.

In Gogol's story, Poprishchin becomes convinced that his boss's daughter is in love with him, and that he is the heir to the Spanish throne: in his case, his delusions are harmless to anyone but himself. These days, when clerks begin to believe they are powerful, they have the internet at their disposal and can disseminate their delusions to a vast number of other, equally delusional clerks. Julian Assange, the founder of WikiLeaks, is a case in point: Andrew O'Hagan, who was commissioned to ghostwrite Assange's autobiography but turned the job down after spending time with Assange, ascribes to Assange "a form of madness" that Assange demonstrated by his colossal internal contradictions, among them a stated desire to make powerful institutions more accountable and transparent while keeping WikiLeaks as unaccountable and opaque as he possibly could. Assange's raving and compulsive lying eventually led O'Hagan to conclude that the man "is probably a little mad, sad and bad."

Assange is not a great man, but his madness is far from harmless: he claimed that it was his intervention, not Vladimir Putin's, that swung the U.S. 2016 election in Trump's favour, and if that's so he has a lot to answer for. As Elizabeth Kolbert wrote in the *New Yorker* (April 22, 2019), madness in minions can now spread like measles in a daycare by means of "the internet, easily buildable blogs, and widely used social media." Something like three billion people watch

YouTube every month, and the more they watch a certain kind of video, the more YouTube lines up the same kind of videos for them to watch next. The internet is no longer a simple tool that can be used for either good or evil, if it ever was; it's more like an assault weapon: yes, you can use an AR-15 to hunt deer, but more often than not it's put to more nefarious purposes.

In *The Economics of Innocent Fraud*, published in 2004, John Kenneth Galbraith noted that terms such as "market economy" and "free enterprise," once advocated by economists like Milton Friedman, have been rendered obsolete now that the influence of online advertising controls not only the way the population shops, but also how it thinks, and therefore how it votes. "Reference to the market system as a benign alternative to capitalism," he wrote, "is a bland, meaningless disguise of the deeper corporate reality – of producer power extending influence over, even control of, consumer demand." As the immeasurable reach of the internet allows the "well-financed management of the public response to extend into the political arena," Galbraith believed that influence over, even control of, voter "choice" has made the concepts of freedom and democracy rather quaint. Our recent realization of the potential of artificial intelligence to not only influence our choices but to render them entirely irrelevant underscores the accuracy of Galbraith's analysis.

I didn't want my version of Gogol's story of a character's descent into madness to be a paranoid political rant. Gogol was not anti-government; he was in favour of the autocracy that ruled Russia in the time of Nicholas I. In my cover of Gogol's story, I am less interested in the cause of Brown's madness – we do not know the cause of Poprishchin's madness – than I am in the form it takes. Poprishchin, perhaps pushed over some edge by the end of his imagined betrothal (an intrusion of reality into his fantasies), sinks deeper into his delusional world and convinces himself that he is the King of Spain, and for that is locked away in an insane asylum. Problem solved.

In the twenty-first century, however, madness is both less obvious (i.e., less specific) and apparently not only tolerated but rewarded. I thought that Brown's belief in a conspiracy theory about chem trails, allied with his casual reliance on various kinds of technological malevolence, would make it clear that his brain has become somewhat porous. Since the pandemic, however, Brown's case has become so common (several people I know strongly believe that airplane contrails are actually chem trails, and that chemicals are being sprayed into the atmosphere by the U.S. government to pacify potential dissidents; others assure me that Covid-19 and even measles vaccines contain secret nanobots that, once in our bloodstreams, will control our thoughts and behaviour) that few readers, I worried, would automatically consider him insane. Recent polls show that half of Americans have endorsed at least one conspiracy theory in the past three years.

And so I have Brown further believe that the Deputy Minister is a cannibal. This comes from Lu Xun's "A Madman's Diary." Lu's main character is convinced that his brother intends to eat him, in fact that the entire population of China secretly belongs to a cannibalistic cult. That, I hoped, would surely convince readers that Brown has crossed a thin line into insanity – until I remembered that every Sunday millions of ordinary citizens line up in their places of worship to eat the body of Christ and drink his blood, albeit symbolically. There is no border between reality and illusion, or delusion, in the deeply religious. Or rather, you can decree a border between madness and sanity, but you will need to build a wall to prevent people from crossing it.

One could argue that Poprishchin's madness was harmless, that even if government agencies failed to clear the streets and offices of Poprishchins, Russia would still be a safe place to raise children and carry out business. There weren't that many Poprishchins about, or people like Collegiate Assessor Kovalyov (in Gogol's story "The Nose"), who woke up one morning to discover that his nose had become a state councillor. Such people weren't threats, they were curiosities; they merely exhibited what George Saunders, in *A Swim in a Pond in the Rain*, calls "strangeness." Yes, I know that, as characters in a work of literature, they are symbolic of a deeper societal malaise; they are bombs with lit fuses, and the fuse finally reached the bomb in 1917. Whereas modern-day madmen wield limitless and immediate power.

Guy de Maupassant's "Diary of a Madman" appeared in 1885, during France's establishment of French rule over Tunis, Madagascar, the Congo, the Niger, and Indochina. The French prime minister, Jules Ferry, justified these exploitative missions by declaring that "it is the right of superior races . . . to civilize inferior races." In de Maupassant's story, the madman is a highly respected judge who has the power to decide whether those who appear before him are innocent or guilty, and becomes obsessed with his ability to kill with impunity. "After all," he writes in his diary, "what is a being? It is a grain of life that moves on the earth, coming from I know not where, that one can destroy at one's will."

These days, madness in great ones seems not so much a warning as the fulfilment of a terrifying prophecy.

THE RING

ON A WARM, fall evening in 1946, a young husband and his wife went for a walk. Their intention was to walk down their street, cut across an open field that skirted a train track, cross the track, and continue along another, longer street that led to Jackson Park. It was October; they had been married since May, and they were still deeply in love. It had not been easy for them, for during the War he had been a sailor from the mainland, not even an officer, and her family was a wealthy Newfoundland trading family, originally from England. There had been no open opposition to their courtship, because it was assumed that when the War ended, he would be shipped back to where he came from. He was shipped back, first to Toronto and then to his home town, Windsor, but by then they were married, not exactly secretly but in some haste, and the family had no choice but to give in. The couple had been in Windsor for a month.

They were wonderfully happy. There was no more secretiveness; no whispered planning, no despairing love letters, no doleful glances over the Sunday dinner table. Nothing now was hidden from her mother and father, whom she loved and who wrote to her every week with news and encouragements from home. They were a married couple; they lived together, walked together arm in arm in broad daylight, slept together at night and woke together in the morning, which amazed them still. They had their own ration books, bills came to the house addressed to Mr. and Mrs. Lewis; the milkman, the iceman, and the bread man all knew her by her married name. Now that he was out of the Navy, Jack looked for work every day, and talked about buying a car. They rented a darling little house that was just the right size for them, with an ice box, a gas range, a porcelain sink and a wringer washer in the kitchen. It was as though the heaven they had dreamed of in St. John's had come to earth in Windsor, with all the things they wanted in it: laughter and late breakfasts and chintz curtains and love-making, sales at Woodworth's, an Anglican church just a few blocks away, with a red-faced minister who smiled when he shook their hands. Jack made it his business to ensure that nothing should ever bring a shadow to his wife's lovely, round, white face. Vivian felt that, for the first time in her young life, she was able to move and breathe in complete freedom. She had never lived unobserved. Her family's love had been confining; Newfoundland was restricting; the War had been a deprivation. Now when she wrote to her mother, it was as one woman to another. She was a married woman; Jack was her life.

And Windsor was a constant source of wonder and delight. St. John's was a city, too, but it seemed so provincial compared to Windsor. Windsor was filled with unknown people whose lives she could only guess at. In St John's she knew the purpose of just about every building; in Windsor there were houses and entire streets that were completely unintelligible to her. What was down that lane? Who could possibly live in a house like that? What would that oddly shaped building be for? And right across the river, clearly visible from the end of Ouellette Avenue, were the soaring towers of the United States! Jack had worried on the train that Windsor would not be good enough for her, that she'd be shocked, or possibly bored, but he was wrong. Windsor transfixed her. It was what she had imagined every time she and Jack had talked about getting married. In a sense, she had married Windsor, and the month they had been here had been like a prolonged honeymoon. Every day she dressed and did her hair as though for an adventure, as though to perform in a movie that had been especially written for her, and for Jack, too, of course. Everything she did she did with a seriousness, almost a studiousness, that Jack tended to mistake for boredom or disdain. But it wasn't, it was just her trying very hard to get her part right.

Back home, Octobers were cold and damp, there would be an icy wind coming down off the Labrador coast. But here in the evening she was still able to wear a light sweater over her summer dress, and white open shoes – imagine! The path they took through the field was bordered by high, wild shrubs and thick thistles, and just before it crossed the tracks there was a shallow ditch filled with sooty water. Someone had thrown a plank over the worst of it, and Jack went ahead and helped her keep her balance. What fun! They were like children in a playground. The tops of the train tracks were shiny with use, two smooth ribbons of light against the dark-red cinders that had been spread between the ties by workers she didn't know. She loved the tracks and the telephone poles beside them, and the smell of creosote; they meant preservation, permanence, the promise of industry. Jack would surely find work here, whereas in post-war St. John's all the best jobs had been taken by the returning sons of Newfoundland.

On the street leading away from the tracks were two houses under construction, in-fills, Jack called them, and they stopped in front of the first one for Jack to light a cigarette. The door opened and, to her surprise, Jack's brother Bennie came out onto the porch and, when he saw them, down to the sidewalk. He was wearing a dark-blue shirt and blue dungarees and a white painter's cap, and was everywhere splattered with white plaster. His dark hands seemed even darker beneath the whiteness of the plaster.

"Dad here?" Jack asked, offering Bennie a cigarette.

"Naw."

She thought how clever Jack was, and how sad. He knew so much about plastering and house construction, he had spent hours on the train telling her about his father's company, how well it was doing. He'd told her a lot of other things, of course. That he had tried to join the army when he was sixteen, but had been sent home because he was too young, and on the day he'd turned eighteen he had joined the Navy. "Anything to get away from Windsor," he said, "and now here I am going back with my tail between my legs." He'd laughed at that, a resigned, sighing kind of laugh, as though the decision had been made by someone else and was out of his hands. There'd been no work for him in Newfoundland, and so he'd had to leave. Until now there hadn't been any work in Windsor, either, but as the two men conversed, she gathered that their father, having secured the contract to plaster both these houses, had left the actual labour to Bennie, who now asked Jack to help him. Jack dropped his cigarette to the sidewalk, stepped on it, and agreed. She knew he hadn't wanted to go back to plastering, that he'd been looking for something cleaner, perhaps in sales. He knew a lot about cars, too. Everyone in Windsor seemed to know a lot about cars. But she also knew that he'd agreed to work with Bennie for her sake, no, for *their* sake, and her heart swelled at the thought; she took his arm to let him know she understood, and that this job would only be temporary until he found something better.

Jack and Bennie talked about plastering for a while, about which yard they would order the materials from and who would pay for it, and Vivian let her gaze wander and her mind dwell on other things. She thought about watching Jack undress at night before going to bed, how shy he had been at first, keeping his back to her until the last second, and then when he turned she was glad he had left the light on. She felt herself blushing happily at the thought, and thought about it again. When her cheeks had cooled, the two men were still talking about plastering. After a while they stopped, and Bennie asked Jack if he'd heard about the chicken thief. This brought her attention back to the present.

"Chicken thief?" she asked. It seemed such a bizarre leap from plastering.

"Someone's been breaking into chicken coops at night and stealing chickens," Bennie said. "Never leaves a trace. He's like a fox."

"Why would he steal chickens?" she asked, mystified, and both Bennie and Jack looked at her.

"Well," said Bennie, "to eat."

Jack laughed. "Vivian thinks all meat comes from a butcher's shop, already wrapped up in butcher's paper. Don't you?"

"No, of course I don't," she said. "We always had chickens in Ferryland, and sheep, and my brother even kept a cow for milk. I've killed dozens of chickens. I just don't know why anyone would steal one. Back home, if you need a chicken you just ask for it, and someone will give you one."

"Ferryland?" said Bennie.

"He a coloured man?" Jack asked Bennie.

"Sure is. Three nights ago he broke into a place up on Wyandott. The owner and his son caught him red-handed, and the thief stabbed the man in the stomach, then punched the kid so hard he broke his jaw. The police are out looking for him now."

"What happened to the man?" Vivian asked.

"The white man? He died, hmm. There was a fight and the thief had a knife on him. The white man broke the thief's arm with a baseball bat and then got himself stabbed. They say there was blood all over the floor of the coop, and out in the alley, too. I don't know where the boy was. Looks like the thief hit him and climbed over the back fence and run off with a chicken, broken arm and all. I sure hope they catch him."

Vivian nodded in agreement. She had never heard of anything so horrible happening back home. She couldn't fathom it. It would be like killing someone for a fish. This was certainly a different place, so close to the United States. She felt a chill run down her spine that was not entirely unpleasant. "Poor devil," she said.

"Poor devil nothing," said Jack. "Wyandott's not all that far from here. Good thing we don't have chickens in our backyard. But you can't be too careful, especially with coloureds. They never had any work. And they never heard of asking, they just take."

"He got a broken arm he likely show up at a hospital sooner or later," said Bennie.

"Aw, they got their own witch doctors," said Jack.

The two men went back to talking about business, and Vivian stood a little apart from them, wondering what the thief might be doing at that moment. She tried not to think about the boy with the broken jaw, his father dead, and the dead man's wife, now a widow. Jack must have seen how distressed she was, because he turned to her and said she should keep walking, he would finish with Bennie and catch up with her in a few minutes, and they would continue on to Jackson Park and sit on a bench to look at the fall flowers. She said all right, and moved off. Soon Jack would be working, and she would have to get used to walking by herself, otherwise she'd be cooped up in the house all day. She wouldn't mind being alone. She liked the way she felt now, her husband and Bennie behind her but not too far away, the fall flowers ahead of her, and the unfamiliar territory between. She'd walk a block or so, then slow down and let Jack catch up. When she'd gone half a block the thought struck her again that she had never in her life been absolutely alone, without someone always knowing where she was. This was another new sensation, and she felt a thrill travel down her once more.

She was in a part of town that was new to her. There were houses and small apartment buildings, and also square, cinder-block buildings with flat roofs that looked like miniature factories. Were they garages? But they didn't have doors facing the street. Chestnut trees arched above the sidewalk, and squirrels chattered at her from the high branches. The sidewalks and drives were littered with green, prickly chestnut hulls, like tiny, exploded mines, as though a sea battle had been fought here, the ships all sunk and the war over. She turned to see if Jack was coming, but he was not, the devil. He would rather stand and talk to his brother about plaster than walk with her to the park.

As she passed a dilapidated, shed-like building set back a few yards from the sidewalk, she was struck by a sudden memory, and stopped to think about it.

There had been a shed like this behind their house in Ferryland. It was before the War, but the shed seemed always to have been there, to have stood forlorn and sagging for so long that no one even noticed it any more. When she and her sisters and brothers and cousins played hide-and-go-seek, she would sometimes hide in it and none of the others would think of looking for her there. It was as if the place were invisible, or existed in some other realm, and what people saw when they passed it was only the faint glimmer of an object that may or may not have been a shed. If anyone but her were asked what was in that spot, they wouldn't have been able to say. Nothing, they would say, or maybe, a big stone? A pile of old hay? This shed in Windsor was thus a direct link to her old hiding place in Ferryland, a kind of portal, and she felt, dizzily, that if she went in and stood very still, when she came out again she would find her sisters and cousins looking for her, someone would call "one-two-three-on-Vivian," and they would all make a dash for home. It was a silly thought, but what if she hid in there until Jack came along, expecting her to be waiting for him at the corner. When he didn't see her, he would look about, not understanding where she could have gone, and for a minute or two, or, if she were particularly cruel, for five minutes, he would experience what an empty, sad, and unendurably horrid place his world would be if she were no longer in it.

At the very least he would know what it was like to have been expecting a pleasant walk to Jackson Park with the person one loved, and to have been robbed of that pleasure for no good reason. To talk about plaster! What was there about plaster that needed so urgently to be talked about?

After he passed by looking bewildered and worried, she would come out of the shed, sneak up behind him and tap him on the shoulder, and they would laugh and embrace.

She walked around to the side of the shed away from Jack, careful not to catch her sweater on the shrubs growing alongside the path. Really, people in Windsor were not as particular about their yards as were the people of St. John's. Everything grew so abundantly here. Her skirt snagged on a nail sticking out of the corner of the shed, and she spent a good deal of time unsnagging it. Still Jack did not appear. The door to the shed, invisible from the street, hung crookedly from a single, rusted hinge, and the dirt floor inside was damp. She held her handkerchief to her nose because of the sharp smell of engine oil and mould. She turned to see if she could push the door closed behind her, but she could not, and when she again looked towards the back of the shed, she found herself staring into the face of a man who was already there.

At first, she could barely make him out in the dark. He had been crouched in one of the obscure corners, but now he was straightening in the weak light coming through a small window on the side of the shed. His face was black and scratched, his hands, which hung by his sides, were balled into fists. Her brother had large hands, a fisherman's hands, but this man's were even larger, and as dark as his face. He was dressed in a ragged khaki shirt tucked into a pair of woollen trousers kept up by a rope that looped around his waist and over his left shoulder. He was barefooted, but had wrapped a pair of puttees around his insteps and partway up his calves. She realized with a start that he was wearing the tattered remnants of an army uniform. His left arm hung like a marionette's empty sleeve, and in his right hand she saw, now that her eyes had adjusted to the gloom, that his balled fist held a knife. The man and Vivian stood calm and still, looking each other up and down, each trying to assess how much of a threat the other was. Neither spoke a word.

It did not occur to her to be afraid. Never in her life had she been exposed to danger; she did not recognize it now. If she had to analyze what she was feeling, she would have said it was curiosity. She was trying to work out what to do next, what he would do next. For it is not the apparition itself that changes the life of the person who experiences it, but what happens after that. So far her life was unchanged. She thought she could hear Jack's footsteps coming up the sidewalk. She imagined the puzzled look on his face, perhaps tinged with annoyance. She did not call out to him. That might provoke a reaction from the man, and that would change her life.

She looked about the shed without, as it were, taking her eyes off the man's face. It was more lair than shed. Two sacks of dried weeds or straw formed a kind of pallet on the bare ground, which was strewn with chicken feathers and small bones. A metal bucket, turned upside down, with holes punched around it, must have served as the man's stove. The only other object she could make out was the knife, which he held tightly in his right hand. She suddenly saw herself through his eyes, a white figure making its way towards him in the darkness, like an apparition of death. He moved his right arm so that it hung down in front of him, and slowly raised the point of the knife until it was aimed at her throat. It was a ridiculous gesture, there wasn't a hint of threat in it. He didn't smile as he made it, but the corners of his wide mouth tightened a little. Then, shaking from the effort, he lowered the knife.

How to interpret this gesture? She had nothing of value on her except her wedding ring, which she had vowed never to remove. She drew it off now. She had a bit of difficulty with the knuckle, and dropped her handkerchief. She held the ring out to him. In her mind, she was not bargaining for her life. She was not afraid. Whatever it was this man inspired in her, it was not fear of what he might do to her. It was more like remorse for what she had already done to him. She was commanding him, she wanted him to vanish, to remove his dreadful figure from her sight so that she could forget it had ever been there. He was not supposed to be there, blocking this passage from her present to her past. Her body was meant to pass freely between the two. She could now hear Jack's footsteps picking up speed and receding past the shed.

Slowly he reached out his left hand to take the ring. His fingers touched hers and she did not recoil. She let the ring go, but he could not hold it, could not close his hand around it. His face grimaced with pain, and the ring fell to the ground beside the handkerchief. They both followed its descent with their eyes, watching it roll a few inches towards the man and stop before his bare foot. Almost without moving he kicked it aside and looked again at her face. They remained like that, looking at one another; she could not say for how long, but she felt that an understanding had passed between them, not the ring but something that had required the ring. Now she was changed.

The man bent and picked up her handkerchief. Still keeping his eyes on her, he wrapped the handkerchief around the blade of his knife. This caused him so much pain that his face tightened and glistened, became almost phosphorescent. With trembling hands he placed the wrapped knife in a sheath that hung from his belt. Perhaps the sheath had been too big for the knife, and now it fit snugly. He looked at her for two or three more seconds, as the pain subsided, and then lifted his face a little, as if to the sun, although there was no sun, only his still-radiant face, and closed his eyes. She had been wrong. She wasn't commanding him. He was dismissing her.

She took a step back. He didn't move. She bent and backed out through the sagging door, slipped noiselessly along the side of the shed to the sidewalk, and stood there for a long time, listening. Then she hurried along the sidewalk to find Jack.

Her husband was waiting at the corner. When he saw her coming the way he had just come, he scratched the back of his head. And when she joined him, he looked at her but did not ask where she had been. Neither did he notice anything changed in her, even though she felt so different now, so exposed, that she was surprised he even recognized her. She took his arm and they continued on to Jackson Park.

Later that night, after they had eaten and she had washed and dried the dishes and put them away in the little cupboard above the sink, she gave an agonized cry.

"What's wrong?" Jack called from the living room. "What is it?"

He came into the kitchen.

"I've lost my ring," she said, tears welling in the corners of her eyes.

"What ring?" Jack asked, as if she had thousands.

"My wedding ring. Look." She held up her hand.

"Where did you lose it?"

"I don't know. It must have come off when I was doing the dishes."

Jack had given her the ring as a symbol of their union, and now she had given it to the thief. She had wedded herself to – but to what, exactly? To his poverty, his persecution, his silent loneliness? To all the sorrow and misery that existed this side of the portal? And yet she did not feel that she had been unfaithful, neither to herself nor to Jack. It was as though she had become wedded to Jack all the more, as though somehow, and she did not yet have the faintest idea how this could have been, although she sensed that it had to do with Jack's brother Bennie, whose hand under its coating of plaster had been as dark in the daylight as the thief's had been in the half-light of the shed, Jack and the thief were the same man, and that being wedded to one was to be forever bound to the other.

"It doesn't matter," Jack said, taking her in his arms. "We're still as married now as we were. And I'll find the ring. I'll get a wrench and take the drain off, there's a trap and it'll be in there. And if it isn't, I'll buy you a new one. Everything will be just as it was before, you'll see."

"Yes, darling," she said, "everything will be just as it was."

ABOUT "THE RING"

"The Ring" is a cover of the short story "The Ring," by the Danish writer Isak Dinesen. Her story was included in her 1958 collection, *Anecdotes of Destiny.* Although Dinesen's first language was Danish and she wrote many works of nonfiction in Danish, all her fiction and her best-known book, *Out of Africa*, were written and first published in English, and only later translated into Danish. She claimed that she wrote her stories and the memoir in English, but there is internal evidence that she at least thought about them first in Danish, so that her English texts can be thought of as a kind of translation.

She was born Karen Dinesen, in Rungsted, Zealand, which is near Copenhagen, Denmark, in 1885. Her family on both sides were wealthy landowners – her father was a politician and a poet with a tragic secret that drove him to commit suicide when Karen (known in the family as Tania, or Tanne) was ten. She wrote a few short stories in Danish in her early twenties, and moved to Kenya in December 1913 with her fiancé, Baron Bror von Blixen-Finecke (they were married a month later, and she became Baroness Karen von Blixen-Finecke), to establish a coffee plantation in the Ngong Hills, above Nairobi. The baron, never an attentive husband, decamped in 1921 (they were divorced four years later), and Karen Blixen ran the plantation herself for the next ten years. Because of its altitude, the land was not favourable to agriculture, and she spent 150,000 kroner of the family-owned Karen Coffee Company's money trying to teach the soil to say coffee. Two years of drought, followed by a severe insect infestation and the softening of the coffee market after the First World War, were the final blows; the family pulled the financial plug in 1931, whereupon she was forced to sell the farm and return to Denmark. There, to earn a living, she returned to writing.

Out of Africa, a nonfiction account of her years in Kenya, appeared in 1937, and a few years later in Danish, translated by herself. In a strange way that she must have found bitterly ironic, her writing ensured that the defunct plantation would actually continue to exist in perpetuity in the minds of her many readers. And the 1985 film based on the book, starring Meryl Streep and Robert Redford, ensured that the book achieved an international renown it might not otherwise have had. I remember watching the film when it came out (I greatly admired Robert Redford's hunting jacket), and retain startlingly beautiful images of Kenya, a strong sense of Dinesen's determination to keep the plantation going — not so much for herself, she has written, because she could have abandoned the farm and returned to Denmark at any time and actually saved money, but because of her concern for the Kikuyu workers she had hired, who had lived on the land for centuries, and who, she said, were happy now to depend on her and the plantation for their livelihood.

These days, it's hard to think of any plantation owned by a white colonist employing Black workers, on their own continent, even — or especially — on their own ancestral land, as the paradise Dinesen imagined it to be. Nowhere in the book (or the film) is there a suggestion that the very idea of a plantation owned by a white colonial master and worked by dozens of underpaid Black workers, whom the white master regards as her "good friends," was a bankrupt notion from the start. In her many letters to her mother, she writes about her feeling of kinship with her "black brothers" in Africa, but there is much familiar condescension tinged by apprehension in the way she writes about them in *Out of Africa*. "Sometimes on a safari, or on the farm, in a moment of extreme tension, I have met the eyes of my Native companions, and have felt that we were at a great distance from one another." She often compares the Kikuyu to wild animals, even to prey species: "What I learned from the game of the country was useful to me in my dealings with the Native people." And she refers to them as "savages," as when, in praising her Kikuyu chef, Kamante, for learning how to make European dishes, she says, "Nothing, I thought, could be more mysterious than this natural instinct in a savage for our culinary art."

The word "savage" is a key colonial marker. It is a transcription, but not a translation, of the French word *sauvage*, which doesn't mean "a brutal or vicious person," as the Oxford English Dictionary defines "savage." *Sauvage* simply means "wild," as in undomesticated. It is possible that a wild person can be gentle and nurturing and, of course, civilized — the Kikuyu, or Agikuyu, had been part of the Bantu nation since the sixth century, and established in their homeland on Mount Kenya since the thirteenth century. They had a well-defined system of government and a strong religious tradition that held that everything in the universe is connected by an inner spiritual force given directly by a single, divine being. They were a peaceful people; certainly, they were not savages in the sense implied by their British conquerors after 1888.

Out of Africa was not intended to be an apology for colonialism; it is primarily a love story. But then, so is *Gone with the Wind*. From 1918, and especially after her separation from Blixen, Dinesen carried on a love affair with a titled Englishman, Denys Finch Hatton (Robert Redford in the film version), an intelligent, handsome but somewhat feckless adventurer such as is often found in "outposts of civilization" (one thinks of Kipling's Kimball O'Hara, in *Kim*, who, for all his Indian ways, was primarily concerned with the continuance of British rule in India, or of Joseph Conrad's Kurtz, whose abandonment of European morality was the darkness at the heart of Africa). Dinesen's affair lasted until Finch Hatton's death in a plane crash in 1931. For ten years, when he wasn't on safari, which he was most of the time, he lived with Dinesen on the plantation, although he took no more active interest in its operation than Baron Blixen had. When Dinesen published her earlier stories, she said she did not want to be a writer because she had "an intuitive fear of being trapped," but she ended up being trapped anyway, first by her marriage to Blixen, then by her love for the largely absent Finch Hatton, and finally by her struggle to keep the plantation going.

All three endeavours failed, although it is only the latter that she writes about in *Out of Africa*. Hers is a most curious love story, in that there is no hint in the book that she and Finch Hatton were lovers. (Neither does she mention the fact that, in 1915, she spent a year in Denmark being treated for syphilis, which she had contracted from her husband.) However, Hannah Arendt is right when she notes, in an essay about Dinesen in the *New Yorker*, that "the connection of an artist's life with her work has always raised embarrassing problems, and our eagerness to see recorded, displayed and discussed in public what once were strictly private affairs and nobody's business is probably less legitimate than our curiosity is ready to admit." Arendt was not alone in decrying the emphasis in English departments and publishing houses these days on a writer's biography (viz. their ethnic identity, and whether they are writing from their own "lived experience") at the expense of an objective or even literary consideration of their work. Philip Roth railed against the trend in his final Zuckerman novel, *Exit Ghost*. "Nobody reads anyone when you think about it," a young biographer tells the aging Zuckerman. "On the other hand, there's a huge popular appetite for secrets." Dinesen kept her secrets to herself.

I have reservations about the politics of *Out of Africa*. I'm not alone in this; Edward Said places the book within "a structure of attitude and narrative that entitles the European authorial subject to hold on to an overseas territory, derive benefits from it, depend on it, but ultimately refuse it autonomy or independence," and Teju Cole recognizes it as another work about Africa's "heart of darkness" written for whites. And yet I find it an extraordinarily sad and powerful work of literature. Its depth is deceptive, and it compels me to look at Dinesen's other writing with sharpened eyes.

I became interested in what these days is referred to as her process: how did she write these stories? When she returned to Denmark after selling the plantation, she took up writing because, she said, she needed to make a living, and all she knew how to do was cook and write stories, and if she were going to be trapped, she would rather it not be in a kitchen, as is the woman in another of her stories, "Babette's Feast." She wrote in English, Arendt says, "out of loyalty to her dead lover's language," and has been justly praised as "an excellent stylist."

The English in which she expressed that stylistic excellence, however, sometimes strikes my translator's ear as a bit stiff—too many "a"s and "the"s—and some of her sentences seem downright odd. For example, in "The Deluge at Norderney," the first story in *Seven Gothic Tales* (1934), she describes the town as being quaint but not backward: "There was even a small casino," she writes, "where the coquetry with the dangerous powers of existence could be carried on in a different measure." What is "coquetry with the dangerous powers of existence"? Flirting with the aristocracy? And does "in a different measure" mean "to a greater degree"? The sentence sounds to me like a bad translation of a sentence originally composed in another language. I suspect that she composed her stories in Danish, first, if only in her head, at the sentence level, and then "translated" them into English as she wrote them down.

Dinesen's "The Ring" is the final story in *Anecdotes of Destiny* – the same collection that contains the magnificent "Babette's Feast" – and concerns a young married couple, the bride's wedding ring, and a sheep thief. It is a wonderfully lucid and yet complex story about secrets, and how a secret, which is after all a lie, can cast a shadow over the happiest marriage, and taint our notions of love and freedom. We remember the terrible consequences of her father's secret love affair, and the secrets Baron Blixen must have kept from his wife that ended in her contracting syphilis. There are still the stilted phrases – "It was not a long time since she had played with dolls" – but the narrative is so compelling that the eye barely snags on them.

I am fascinated by the interplay of secrets and freedom, by their mutual exclusivity and their connections to race, having written two novels that explore their various manifestations. I was also struck by the way Dinesen's story intersects with my own life: like Dinesen's Lovisa, my mother lost her ring in the first year of her marriage to my father – although it was her engagement ring, not her wedding ring. She always claimed that it slipped off her finger while she was washing dishes, but it was never found, rarely even alluded to, and my father never bought her a new one. Dinesen's story made me wonder if there weren't a deeper story behind my mother's lost ring, and somehow this shadow story became connected in my mind with my father's secret identity as an African Canadian. And both these stories, Dinesen's and mine, are focused on the figure of the thief. It is because of him, or of their symbolic marriage to him, that both Lovisa and Vivian tell their first lies to their husbands. Dinesen's attitude towards her African workers in Kenya corresponded, in my own creative reality, with my father's (and therefore my) African heritage, and so I made the thief in my version a Black man, and Vivian's lie to her husband part of the larger lies whites continue to tell Blacks.

Dinesen thought of herself as a storyteller: "*Moi, je suis une conteuse,*" Arendt quotes her as saying, "*et rien qu'une conteuse.*" But the stories she told aren't love stories. Like *Out of Africa*, beneath their harlequinesque surface they are stories about race and class and privilege.

THE CARTEL

ON JANUARY 15, the Mexican national newspaper *El País* ran the following story in small type on page one, tucked safely below the fold:

> The well-known environmentalist and human rights activist Sylvia Gonzalez, director of El Rosario Monarch Butterfly Preserve in the free and sovereign state of Michoacán, has been missing since last Tuesday. It is widely suspected that her disappearance has to do with her strong opposition to illegal logging in El Rosario, which threatens the survival of the Monarch butterfly, an endangered species that migrates annually to Michoacán and hibernates in the pine trees of the reserve. El Rosario is a UNESCO World Heritage Site, and the largest butterfly sanctuary in the world. In addition to being at the forefront of the anti-logging movement, Señorita Gonzalez has also been an outspoken opponent of the many illegal avocado farms appearing in the region. In spite of their best efforts, the police have so far failed to trace the whereabouts of the missing environmentalist.

Of course, everyone in Michoacán knew about Sylvia Gonzalez. Before becoming El Rosario's director, she'd been a popular community leader who, several years before, had led a protest march from Angangueo all the way to Morelia, the state capital, to demand government protection for Michoacán farmers. Drug cartels, which had been trying to take over the state's avocado industry, were threatening farmers' lives. She had been elected as state deputy, the first woman in Mexico to hold such a position, but had stepped down to assume the directorship of El Rosario when she realized that the illegal logging was being carried out to clear land for avocado farms. On top of everything else, her fiery spirit, her tireless devotion to the people, her fearless opposition to state-sanctioned violence, she was a young and beautiful woman. Always well dressed, her long, black hair held by a simple cloth band, she wore plain, white blouses and designer jeans that somehow did not make her look vain or faddish. Her parents were wealthy landowners, members of Mexico's privileged class, and Sylvia had been raised well, educated in the United States – at Harvard University, in environmental law, with a second degree in biology from the University of California in San Diego. Her blue eyes, the same blue, it seemed, as her El Rosario vest, stared out from the pages of Morelia newspapers with a defiant pride. She knew she was endangering her life by opposing the narcos and the local police, who were on their payrolls, but it wasn't her life she was concerned about so much as the lives of the people she was standing up for. There was the glint of blue steel in those eyes. When she addressed a group of labradors or a meeting of community organizers, her voice was at once soft and penetrating. She would raise herself on her toes, the cords in her lovely neck throbbing with passion, her slender fingers gripping the microphone as if it were a stick with which she would beat off a horde of attackers, and she would shout a slogan that the people would pick up and repeat like a mantra. The next day, the headlines would print the mantra in forty-six-point Copperplate: DECIMOS QUE NO! (WE SAY NO!) And in the photo below the headline her coppery arm would be flailing the crowd with the slogan as if with a whip. Decimos que no! Decimos que no! Such was Señorita Gonzalez.

Beyond Michoacán, she was less famous but still well known. The avocado sellers in Morelia and Guanajuato and San Miguel de Allende knew that the price of avocados had risen, and they knew why, but they would not have known that opposition to the cartel takeover existed, nor would they have supported it if they had. Cutting down trees? What was wrong with cutting down trees? People have to live. Farmers have to grow avocados. People are more important than butterflies. And growing avocados is better than growing poppies for heroin, wouldn't you say? So you have to pay a few more pesos for your avocados. They're still cheap. What does it matter where they come from? Mexicans have become careful about enquiring into such things. There is the story of the patient weasel and the hen who stuck her neck through the chicken wire to reach a tasty bug.

Farther away, in Mexico City, Sylvia Gonzalez was not some obscure rabble-rouser marching at the head of a clutch of campesinas. In the judicial halls of the capital, in the courtrooms and the judges' chambers, Sylvia Gonzalez was a force to be dealt with. She was synonymous with victory. She breathed victory. Her knowledge of the law, both American and Mexican, though they were so different that to categorize them both under the same heading was hardly accurate, had stymied the most sycophantic opposition to her accusations. Even President Sheinbaum, who had campaigned on a platform of ending gang violence, corruption, and the drug trade, but who, once elected, had found the pathways to ending violence, corruption, and the drug trade blocked by one impasse after another, had had to concede to *El País* on several occasions that she and Señorita Gonzalez agreed on many important issues, and that she was working closely with Señorita Gonzalez and the board of directors of El Rosario to see what measures could be taken that would satisfy all sides of this very delicate question. Several professors from the National Autonomous University in Mexico City had voiced their support for Señorita Gonzalez since, after all, her cause was the future survival of Nature, the protection and preservation of the nation's natural heritage. Americans, but no Mexicans, interviewed Sylvia Gonzalez on television. And just two months before her disappearance, Pedrito dal Costo-Caval, the world-famous bullfighter from Portugal, had arrived in Mexico, met Sylvia Gonzalez at a community meeting in Morelia, which had been held in one of the city's largest bullfighting arenas because she drew such large crowds, and been so enthralled by her rhetoric, and so charmed by her personal attributes, that he had put the full weight of his popularity behind her anti-logging campaign.

And now Sylvia Gonzalez had vanished! Except for the little that was reported in the brief announcement in *El País* in the middle of January, and despite what anyone might privately suspect about her disappearance, nothing further came to light about what had befallen her.

IN THE CAFÉ DE TACUBA in Mexico City, in one of the smaller, windowless rooms at the back, barely more than a double row of tables between the staircase leading up to the main dining area and a second, smaller staircase leading down to the pastry kitchen, sat three gentlemen whose bylines were known to most of the gringos and a great many chilangos. Their names ran off the tongue like those of a double-play combination for the Yankees: they were Messrs. Washer, Pumper, and Klingson.

Flip (short for Philip) Washer was a reporter for the *Hark*. Not just a reporter; he was chief of the paper's Mexican bureau. In fact, he *was* the *Hark*'s Mexican bureau. He had a wife whom no one but he had ever seen, and a small office with a single bare lightbulb, one large desk, a wooden swivel chair, a laptop computer, and a metal file cabinet that he locked even when he went down the hall to use the toilet. In the café, he wore a frayed, wide-brimmed, sweat-darkened Panama hat that may have predated the digging of the Panama canal, and western cowboy boots, not true Mexican vaquera boots, mind you, but real American cowboy boots that he'd bought many years before in Boston, when he was attending a journalism convention and wanted to advertise the fact that he was the *Hark*'s Mexican bureau chief. Below his hat and above his boots, he was a small man. His most noticeable feature was a large silver belt buckle that he actually had bought in Mexico City, at a Roots store on Cinco de Mayo, about which he complained constantly. It was a Mexican buckle affixed to an American belt; it was made wrong; it cinched either too tight or too loose. Since he weighed hardly more than his boots and the buckle combined, the belt always cinched loose, and his pants hung down on what ought to have been his hips, and his pant cuffs hid the fancy toolwork on his boots. But if he cinched it to the next hole, his waist was drawn in like the tied-off end of a Mennonite sausage. He felt he couldn't win. He was defeated by his belt buckle. His face was as crumpled as an unsatisfactory first draft. He wore oversized glasses that became sunglasses according to some prismatic whim of their own, and it was impossible to say whether they rested on the bridge of his nose or on his cheeks. Probably the latter, but one didn't like to stare. As he sat at the table, he removed his hat and his glasses and rubbed his eyes with excessive zeal. Tears formed in them and wet his knuckles.

Even so, Flip Washer was a formidable news man. Although his beat was to cover anything of interest that might happen in Mexico, his special interest was crime. Not any particular crime per se, but in the background to the crime, the circumstances in which the crime had been committed. He was, at heart, a superb features writer. He eschewed the inverted pyramid, in which all the vital details of the crime were announced in the opening sentence, and each succeeding sentence contained less and less pertinent information until the final paragraph conveyed nothing more than that Oaxaca, let us say, was a city located two hundred and eighty miles southeast of Mexico City. Washer would begin his dispatches with just such a lesson in geography. He would then proceed to give the most detailed information about the principal characters in his story: their parentage, their educational backgrounds, their family circumstances, where they worked, how much they earned, whom they were seeing publicly, and whom they were seeing on the side. He would turn all this assiduously gleaned information into an artful structure, a small but telling detail here, an informed innuendo there, that built slowly towards the inevitable climax, which was the actual crime. His editors were grudgingly acquiescent, because his readers were transfixed. Occasionally, if his careful construction lacked a confirmation, or opened a door Washer did not enter, he would follow it up the next day with an interview with the victim's pregnant girlfriend, the one his wife didn't know about, or with the suspect's sister, and that would finish the story, the way installing wall-to-wall carpet finished a room. Washer thought of himself as a portrait artist. He did not believe that a photograph was worth a thousand words, but a portrait, yes, a portrait could reveal aspects of a character's inner workings that a photograph could never capture. Crime itself was mundane, even murder could be boring. But a portrait of a murderer, or the laying out of the events leading up to the crime like exhibits in a museum of the imagination, that was what had made Flip Washer famous.

Frank Pumper was a different quintal of fish altogether. He was a large man with a bald head and a tight suit. He'd always been large and was accustomed to thinking of himself as large. He'd been a lineman on his college football team and had a couple of trophies stashed away somewhere to remind him of his younger self. The brass football-wielding figures atop the trophies were a lot thinner and looked more agile than Frank Pumper had ever been, but Pumper still gave the impression of being fit. He was, however, no longer agile, and lately he'd begun to sag in places. Under his chin. His glutes. The soft stretches between his armpits and his clavicles. He avoided running because he didn't quite trust his legs anymore. He couldn't fasten the top button of his white cotton shirts, and so his ties were perpetually loosened. He took them off that way at night and hung them on a hook on the inside of his closet door.

Still, he looked reliable, almost respectable. He did not have a moustache. His eyes were steady and trustworthy, with none of the glazed indifference so often seen in the eyes of most of the gringos in Mexico, who saw things every day of their lives that they would rather not look at, and so they didn't. Frank Pumper looked. Looking was his livelihood, and it was also his nature. He said he didn't feel, because feelings got in the way of understanding, but he did feel. The stories he wrote for the *Bay-Times* were hard-hitting, pull-no-punches, look-away-if-you-can stories that could not have been written as well as they were by a person who didn't feel, and feel deeply. He was the man sitting quietly in the darkest corner of the bar at three in the morning, still on his second mezcal. His Spanish was flavoured and flawless. He had read everything to do with Mexico, even the Mexican novelists, even the Mexican poets. In fact, he was a devotee of poetry in general. He had his own idea of the classics, but he read widely. Flip Washer's wide-brimmed Panama hat, now perched on a hat-tree beside their table, always reminded Pumper of a line from a poem by Elizabeth Bishop: "The whole shadow of Man is only as big as his hat." That was certainly true of Flip Washer, but only Frank Pumper would have thought of it. Poetry notwithstanding, he was on as good terms with killers and police informants as he was with lower-ranking politicians and assistants-to-the-mayor. He knew things about Claudia Sheinbaum that she didn't think anyone knew but her confessor. He knew things the president had never told her confessor. He knew what had happened before it happened. He would have been great at writing obituaries, but the *Bay-Times* wouldn't have paid him a thousand a week to write obituaries.

And then there was Klingson. Tall, thin, silent-as-the-grave Walter Brickhurst Klingson. The Brickhurst betrayed his Southern origins; that his family once owned slaves was among the things Klingson never talked about. News entered Klingson and didn't come out until the morning edition. Ask him what was going on and he'd shrug his padded shoulders and say, "You tell me." Meanwhile, an hour ago he'd have written five hundred words about what was going on and emailed it in from his phone. It was no use asking Klingson anything, but he was useful as a kind of Ouija board for sounding out the reliability of certain kinds of information. The tighter-lipped he was about something, the more likely it was that it was going to be a big story in the *Banner-Tribune* in three days' time. He was like a tightly stoppered, dark green bottle, but there was good stuff in him, and it was always wise to keep a bottle of good stuff around.

The three staunch newspapermen made up what they called, among themselves, the Mexico Cartel. The name was a kind of dangerous joke, because no one who knew Mexico used the word "cartel" lightly. But at the same time it was apt, because Flip Washer, Frank Pumper, and Walter B. Klingson more or less controlled the bulk of the news flowing north across the border from Mexico to the rest of the world, as surely as the drug cartels controlled the flow of heroin and cocaine from Jalisco and Guerrero into California and Arizona. The few lines about the disappearance of Sylvia Gonzalez that had slipped into *El País* had reappeared the same day, augmented with patches of local colour and two or three sidebars, in the *Hark*, the *Bay-Times,* and the *Banner-Tribune.* The *Hark* reported, possibly inaccurately, that Sylvia Gonzalez had been born in Colorado, and so was an American citizen, and after that a dozen other newspapers picked up the story and ran with it. An environmentalist disappearing in Mexico was page eight; an American environmentalist disappearing in Mexico was a headline. The *Herald* and the *Guardian* sent their own reporters down, a young man and a woman, both of whom fairly vibrated with energy. The duo showed up at the Café de Tacuba and asked the Cartel, although they didn't call them that, if there'd been any follow-up on the missing American activist. "You tell me," Klingson said. Whom should they talk to? Where should they go? Pumper gave them the name of a minor official in the Department of Justice. Washer told them they could take a bus from Estación Norte to Querétero, then another to San Miguel de Allende, and from there switch to a third bus to Morelia. He waved his right arm as if drawing a map on a large canvas, making half of Mexico seem like a *New Yorker* cover. "Primera Plus is cheaper," he said, "but the ETNs are more comfortable. They have little television screens in the seat-backs, like in airplanes." The duo said they'd rent a car. "Suit yourselves," shrugged Pumper. "You can't see anything from a car." There was nothing more to be had from the Cartel.

When the duo left, Pumper, Washer, and Klingson sat quietly for a few minutes, sipping tequila, then Washer asked, "Are we getting older, or is the world just getting younger?"

No one knew where the Cartel got its information. It was almost as if they manufactured it themselves, except of course they didn't. No sooner had the two intrepid newshounds from the *Herald* and the *Guardian* secured their rental car and headed off on their three-day wild goose chase to Michoacán than the *Bay-Times* ran a story, on page three, bylined Frank Pumper and date-lined Mexico City, stating that although there was no further information concerning the whereabouts of the missing Sylvia Gonzalez, sources close to the young woman's family claimed that a reward of a hundred thousand pesos was going to be offered for any information leading to the rescue of the couple's only daughter. In the *Hark*, Washer noted that no ransom had yet been demanded, and quoted a source "in Sr. Gonzalez's immediate circle" saying that "Sylvia has been estranged from her parents for several years, but Señor and Señora Gonzalez are devastated by the tragedy that seems to have befallen their daughter, and will do anything in their power to restore her freedom." Pumper's article in the *Bay-Times* ended with the information that a hundred thousand Mexican pesos was the equivalent of five thousand American dollars, and represented the annual income of the average Mexican working-class family.

Pumper wasn't happy with his story. "They cut it in half and turned it upside down," he complained to Washer and Klingson, who nodded in sympathy.

"What can you do?" said Pumper.

"You tell me," said Klingson.

"What are you doing with the other half?" asked Washer.

ONE DAY, a new face turned up at the café, a fresh, young freelancer named John Baker. He was from Chicago. He used to work for the *Aurora*, he said, but now he did most of his writing for magazines. He sometimes sold stories to newspapers to help pay for his investigations. He might send a few things to the *Aurora*. He was as long and lean as Klingson, had a pile of thick hair and Pumper's deep-set, brooding eyes, and he had Washer's nose for a good story.

He'd blown his life savings to come down to Mexico to find out what had happened to Sylvia Gonzalez. He'd queried *National Geographic*. He might write a book. He was going to be in Mexico for three weeks, maybe four. He even had a title for the book. "*The Mariposa Project*," he informed them. "*Mariposa* is Spanish for butterfly." The Cartel regarded Baker speculatively. The creases in Washer's face deepened. Pumper smiled. Klingson's face was an unreadable mask. Baker cleared his throat.

"Anything you can tell me," he said, "anything at all, I'd appreciate it."

"We don't know anything," said Klingson.

"We heard she's in Chiapas," said Washer. "On a rest cure."

"Chiapas? Where's that?"

"Or maybe Guadalajara."

"How do I get there?"

"There's a guy in the Department of Justice you could talk to," said Pumper.

"What about this bullfighter guy from Portugal?" said Baker. "Is he still around?"

"Pedrito."

"Yeah. Have you heard anything about him?"

The three Cartel members looked at each other. "Good question," said Klingson.

"Maybe I'll try to track him down."

"If he was smart, he'd be back in Portugal by now."

"I don't know," said Baker. "Are bullfighters smart?"

"They're quick."

Baker caught up with Pedrito in Morelia, where the bullfighter had been living for a month, participating in the search for Sylvia Gonzalez. Pedrito told Baker he'd been to all her rallies, sitting in the front row and clapping his hands wildly whenever she made a forceful point or gave an opponent what-for. Since her disappearance, he'd bribed every police officer and government official in the city, of whom there were many. Baker and Pedrito became fast friends, united by a common concern. Stories about the ongoing investigation by special correspondent John Baker began appearing in the *Aurora*. The search was now in its fifth day, then in its second week, hopes were fading for a speedy end to the tragedy, worries were mounting that she wouldn't be found alive. An interview with Sylvia's mother, another with a tour guide at the El Rosario Monarch Butterfly Preserve. The story shifted from Morelia to Mexico City, then from Mexico City to Angangueo and Ocampo, two villages close to El Rosario. John Baker visited them both, talked to local citizens, to tour operators who brought American tourists in from the airports and put them up in local hotels, to the American tourists themselves, most of whom were unaware of the alleged kidnapping until Baker informed them of it. When Pedrito disappeared, the *Aurora* reported that the matador had returned to Portugal to raise money to continue the search. While he was gone, Baker started a GoFundMe campaign for the butterfly preserve, which was desperately under-financed and short-staffed. He called it "the Mariposa Project." He wrote a feature for *The Atlantic*. He signed a book deal with Simon & Schuster. He booked a suite at the Santa Maria Hotel in Morelia for a month.

Back in Mexico City, Washer, Pumper, and Klingson ordered a bottle of Centenario. The waiter brought the tequila, three glasses, and three shots of sangrita. The Cartel told the waiter to tell anyone who asked that they weren't there. They were in conference. They were putting their heads together. They knew what was going to happen, and they wanted to make sure they agreed on what they were going to do about it. They knew that their respective papers would no longer be satisfied with dispatches about possible sightings in Chiapas or telephone interviews with Señor Gonzalez's gardener. The disappearances of Sylvia Gonzalez and Pedrito dal Costo-Caval had become a bigger story than that, bigger than a recycled piece about a health department official caught taking bribes from a Chinese pharmaceutical manufacturer, bigger than an exposé of construction irregularities in apartment buildings revealed by the 2017 earthquake, which killed, yes, we know, many thousands of people. Old news. Old news was not news. Their editors wanted new news. They wanted dirt. Dirt was news.

Frank Pumper's phone buzzed. The chief of police in Morelia was returning his call.

"Chief," said Pumper, putting his phone on speaker. "I've got a line of enquiry for you concerning the Sylvia Gonzalez case."

"Yeah, you and everyone else," said the chief. "Well, what is it?"

"I'm guessing a colleague of ours from the States, a Mr. John Baker, you've heard of him?"

"Yeah, he's been around. What about him?"

"I have a hunch he's behind this so-called kidnapping. He's unconscionable. He's unscrupulous. He'd kill his great aunt if there was a good story in it." Across the table, Washer nodded in agreement. The killing of a great aunt would be a great story. Klingson lit a cigarette. "My guess," said Pumper, "is that Baker has Señorita Gonzalez holed up somewhere, somewhere nice and comfortable, for example in a suite in the Santa Maria Hotel, and in a week or two he'll haul her out and claim he found her in a logging camp in El Rosario."

"Is this what you're writing in your newspaper?"

"I will as soon as you find her. I could say you were acting on an anonymous tip."

The police chief sent a patrol car around to the Santa Maria, but John Baker had already checked out. He was, at that moment, on an ETN bus heading for Mexico City, travelling alone. He had received an email, through his account at the *Aurora*, from a woman who said she was aboard the cruise ship *Atlantis*, bound for Lisbon.

"There are two passengers on the ship," the woman wrote, "and I'm positive they are the famous Portuguese bullfighter Pedrito and a young woman who speaks Spanish and looks an awful lot like the woman your paper said was kidnapped in Mexico. I'm attaching a photo I took with my phone. Thought you'd like to know." It was signed, "A Friend."

The photograph showed a couple in formal attire sitting at a table in the *Atlantis*'s first-class dining room, along with a man in the ship's uniform. Baker stared at the photograph. He tapped it and enlarged it. The resolution was fuzzy, probably because the dining room lights were low or the woman who took it had the shakes. Baker tapped again and squinted. The couple might have been Pedrito dal Costo-Caval and Sylvia Gonzalez. The bottle on the table might have been champagne. The man in uniform might have been the ship's captain. After studying the photograph for a long while, Baker sent an email to Pedrito, asking him to confirm he was really on a cruise ship called the *Atlantis* with Sylvia Gonzalez. He waited an hour without receiving a reply. Then he composed a second email and sent it to his editor at the *Aurora*.

THE NEXT DAY, the *Aurora* ran the following story on its front page, below a reproduction of the blurry photograph with the champagne bottle on the table but the ship's captain cropped out. The headline was: MISSING ACTIVIST SAFE, MYSTERY IN MEXICO SOLVED!

Morelia, February 12
By John Baker, special to the Aurora

> The mystery has been solved surrounding the disappearance of Señorita Sylvia Gonzalez, the environmental activist in Michoacán, Mexico, who was reportedly abducted by a Mexican drug cartel on January 15 of this year. It has been learned by this correspondent that the missing woman has eloped with the well-known Portuguese bullfighter Pedrito dal Costo-Caval. The two have been identified as passengers aboard the luxury cruise liner Atlantis, which two days ago sailed from Veracruz, Mexico, bound for Lisbon, Portugal. (For more on this story, please turn to page A8.)

THE ATMOSPHERE IN the Café de Tacuba was glum. The day's copy of the *Aurora* lay on the table, its front page with the blurry photograph and the thirty-six-point headline forming a silent centrepiece, surrounded by three half-empty glasses of tequila blanco and three full glasses of sangrita. No one had turned to page A8. They all knew what was on page A8. Old news. Flip Washer sat slumped in his chair, his face hidden in the shadow of his Panama hat. He might have been unconscious. Klingson lit a cigarette and coughed, took in a lungful of smoke, coughed again, and looked at the sangritas as though they were Horsemen of the Apocalypse. Frank Pumper was reading emails on his phone from his editor. He had been reassigned to the obituaries section, effective immediately, and was to return state-side on the next available flight. What was he going to do with his apartment? His books? He wrote back to his editor: "No, thanks. I'm staying here. Fire me." Two minutes later he received another email: "You're fired." Two minutes. His editor must have consulted with the section manager. Pumper wrote back: "Let me write one more piece. Then I'm done."

IN HIS APARTMENT that evening, Pumper turned on the goose-necked lamp, pulled his chair as close to his desk as his midriff allowed, took a book down from the bookshelf, and opened his laptop. "The Heart and Soul of Mexico," he wrote.

> Lately, I have been reading poetry. Mexican poetry. I know that is a strange sort of activity for a crime reporter, but that's what I've been doing. Poetry isn't the opposite of crime; poets have been compared to detectives, and detectives solve crimes, they don't commit them. Poets solve crimes by revealing souls. And sometimes those souls are dark.
>
> Mexico has a dark soul. On the surface, perhaps, to many Americans, it may seem that Mexico is all about sandy beaches and tequila sunrises and romantic songs in which the word *corazon* all-too-frequently appears. *Corazon* means heart. And it's true that Mexico has a light heart. Mexico has a light heart and a dark soul. I know that from having lived

in and written about Mexico for the past twenty-five years as a crime reporter. And from reading Mexican poetry.

I recently read a poem by a Mexican poet that I think sums up exactly what I mean when I say that Mexico has a light heart and a dark soul. The poet's name is Margarito Ledesma, which was a pseudonym for a lawyer named Leonbino Zavala, who died in 1974. Zavala published his book of poems, purportedly by Margarito Ledesma, in 1950. He referred to himself as a *humorista involuntario*, an involuntary humorist. For a long time I asked myself what an involuntary humorist could be. Someone who didn't want to be a humorist but found himself writing humorous poetry in spite of himself? Or someone who didn't think the world was all that funny, but who found himself laughing at it anyway? That sounded to me more like the Mexico I have come to know.

The poem I have in mind that best illustrates this involuntary humour is called "My Cinnamon Dog." In it, Ledesma tells us he once had a dog "who was sharper than any thistle." Ledesma's dog obeyed him when it felt like obeying him, and ignored him when it didn't want to be bothered fetching sticks or shaking paws. Ledesma took that as a sign of the dog's superior intelligence, and he learned to give the dog commands that made him feel as though his dog were obeying him when in fact the dog was just doing what it wanted. If the dog was lying quietly, Ledesma would say, "Don't get up," and it wouldn't. And if the dog was running in a straight line, Ledesma would say "Don't turn to the right," and the dog would keep on running straight. Ledesma and his dog reached an accommodation by which they were both happy, and both felt they were in control of their relationship. Everything seemed fine, Ledesma had an obedient dog, and the dog had an appreciative owner. Then we get to the last stanza:

> Oh, he was a good little laddie,
> And he made my poor spirits rally,
> Until a municipale,
> Threw him a poisoned meat patty.

You see what I mean, don't you? Ledesma gets a dog that, after a period of mutual adjustment, raises his spirits. That is Mexico's light heart. And then, *wham!* Reality sets in, darkness descends. His dog is killed by a city policeman. Who knows why? What difference does it make? Nothing to be done. That is Mexico's dark soul.

And that is why I don't believe the news, reported yesterday, that Sylvia Gonzalez, the environmental activist who disappeared three weeks ago, has run off to Portugal with her lover, the handsome bullfighter Pedrito dal Costo-Caval. I don't believe that they are, at this moment, sipping champagne on the luxury liner *Atlantis*, somewhere between Veracruz and Lisbon. That report, based on a blurry photograph from an anonymous informant, doesn't gel with what I know about Mexico. It's too lighthearted. It corresponds to only one side of the Mexico I know.

> In the Mexico I know, people do not disappear for three weeks and then turn up sipping champagne on a luxury cruise ship. Especially people who have offended one of the country's major drug cartels. Pedrito and Sylvia eloping on the *Atlantis* are Ledesma's cinnamon dog. Cartel soldiers are the municipales.

Pumper read the story over a couple of times, changed a word here and there, attached the file to an email and hit send. His editor at the *Bay-Times* chopped it up into shorter paragraphs, ran it as an op-ed piece, and told Pumper he could stay in Mexico City for a while longer.

TWO DAYS LATER, the following story appeared in the *Banner-Tribune*:

> **Mysterious Mexican Disappearance Ends in Tragedy**
> **By Walter B. Klingson**
>
> Mexico City, 14 February. The body of Portuguese bullfighter Pedrito dal Costo-Caval, who disappeared last week and was presumed to have returned to Portugal, has been found at the bottom of a holding pond on an avocado farm in the Mexican state of Michoacán. Costo-Caval had been assisting police with their investigation into the disappearance of environmental activist Sylvia Gonzalez, director of the El Rosario Monarch Butterfly Preserve in Michoacán. Señorita Gonzalez's whereabouts are still a matter of conjecture. However, the discovery of Costo-Caval's body on an avocado farm strongly

> suggests that her disappearance is connected to her well-known opposition to increased logging and avocado farming in the El Rosario preserve. State authorities in Michoacán have renewed their search for Señorita Gonzalez. According to Hector Martínez, chief of police in Morelia, Michoacán's capital, who found Costo-Caval's drowned body after responding to an anonymous tip, "We are doing everything in our power to solve this mystery. We will find out who is responsible for both the death of the matador and the fate of Señorita Gonzalez."

That day, the atmosphere in the Café de Tacuba was almost cheerful. Washer and Pumper were drinking coffee. Pumper was making telephone calls for a background story he was writing about the avocado industry. Klingson was off somewhere chasing down a rumour about corruption at the head of the Mexican teachers' union. Washer was talking to John Baker, who was no longer a special correspondent to the *Aurora* but claimed to be working on a feature about monarch butterflies for *National Geographic*.

"You should speak to my wife," Washer said. "She's an authority on monarchs."

"Is she a lepidopterist?" asked Baker, half-mockingly.

"No, but she does a lot of volunteer work," said Washer. "In any case, she isn't here. She's out of town."

What Washer didn't tell Baker was that his wife was on her way to their winter residence on the Algarve, in Portugal, where Washer would join her in a week or two. In fact she was, at that moment, aboard the cruise ship *Atlantis*, bound for Lisbon.

ABOUT "THE CARTEL"

This is a cover of "The Cartel," a short story published in 1920 by the Austrian writer Joseph Roth. I first heard about Roth from the late Canadian novelist Matt Cohen. Matt planned to write a biography of Roth but, like Roth himself, he died young. When I read Roth, I realized at once why Matt admired him. Both he and Joseph Roth accepted the absurdity of daily life, which they regarded as the real business of the short story. They saved their deeper investigations into the consequences of life's absurdity for their novels. For them, novels were humorous tragedies, while short stories were more like tragic jokes. No need to explain, in a short story, why the assistant stationmaster is an idiot; he just is. Or how Christopher Columbus ended up as a side-show in an American travelling circus; he's just there at the beginning of Cohen's short story, "Columbus and the Fat Lady." The how of it is either unimportant or would take a novel to explain. Matt used to say that he wrote short stories as warm-ups to his novels, or as frame stories for them, and Joseph Roth's stories give a similar impression. Roth's characters tend to drift into situations and then leave before the situations expand into novels. Michael Hoffman, Roth's translator, calls the stories "a sideline, a by-product, or part of [Roth's] apprenticeship." The stories may be important, but they aren't serious. Roth's story "April," written in 1925, ends the line: "'Life is very important!' I laughed." That sounds like something Matt would have written if Roth hadn't beaten him to it.

Roth was born in 1894 in the shtetl of Brody, in Galicia (then Austro-Hungary, now part of Ukraine). Galicia, once a centre of Jewish culture and learning, had become a backwater by the time Roth was born. Roth's father, whom Roth did not know, died in prison when Roth was sixteen. Three years later, Roth left Brody to attend the University of Vienna, where he studied German literature. In 1916, he joined the Austrian Army. He served on the Eastern Front, where, like his character in "Stationmaster Fallmerayer," he was "surrounded by the stink of gas and the smell of blood, in the rain, in the swamp, in the mud, in the sweat of the living, in the reek of the moldering dead." In 1918, after witnessing the Russian Revolution, he returned to Vienna, converted to Catholicism, and began writing for leftist newspapers like *Der Neue Tag.* He then moved to Berlin where, from 1923 until Hitler became Chancellor of Germany in 1933, he wrote for the *Frankfurter Zeitung*, a large, Jewish-owned, liberal daily that was anti-fascist and, in its *Feuilleton* section, published longer features and even short fiction by such writers as Thomas Mann, Walter Benjamin, and Stefan Zweig.

In 1928, *The Panopticum on Sunday,* a selection of Roth's journalism, was published. (A *panopticum* is an exhibition of historical or topical curiosities in wax, something like Mme Tussaud's wax museum in miniature. Roth was fond of them, presumably because, like a novelist, the designer could make subtle inferences simply by placing one exhibit beside another. In one of his *Feuilleton* pieces, "The Philosophy of the Panopticum," Roth wrote: "Thanks to a cannily symbolic layout, the Chamber of Horrors was just one step away from Fairy-tale Hall, and the Rulers of Europe was a curtain's thickness from the Fun House.")

Two years later, Roth's wife, Freidl Reichler, was placed in a Viennese sanatorium (the Nazis later sent her to a gas chamber). In 1932, Roth published his masterpiece, the novel *The Redetzky March*, which follows the collapse of the Hapsburg Monarchy, and the next year he moved to Paris, where he continued to write novels and anti-fascist articles for a variety of publications. But his fortunes declined. He moved to a new hotel whenever the bill for the old one came due. He drank monumentally, borrowed from friends, became disillusioned and nostalgic for the glorious Hapsburg past. His last work of fiction, a novella published in 1939, the year of his death, was *The Legend of the Holy Drinker,* about an alcoholic struggling to pay off his debts.

Roth's "The Cartel" is about three seasoned journalists in New York who are covering the abduction of a well-known suffragette, Sylvia Punkerfield. It's the only one of his stories that takes place in the United States. Roth was fascinated by America, like Kafka when he wrote the novel that in translation is called *Amerika (*Kafka's title was *Der Verschollene,* or *The Lost One*), which he had never visited, but to the idea of which Roth was morbidly drawn. He saw America as the antithesis of the old, pre-World-War-One, royalist Europe, a moral and cultural hell that had replaced the Austro-Hungarian heaven. And he regarded Americans as uncouth and boorish – in "America over Paris," a 1925 article Roth wrote for the *Frankfurter Zeitung,* he characterizes Americans visiting the French capital as "a great crowd of anonymous and desperate opportunists" and "swamp-born Myrmidons" who come to Europe to gawk and haggle: "In the Louvre, in front of the Venus de Milo or the Mona Lisa or the slaves of 'Michael Angel,' they sing out their 'Wow!'"

Roth's characters travel to America only to be rebuffed and defeated. In "April," the narrator tells a cautionary tale of his friend Abel, who "yearned for New York" but "had a low opinion of beauty and he loved crippledom and distortion." One day, "he was able to travel to New York. On the boat he saw, for the first time in his life, a beautiful woman. When he reached port, the beautiful woman vanished from his sight. He took the next ship back to Europe." Hans Pauli, the young musician in "The Honors Student," actually makes it to the New World. When in Germany he was supplanted from his love affair with Mizzi Schinagl, Pauli "grasped his tragic destiny as an artist" and "bought a ticket, sailed to America, played in cinemas and nightclubs, became a dissipated genius, and finally died of hunger on the street." That was Joseph Roth's America: Europe's tragic destiny. In 1939, he learned of the fate of the German Expressionist playwright Ernst Toller, who hanged himself in a cheap New York hotel room. Michael Hoffman reckons it was news of Toller's death that "precipitated [Roth's] final collapse." In W.H. Auden's poem "In Memory of Ernst Toller," Auden saw in the playwright's suicide the final end of "the Europe which took refuge in your head," and also in Roth's head, a Europe that was "already . . . too injured to get well." PEN U.S.A. invited Roth to America in 1939; after Roth's death, the invitation was found among his papers, unanswered.

So what does it mean that Roth set "The Cartel" in New York? The story, as Hoffman says, is "boisterous but faintly embarrassing," like America itself to those looking at it from the outside (say, from Europe or Canada). In the story, the three seasoned journalists who refer to themselves as "the Cartel" are outwitted by a young freelancer who shows up and scoops them by exposing, in print, what really happened to Sylvia Punkerfield. I chose to re-set the story in Mexico – a hard setting to resist for a story called "The Cartel" that involves a disappearance. I metamorphosed

Punkerfield from a famous American suffragette into Sylvia Gonzalez, after Homero Gómez Gonzalez, the Mexican environmental activist who disappeared following his well-publicized opposition to logging in El Rosario, the world's biggest monarch butterfly preserve. Mexico, where I have been living for half of each of the past fifteen years, remains as exotic, and sometimes as frightening, to me as the United States was to Roth, and although there are still many battles to be fought, the matter of environmental protection is one to which I hope the world will return once the current spate of climate-change-denialism has run its inevitable course.

That's a more optimistic view than Joseph Roth's. His "The Cartel" is a detective story, in which he adopts the voice of a hard-boiled American detective writer, say Dashiell Hammett, who, coincidentally, was also born in 1894, and who published his first short stories in 1922, three years before "The Cartel." Roth's story was, in a way, a kind of approximation of Hammett, written in a German that tried to sound hard-bitten and tough. By moving it ahead a hundred years and transporting it to Mexico, I felt that a gumshoe voice was no longer appropriate (I've never liked it anyway). And Roth ended the story so abruptly that it almost seems as if he, too, grew tired of it, or else had already accomplished what he'd set out to do, although it was unclear to me what that was, and so he just stopped writing. (He does the same thing in "Stationmaster Fallmerayer.") Three older, experienced journalists out-scooped by a young freelancer – could that be what Roth wanted to show? Possibly. At the time he wrote it, Roth was thirty-one and trying to break into the tight field of political journalism; he might have wanted to elbow aside the previous generation of self-satisfied newspapermen who sat in cafés all day and waited for the news to come to them. Then he may have realized that was never going to happen.

In Roth's story, the young freelancer wins by playing an unscrupulous trick. He knows all along that Sylvia Punkerfield hasn't been kidnapped, because he himself arranged for her to elope with her Portuguese bullfighter. The absurd meets the unethical. The result is a story with a not very satisfying twist at the end. I've added a second, restorative double-take that I like to think Roth would approve of, or at least accept. I think Matt Cohen would, too, and possibly even Dashiell Hammett. My "The Cartel" is a cover with the final, minor chord changed to a major, bringing it around full circle to the opening. It is thus the same as Roth's and different. After all, as Roth wrote in "April," "all stories are related. Either they resemble one another, or else one turns out to be the opposite of the other."

THE QUESTION

THE QUESTION CAME UP during a Wednesday afternoon seminar, part of the graduate course I was teaching at the university. I'd been talking about three of the works on the syllabus – Agatha Christie's *By the Pricking of My Thumbs*, Michael Innes's *Appleby at Allington*, and Tom Stoppard's *The Real Inspector Hound*. My students were surprised by the choice of texts, but I like mystery novels, I told them, and think they tell us a great deal about the society that produces them. They can be useful for identifying the things people worry about, and when those worries shift to different concerns. When the question arose, I was trying to make the case that the stories had more in common than the fact that they were all published in 1968. The question came from one of my students, a young woman in her early twenties who always read the texts and raised most of the interesting issues.

"Where were you in 1968?" she asked.

"Just let me finish this thought," I said. She knew I was putting her off. The question had taken me by surprise.

"These three works represent the conjunction of three distinct ages in mystery writing."

"Not just in mystery writing," the young woman said, as though to ask when was I going to make this part of the course relevant to something. Most people don't take mystery novels seriously. They dismiss them as genre fiction. Beach reading. That's why I put them on the syllabus. Through the open windows the raucous call of a lawn tractor drowned out my words. I paused until the noise abated, taking advantage of the time to think about the question. My top-of-the-head thought was that none of these students had been born in 1968 – in fact, many of their *parents* hadn't been born in 1968 – so in a sense the classroom also represented the confluence of three generations, and all of us, in our own ways, have been affected by the literary, political and philosophical spheres of half a century ago. I thought that was a discussion topic I could come around to.

"You're right," I said to the woman when the tractor had passed. "That year was a fulcrum in many ways. 'A nice trichotomy of forces,' as Stoppard puts it in his play."

In 1968 I was a second-year English major at this same university. Instead of returning to classes that fall, I went to Europe. These days it would be called a gap year. I'm aware now, of course, of what a momentous year it was in which to have been a student in Europe, but at the time I knew little of that. Oh, there was Sir George Williams University, in Montreal, where students tossed the university's hard drives from the ninth floor of the Henry Hall Building. I knew about that at the time, but had no idea what caused the riot. I wasn't political, and I wasn't in Montreal. I'd taken part in a couple of anti-Vietnam-War demonstrations in front of the American Embassy in Ottawa; I remembered linking arms with draft dodgers (who included a large number of our professors) and marching along Wellington Street, shouting slogans such as, "Hey, Hey, LBJ, how many kids have you killed today?" and "Hell No, We Won't Go," which I thought was safe because we were in Canada and no one was asking us to go. I also attended one or two Students for a Democratic Society meetings on campus. I called myself an existentialist, in the sense that I was certain my existence was meaningless, and I was in retreat from anything that smacked of the real world, which I regarded not as context but as pretext. Whatever that meant. I was, however, romantically interested in a student in my English class, an American from Washington, D.C, who was involved in student activism, and I tagged along to the SDS demonstrations with her. When she went home for the summer, I remained in Ottawa, got a job doing something meaningless for the federal government, and at night barricaded myself in my apartment, reading books and listening to Leonard Cohen albums. I missed the St.-Jean-Baptiste Day riot in Montreal, when Ginette Reno led the parade down rue Ste.-Catherine naked from the waist up except for a blue-and-white Québec flag painted across her breasts. I was at a desk in Ottawa, reading mystery novels and the collected plays of George Bernard Shaw at night. If asked what the most memorable events of 1968 were, I probably would have said the publication of Alice Munro's *Dance of the Happy Shades* and Margaret Atwood's *The Animals in that Country*. I'd still say that today, although a little sadly, and not here, not to this seminar group.

"Yes, it was a turbulent time," I said. "A violent time." Protests in Prague, Paris, Berlin, Madrid, Mexico City, students arrested, beaten, shot, Soviet tanks in the streets, barricades and Molotov cocktails. "I was in Europe. I took a train to Geneva. Don't ask me why. I was twenty; I was reading Freidrich Dürrenmatt." Snickers from them, but it was true, I went to Geneva because I was reading Fredrich Dürrenmatt, just as now I might go to Venice after reading Donna Leon. "On the train I overheard four Americans my age talking about what they were going to do when they got to Madrid. They were going to join the demonstrations against Franco, who'd ordered a special mass to be said in honour of Adolf Hitler. I didn't tell them they were going the wrong way, that they were on the train to Geneva. When the conductor came to take my ticket, I spoke to him in French, and relaxed when the Americans left at the Swiss border, saying 'Where the fuck are we?'" I thought it was safe, making fun of Americans. I didn't tell my students there'd been payback: leaning through the car window while the train was stopped, I bought a sandwich and a beer from a vendor on the station platform, feeling like a seasoned traveller. The bill was five francs. All my cash was in 500-franc banknotes. I handed one through the window, and as I waited for my change the train slowly began pulling away from the station; the vendor, my 500-franc note in his hand, smiled up at me and waved goodbye.

"I suppose, " I said, "if I'd been asked at the time to articulate my state of mind, I would have said I chose to oppose injustice with words rather than with swords." That sounded noble enough, and might even have been true. "Has anyone here read Paul Valéry's *La Soirée avec Monsieur Teste*? Anyway, I agree with Wendell Berry (another old codger none of you has read) that 'the resort to violence is the death of imagination.' When you enter into a violent relationship with someone, you can no long imagine each other. You become symbols, not real people. Words are more effective than bombs," I said. "We still quote Shakespeare when denouncing antisemitism."

"*We* don't," said my student. "We quote Noam Chomsky."

"A classic mystery novel," I went on, "follows the same structure as a Shakespeare comedy: the social order is upset at the beginning by a death, then at the end, through the efforts of a good agent, order is restored."

"So you're saying riot police are agents of good?"

"No, I'm not. Riot police don't solve murders. Most often it's a lone detective working within a corrupt institution, or a private citizen, a journalist or forensic scientist or an amateur detective, someone acting outside the establishment."

In Geneva, I took a room in a depressing hotel near the train station, where, when I signed in, the young desk clerk borrowed (or so I thought) twenty francs, my French wasn't very good, claiming (so I thought) he needed it for his sister, and he would pay me back (I thought he said) later that day. I gave him the money. After a sleepless night on a sagging bed (no twenty francs, no sister), I moved to a better but more expensive hotel in the upper town. I spent my days walking in the old city and my evenings at the Nouveau Théâtre de Poche, where I watched Beckett's *Oh les beaux jours* every night for a week. I found a used bookstore that had a few shelves of English books, and read every green Penguin on them: Dorothy Sayers, Marjory Allingham, Ngaio Marsh, Michael Innes. They all warned me to be careful, to watch for sharpers, charlatans, psychopaths, false prophets. I also read all the orange Penguins the store had, trading one for another until I'd gone through most of Graham Greene, Iris Murdoch, Kingsley Amis, Evelyn Waugh, and Anthony Burgess, who warned against the same things. I was vaguely aware that the Europe I was reading about was having its knees knocked out from under it, that governments were either caving in or retaliating with force, that universities were no longer sanctuaries for stepping away from the fray, but launch pads for jumping (or bumping) into it. I lamented (I still lament) their loss. Reading Dürrenmatt's unsettling mysteries by day and bathing in Beckett by night turned my eyes away from what was going on in the world, the world not of being but of nothingness. Geneva was my substitute for the university, my bastion; I could be *engagé* there, but in less immediate, more serious matters. It was the home of Jean-Jacques Rousseau, for Christ's sake, there was a statue of him on an island in the lake, just past the flower clock. After the performances, I retreated to the Café des Artisans et Artistes du Nouveau Théâtre de Poche, hoping someone would speak to me — "Oh, didn't I see you at the play? Come and join us!" — but no one did. I wasn't part of the new order, and the old order was making its last stand without me.

"In 1968, Agatha Christie, the doyenne of the Golden Age of detective fiction, was a throwback to the vanished England of country houses, quaint villages and gentlemen murderers of people no one liked very much in the first place. She was more closely connected to the First World War than to the Second, let alone anything to do with Vietnam. Taken as a whole, her opus may be compared to that of Virginia Woolf."

The inquisitive young woman looked shocked that I would mention Virginia Woolf and Agatha Christie in the same breath.

"In 'The Shooting Party,'" I said, "thirty years before Christie, Woolf writes about 'the ghost of a family, of an age, of a civilization dancing over a grave.' By the sixties, Christie and England were long past their glory days. England, Europe, the old world, were crumbling, and there she was wandering around in it, writing as if the era of stately, unlocked homes with trusted servants and the family jewels left lying about were still the norm. Innes showed us that the old England deserved to die; Stoppard showed us that the villain didn't get caught. Christie's hold on mystery writing was fading by then. Other, tougher writers were coming up to knock off her crown. P.D. James, whose third Adam Dalgleish novel came out in 1967. Ruth Rendell, who'd begun the Reginald Wexford series in 1964, and who also wrote psychological novels under the pseudonym Barbara Vine: the first one, *Wolf to the Slaughter*, also came out in 1967. In a rather cruel review of *By the Pricking of My Thumbs* – by the way, who can tell me where that quote is from? No? – Robert Barnard, himself a mystery writer of note, wrote that Christie's novel 'declines rapidly into a welter of half-realized plots and a plethora of conversations that meander through irrelevancies, repetitions and inconsequentialities to end nowhere, as if she had sat at the feet of Samuel Beckett.'"

I thought that nothing of any international importance happened in Canada. Sir George Williams wasn't part of anything international, just a bunch of disaffected hippies acting up, the kind of students I avoided. I was wrong about Canada, though. In 1968, a young man from Dominica named Roosevelt Douglas was an agriculture student at Sir George Williams. When final grades were announced in May, Douglas was convinced his biology professor had failed him because he was Black, and he became part of the student protest that destroyed the university's computer centre.

He was one of three students arrested when Montreal's riot police evacuated the Henry F. Hall Building. He spent eighteen months in jail; he taught illiterate prisoners to read, and he befriended members of the FLQ. When he got out, he switched his major to political science. When he returned to Dominica, he entered politics and, in 2000, became the island's prime minister. "The truth is," he said, much later, "I didn't become committed to the movement in Dominica. I became committed to the movement in Canada." So we didn't have to leave Canada after all.

"Words are powerful weapons," I said. "I know you've heard that before, but who's to say I wasn't more deeply radicalized by Beckett – by Winnie, in *Happy Days*, prattling on while half-buried in a pile of rubble, and her husband Willie, who shouts newspaper headlines to her from the other side of the heap – than I would have been had I been tossing computers from the Henry Hall Building in Montreal, or Molotov cocktails at Soviet tanks in Prague? Who's to say that Stoppard's disregarding the fourth wall in *The Real Inspector Hound* in 1968 didn't make possible the tearing down of the Berlin Wall in 1989? Do we think Gorbachev tore it down because Ronald Reagan told him to? I'd have said the world has been as radically changed by literature, and that those changes are reflected in detective fiction, as by jackboots and tear gas, or, for that matter, by bricks and barricades. What we sought was a connection between the past and the future, not a division between them. The past doesn't die, it evolves. Consider where Beckett might have got his image for Winnie's predicament. Consider that, in 1930, Freidrich Dürrenmatt had written, 'Our earth, by which I mean everything that creeps and crawls and takes itself seriously, is nothing but a pile of rubble.' I mean, in 1968, much of the earth *was* a pile of rubble!"

The thought still made the back of my neck tingle, but I could tell the students weren't buying it. When the seminar dispersed, the inquisitive student remained in her seat. I knew that power had shifted since 1968, that language was now seen as a dialect with an army behind it, a weapon wielded by the colonizers. Literature as an alternate but equally valid reality had died on the barricades of Berlin and Paris. Professors shamed and ejected, writers vilified for being born in the wrong place at the wrong time. Blows to the head. I waited to see what she would say, checking to be sure the classroom door had been left open. Neither of us spoke. After a while she stood.

"I'm dropping the course," she said. "There's nothing more you can give me."

"What will you take instead?" I asked.

But she didn't say. She gathered up her papers and books and, holding them against her chest, stood looking at me. Like Winnie, I thought, safe in her pile of rubble.

ABOUT "THE QUESTION"

"The Question" is a cover of "1968," Günter Grass's story for that year in his book *My Century*, which contained a story or essay for every year of the twentieth century. I read the book to see what he would say about his part in the Second World War, when he served in the Waffen-SS "somewhere far off in the Bohemian woods," as he wrote in the *New Yorker* in 2006. But he'd kept fairly quiet about those years in *My Century*, which had come out in 1999. I was also interested in his take on what had happened in 1968, the year a generation of students tried to change the world, and very nearly took it over. A year very much like 2025.

I've always felt guilty about the sixties. There's a question from that decade, I think posed by John Lennon, that haunts me still: "What if they held a war and nobody came?" Well, they held a revolution, and I didn't go.

If the revolution had succeeded, I probably wouldn't feel so bad. I could tell myself they hadn't needed me after all. But it didn't succeed, although it looked good for a while. The United States wasn't so bellicose about Vietnam after the demonstrations of 1968, but it didn't pull out until 1975, and by then the damage was irreparable, in Vietnam and Cambodia as well as in the United States. After 1968, the Soviets invaded Czechoslovakia and put out that ground fire; France repaired its cobblestoned streets and students went back to their classes. In the U.S., two significant events took place in 1968 that effectively spelled the end of the revolution in that country: Martin Luther King, Jr., was assassinated, and the Democrats held their National Convention in Chicago. Both King's funeral and the DNC were marked by an overwhelming display of military force, an almost Soviet-style parade of National Guardsmen and special police. The many long-haired heads that were clubbed, the thousands of protesters arrested and beaten, "spoke almost of a sort of psychotic imagining," wrote Elizabeth Hardwick, who witnessed both events, "as if by some cancerous multiplication the sensible and necessary had been turned into a monstrous glut." This aura of brutal, police-state control ended any positive, peaceful advances that had been made in the area of civil rights, or indeed human rights. From then on, the battles were between the militants and the military, to neither of which I belonged.

There's a beautiful but sad novel by Andrew O'Hagan, *Be Near Me*, the pathos of which has its source in the section that deals with the narrator's time at Oxford in the 1960s. In David Anderton's final year, he participates in an anti-war demonstration in London (halfheartedly, as I did in Ottawa), and his recollection of the event pretty much sums up my experience as well: "It looked for a moment as if the Tower of Babel might fall to a group of flowery innocents. The comic songs. Policemen scampering after their helmets or pressing the faces of curly-haired youths to the pavement. The whistles and shouts. The armbands and the shoving and the sense of outrage." Anderton felt, for a moment, as though he were actually, finally, participating in something real. But the feeling was short-lived. The elation "appeared and departed over a blossoming two hours, my life as a radical, and then the day dissolved into an afternoon of pubs and forty years of chatter." That was the sixties. I didn't run away, and I didn't get stoned. I just didn't pay much attention to what was going on around me. I was not what Sartre would have called *engagé*.

There was, in the end, no solution, or at least, as Grass points out, no short-term solution that literature could offer. I agree now with Chekhov and others that literature doesn't exist to answer questions, but does a far more lasting job by continuing to raise them. That isn't of much comfort, however, when every mindful gain made in the battles against racism, sexism, fascism, environmental degradation, and global warming have been eroded and reversed by the dull determinations of the corporate and religious right. It ought to be no surprise that a country that has been called "a nation of shopkeepers" should place a high value on commerce, and twice elect the biggest shopkeeper of them all its president. But it still astounds me, and I can't help wondering if, in the 1960s, one more fist raised against the military-industrial complex, one more brick thrown from the barricades in Paris, one more body lying in front of the tanks in Prague, would have made a difference.

As effective as rational protests, even revolutions, may seem, ultimately they fall short of their goals. What did the Occupy movement accomplish? After Black Lives Matter, have Black lives mattered more? Have fewer women been assaulted because of #MeToo? Will No Kings bring down Donald Trump? It remains to be seen if the Gen Z protests of 2024 and 2025 will accomplish more than those of 1968. Certainly they have succeeded in bringing down corrupt regimes in Bangladesh and Nepal. But Gen Z protests against cartel violence and political inaction in Mexico, in response to the assassination of Carlos Manzo, the mayor of Uruapan in the state of Michoacán, are unlikely to stop the drug cartels from killing their enemies. I am not a futilist; I don't see how any writer can be. I remain convinced that words are effective and lasting tools for change. Even Sartre wrote that "words are loaded pistols."

In his essay "Reflections of a Nonpolitical Man," literary critic Sven Birkerts asks why he feels guilty about the 1960s, why he wasn't more politically active then, and why he still isn't the kind of person who would chain himself to the doors of the Monsanto Corporation until they stopped genetically modifying our food. "What is wrong with me," he asks, "that I cannot bestir myself to do anything more than sign an occasional petition, write out a small check?" After examining and rejecting the more obvious reasons for his passivity – laziness, selfishness, a sense that small protests are of little use in stopping big machines – he comes to the conclusion that the best thing he can do to protest the enemies of our generation is to go on doing what he does best, which is to think, to read, and to write. The political activist in the street and the writer in his study are not separate entities, but equally effective points on the continuum of human resistance – the person who writes the pamphlets and the person who distributes them are both doing valuable work. Through writing and thinking and teaching, Birkerts tries in his own way to influence the perspective of others, to open others' eyes to the atrocities committed "by our common enemies: the liar, exploiter, polluter, rhetorician . . ." That's pretty much how I feel about it, too, hence my version of Grass's story. Although it sounds a bit like self-justification – I have friends who have gone to jail for their beliefs – it does partly assuage my guilt. But it may not sound like much to a generation raised on a daily stream of televised atrocities and social media.

Grass's "1968" is an account of that year related from the perspective of the 1990s by a narrator who is now a university professor of literature – i.e., employed by the institution the 1968 riots had targeted. In Grass's story, the narrator's disappointed student leaves the seminar, saying, "You have nothing more to give," and that's the last line of the story. I thought that was unnecessarily harsh of her, and so abrupt that it seemed even an older and wiser Grass had no reply to it. But while writing "The Question," I realized we are giving all we have to give, and the current generation is disinclined to take what we have to offer. It isn't that we have nothing more to give, it's that we have nothing *else* to give. Is that because our revolutions have failed while the outcome of theirs is still undecided? Is contact with us useless to them, or perhaps even tainted?

Art won't answer these questions. History will.

MINISTRY TO THE DYING

UNABLE TO RETURN to Mexico because of Covid, my wife and I kept in touch with our friend Michael, who lived in San Miguel year-round and was a conscientious letter-writer. Some people are like that, I find; they write letters to friends as part of their daily routine. Michael didn't just answer emails, he composed long, friendly, informative missives that kept his many friendships alive and functioning. It's more accurate to say that Michael kept in touch with me, as I am not good at keeping friendships going, a trait I attribute to having grown up in a military family and being uprooted and replanted to a new posting every four years. I learned how to make friends quickly, but not how to keep them.

Michael wrote that he was binge-watching *The Mary Tyler Moore Show* on YouTube. It was a bold admission, he said, because most of his friends wouldn't get the attraction. They would think he was either slumming or losing his marbles. But he thought I would understand. I wrote back that I watched *The Mary Tyler Moore Show* faithfully when it was on regular TV, and clearly remembered many scenes and whole episodes, which still made me laugh. Michael and I began analyzing why we liked the show and why he was liking it again, even though it was clear to both of us that the world Mary Richards had lived in during the 1970s was long gone. Perhaps that was the appeal. Because the world we were living in was also on its way out, and we wanted to assure ourselves that some things survive.

Michael was one of those people who knew a lot about a lot of things. He read widely, not many novels, he said, but biographies and works of contemporary history, many of which he took out of the bilingual library in San Miguel. He preferred to watch documentaries rather than movies, although he always knew which movies and actors were up for Oscars. A few years back, he took a French course and read all of Proust in the original, thinking it was time he developed an appetite for fiction. He said afterwards that he didn't like the Scott Moncrieff translations, because he thought Moncrieff took too many liberties with Proust's text, sometimes in ways that obfuscated what Proust was saying. Proust, he said, was a precise writer, and Moncrieff made him sound heavy and obscure. Before retiring to Mexico, Michael had been the director of a large art museum in the United States, and he knew a great deal about visual art and artists. Since retiring he was expanding his interests into other areas of art. He subscribed to the Met's *Opera on Demand*, and read up on each work for a week before watching it on his fifty-inch flat-screen monitor on Sunday afternoons. He said he wanted to know in advance whether he was going to like the performance.

In his letter, he mentioned that he'd recently read that Glenn Gould had also been a fan of *The Mary Tyler Moore*

Show, and that was partly why he began watching it again (and confessed to watching it at all), to see what those two worlds — Gould's and the fake world of Mary Tyler Moore — could possibly have had in common. He'd always assumed that Gould, like himself during the time he was a museum director, lived entirely in his head, completely absorbed in his work. He'd thought Gould isolated himself in his musical world, having little time for or interest in anything outside that concentrated sphere. Certainly nothing as mundane and transitory as a television sitcom. Apparently he'd been wrong about that.

In my reply I wrote that I wasn't surprised that Gould watched television, and related a story I was told years ago by a friend who worked as a sound engineer at the Canadian Broadcasting Corporation. When Gould died in 1982, his Park Lane apartment on St. Clair Avenue, in Toronto, had contained hundreds of eight-track tape recordings Gould had made of himself playing on his favourite Steinway piano. The CBC had acquired the tapes (and, later, the piano), and given them to my friend to go through with an ear to releasing a remastered CD of Gould's recording of the *Goldberg Variations*. My friend's job was to identify the best of the recordings, and to edit out any sounds that were not part of the music: buses going by on the street, the telephone ringing, a whistling kettle, the pizza guy knocking at the door. One day, my friend said, he was listening to a particularly fine recording of Bach's *Canone alla Settima*, but could hear the faint sound of a television in the background. It sounded like someone delivering a long monologue, he said, and when he strained to make out what it was he suddenly heard Foster Hewitt shouting, "He shoots! He scores!" Glenn Gould had been watching *Hockey Night in Canada* while flawlessly playing Bach.

Even at that, I said, I thought the worlds of Glenn Gould and Mary Richards seemed vastly different from each other, and also different from the world the rest of us inhabited. Michael wrote that what he found soothing about *The Mary Tyler Moore Show* was its innocence. A single woman living in Minneapolis, interesting job, spacious apartment always immaculately kept if somewhat tastelessly decorated. She had no apparent worries; the news program she worked for almost never broadcast bad news. If the world was falling apart, it was doing so somewhere other than in Minneapolis. 9/11 hadn't happened, Covid hadn't happened, ICE hadn't happened, mass shootings and illegal border detentions hadn't happened. Kent State, Watergate and the end of the Vietnam War all happened during the program's seven-year run, but if you watched only *The Mary Tyler Moore Show*, you'd never have known any of those epochal events had taken place.

The more I thought about it, though, the more I realized that the worlds inhabited by Glenn Gould and Mary Richards were in fact quite similar. You wouldn't know there was a Vietnam War if you listened only to the *Goldberg Variations*, either. If Glenn Gould could play flawless Bach with a hockey game going on behind him, he could also play flawless Bach with a war taking place on the other side of the world. If he ever wondered what kind of woman he would have been able to live with, or what kind of world outside his apartment he could have inhabited without going insane in five minutes, Mary Richards and her hermetically sealed life would have fit the bill perfectly. Mary was smart, single, beautiful, extremely tidy, had a good income and a warm sense of humour, and there was plenty of room in her apartment for Gould's Steinway. She was even the kind of woman who would, in time, have learned to enjoy watching hockey.

During the early days of the pandemic, my wife and I spent most of our time in our house in Canada, following the self-isolation measures recommended by the provincial health authorities. We went out early in the morning to shop for groceries, and, in the evenings when few people were about, took long walks in the neighbourhood to get some exercise. We held hands during these walks, as though we were explorers entering strange and possibly dangerous territory. There hadn't yet been any Covid deaths in our town, but elsewhere — in Mexico, for instance, as Michael reported — the toll was mounting; already two people had died on his street, and we knew it wouldn't be long before the tide reached us. We had friends and family living in larger cities, where Covid deaths were becoming common, and we felt lucky and a bit guilty that so far, except for our not being able to return to Mexico, our daily lives were so little affected by the pandemic.

In my next letter to Michael, I imagined Glenn Gould married to Mary Richards. Mary would spend the day at the television station, redacting features about charity fundraisers and the city's new traffic lights, while Glenn stayed home recording Bach sonatas. Occasionally he would spend a day writing. He wrote about many things besides music: he wrote about Toronto, calling it "a complicated, unpleasant mix of sounds," a phrase he also used to describe the music of Mozart. Perhaps after reading Marshall McLuhan, he wrote about television, which he viewed as a kind of controllable window: when the view became disturbing, he could switch it off. He had stopped giving public performances in 1972 so he could devote himself entirely to recording, but when he had travelled, he preferred staying in motels rather than large hotels. He liked small towns, especially in the parts of Ontario north of Lake Superior, where a town appeared every fifty miles or so along the Trans-Canada Highway. They were mostly small, single-industry towns, he wrote, forestry or mining towns, and that gave them distinct identities, loyalty to a corporate patron, or at least to the *idea* of an owner. He seemed interested in the political aspect of that, and greatly enjoyed his concert tour to the Soviet Union.

Whenever Gould was in an elevator with another person (his apartment was on the ninth floor), he covered his face with a handkerchief; he was thought to be a little odd, even paranoid, but during the pandemic most people wore face masks, and Gould's behaviour no longer seemed so eccentric to us. Walking the trails in our city's parks, we encountered groups of unmasked joggers and could almost feel their heavy, virus-laden breath landing on us as they passed. In one of the episodes of *The Mary Tyler Moore Show*, Mary comes down with a severe cold and stays home from work for a few days; Glenn would have admired her for that, except Mary being in the apartment all day would have interfered with his concentration. He could hardly be angry with her for being ill, but after a day or two he might have been unable to hide his frustration. He might have unintentionally made her feel guilty of stifling his creativity, and he, in turn, would feel guilty about making her feel guilty. Occasionally, their marriage would stumble over that knot of guilt. Perhaps that was why he never married, out of consideration for the woman he didn't marry. And why Mary Richards herself so determinedly avoided becoming involved in any long-term relationships.

Our town in Canada is about the same size as San Miguel, where we spend half of each year. When Covid kept us in the north, Michael wrote to us about what we were missing. A new restaurant opened near where we rented our house; another closed because so few tourists were travelling. The Day of the Dead celebrations had been particularly poignant. Our town in Ontario was not a single-industry town, unless the government could be considered a benefactor. The town had two universities, a college, several federal prisons, and, across the river bridged by a busy causeway, a large military base. Most of the smaller businesses serviced those larger concerns: a bakery, a soft-drinks bottling plant, four or five building supply companies, several car lots. These were in the periphery, surrounded by new housing developments built in a variety of modern styles. The houses in the old part of town, where we lived, were large and stately red-brick or limestone dwellings arranged along broad, tranquil – you might almost say self-satisfied – streets. There were ancient trees on the lawns, but in the spring, before they leafed out, they were almost unnoticeable. Many of these older houses had interesting architectural details, rose windows, fancy cornices, gingerbread moulding around expansive porches, and my wife and I talked about them on our walks. She said they would be dark inside; I agreed, but thought that wouldn't be a problem. I also thought they would be quiet. A few had what must once have been coach houses behind them, now mostly converted to garages or renovated into small apartments set back from the street. Some of the yards on the side streets had become overgrown with shrubs and vines, ugly and grasping in winter, their leafless branches resembling bones rising from the frozen earth. A few of the sidewalks and porch fronts were in need of repair.

We crossed the streets to avoid other pedestrians, especially near the older of the two universities, where most of the students remained steadfastly unmasked.

A Starbucks was nestled in a residential area near the university, and before Covid we sometimes stopped there for a coffee. If the weather was agreeable we would sit at one of the outside tables, among the students and their dogs. But now we passed it by. Across the street had been another coffee shop, privately owned, which eventually became a frozen yoghurt emporium and was now a computer repair shop. The houses here were old but had been broken up into student apartments. Since it was the end of winter, the students were preparing to move out, and the front lawns were littered with discarded furniture — desks, sodden sofas and mattresses, rickety bookcases. One house looked as though a fire had gone through it recently: two of the upstairs windows were covered with plywood, others were cracked and blackened, and the roof was patched with a large, blue, plastic tarpaulin that made a crackling sound in the wind coming up from the river.

On our way home, we passed Christ Church Anglican, a large, white, modern building with a wide, gently sloping roof, fronted by a high steeple that, at the top, was louvered to emit the notes of an electronic carillon on Sundays. It was the church my mother went to before she died. Beside the church was the manse which, when my mother was a church member, was the home of Ruth Webster, the congregation's first woman pastor. Reverend Ruth was a large, red-faced woman, a former opera singer, she informed us, who went into the ministry when a virus of some kind attacked her vocal chords and she could no longer sing professionally, although she could still belt it out. I remembered her as a rather loud force during the hymn-singing, formidable in her battleship-grey surplice, with a large, gold, stylized crucifix around her neck.

As we passed the church, I looked away, pretending to follow the flight of a flock of starlings that had been sunning themselves on the church's black roof and now, as if obeying some mute command, had decided en masse to shift to a bare tree across the street. My wife was not fooled.

"Don't worry," she said, squeezing my hand, "she's moved on."

I wondered briefly whether she meant my mother or Reverend Ruth. It had been twenty years.

When my mother was dying of stomach cancer she refused to go into hospice, and my wife and I moved into her house to care for her during her final months. We sat up with her in the evenings, after my wife had made dinner, which my mother couldn't eat, and talked quietly as we watched television. My mother had her shows, *Wheel of Fortune, Jeopardy*, shows that required just enough intellectual input to make talking difficult. When she was still strong enough, we asked her to go through boxes of old photographs and tell us the names of the people in them. I didn't know most of my relatives on either side of the family. My father had, as he said before he died, turned his back on his family when he left home during the War, and had rarely gone back. There were a few books of crinkled photos, taken with a Brownie box camera, with the years printed in the scalloped margins. My mother had left her family in Newfoundland when she married my father. She would write, "Jack, Mother, Sheila" on the back of a photograph, and I would have to ask her who Jack and Sheila were. Her sister and brother-in-law, she'd lived with them in St. John's during the war. I was never quite sure what her mother's name was. In an old Navy trunk, along with a small trove of Newfoundland coins and stamps, we found stacks of letters sent to my mother in the 1940s, after she had married and moved to Toronto. Most were written in purple ink and signed, simply, "Mother." Others were typewritten and ended, "Your loving Father." The letters were filled with the daily happenings in the small outport my mother had left when she moved to St. John's: "Billy has taken his car apart and there are oily bits lying all around the kitchen so there's not an inch of clean space for me to bake." And some lively humour: "Freddie's horse broke a leg and Father had to take him out to the sheep pasture to shoot him. The horse, I mean, not Freddie."

Gradually my mother became too weak and disoriented to leave her bed, and we sat at her bedside and talked. Her doctor came and put a medical port in her arm, and left us with a supply of morphine. Various social workers and VON nurses came and went. When it looked as though she was close to the end, my brother came and stayed with us, and he and I sat with her, he on one side of the bed and me on the other, talking to our mother about whatever came into our heads while my wife slept in the next room until it was her turn.

At one o'clock in the morning, my mother raised her hands to form an obtuse angle above her chest, and looked inquiringly at my brother and me. We asked her what she wanted, but there was fluid in her lungs and she couldn't speak. She kept her hands at an angle and shook them. We tried to guess what she wanted. Something from the attic? She shook her head. Some paper to write on? No. Our guesses became wild and ridiculous. A sandwich? A tent?

Her suitcase? After a few minutes we fell silent, and our mother sank back onto her pillow and sighed with resignation. Her arms fell to her side, my brother and I looked at each other, and when we looked back at our mother, she had died.

It wasn't until weeks later, when my wife and I had returned to our own routines and were walking past Christ Church Anglican, that I looked up at its gently sloping roof and recognized the angle my mother had been making with her hands. She had known she was about to die, and had wanted us to call Reverend Ruth to deliver the Ministry to the Dying, the Anglican version of last rites. How could we not have deciphered that silent plea? Our incomprehension had condemned her to enter whatever afterlife she believed in without the spiritual preparation Reverend Ruth would have provided. She might have to spend eternity in limbo because of us. I avoided walking by the church after that, and still tried not to pass it when we went for our life-enhancing walks during Covid. But that evening I'd been distracted by the burned-out apartment building, and as I looked at the church and the manse the feeling of helplessness and inadequacy came flooding over me again.

In my most recent letter, I told Michael that I had begun collecting words and phrases associated with the pandemic. When I had enough of them, I said, I would make a book, perhaps a dictionary. What is a virus? Where does the word "vaccination" come from? When was the first quarantine imposed? Hadn't psychologists always told us that self-isolation was a dangerous thing? What was an "uptick" before it came to mean a slight increase in the number of Covid deaths? I looked for these words in media reports and scientific papers, and kept a careful record of them, trying in some way to understand how something as traumatic and predatory as a pandemic could be subsumed so easily into our language and become normalized. How we could look away from death, and slip so unconsciously from one era to another.

Michael told me that long before the pandemic, the American poet John Ashbery had written a poem called "Uptick." The poem is included in a posthumous book of Ashbery's called *Something Close to Music*, which made me think of Glenn Gould. In the poem, Ashbery proposes that time "doesn't dovetail," seconds don't smoothly flow into minutes and hours; real time incorporates gaps and holes, ". . . one minute running out / faster than the one in front / it catches up to." Time measured by a ticking clock is slower than the time that whispers past us as we walk along our town's quiet streets, holding hands and looking elsewhere, each of us thinking of other things. In real time, a second is very slightly longer than the movement of a clock's second had, so that there is a gap between the end of a clock's tick and the beginning of the next second. I thought about those gaps accumulating until, after a hundred clock seconds have passed, or a thousand, a second of real time has gone by unmeasured, and how it must be during those isolated, unrecorded seconds that people die.

In 1967, Gould began a five-year love affair with a woman named Cornelia Brendel Foss, an American painter who was born in Germany in 1931 and escaped to the United States with her mother in 1939. She was married to Lukas Foss, who at the time was the music director of the Buffalo Philharmonic Orchestra. Cornelia left her husband and, with her two children, moved to Toronto to be near Gould. Perhaps it was she who introduced Gould to *The Mary Tyler Moore*

Show, and he in turn aroused in her an interest in hockey. Who knows? In any case, they never lived together, and every weekend she took the children to Buffalo to visit their father. After four years she left Gould and returned to her husband, who was then the music director of the New York Philharmonic. She later told an interviewer that she and Gould had loved each other, but that his weirdness made it impossible for her to stay with him. "Apart from the paranoia," she said, "he would have been a good husband and father. But his phobias got worse. He was just too ill." After she left, Gould gave up performing in public and retreated into the fastness of his apartment. He became a recluse, rarely venturing outside, never even opening his windows. He would sleep during the day, and talk to friends and colleagues only over the telephone, usually after midnight. Then, when the complicated, noisy world around him was finally quiet, he would settle down to work.

ABOUT "MINISTRY TO THE DYING"

"Ministry to the Dying" is a cover of Lydia Davis's story "Glenn Gould," which appeared in her second short prose collection, *Almost No Memory*, in 1997. *Kirkus* called *Almost No Memory* "a probing, quietly compelling series of meditations in story form," a form I like because it emphasizes the delicate poise between fiction and nonfiction. Davis is a master of the short lyric essay, which exists in the grey zone between creative nonfiction and prose poetry. Some of her stories are a single paragraph long, most no more than a page or two. Many are about death, in particular the death of relationships. Her writing is spare and straightforward, which means every word counts and the emotion they convey builds steadily to a shattering crescendo that leaves the reader briefly struggling for air. Her writing is marked by precision and concision; in that, she is much like Glenn Gould, who thought Mozart too verbose and preferred the tightly controlled, precisely articulated notes of Bach. Davis writes like a poet for whom words are too hard-won to waste — as did John Ashbery, whose poem "Uptick," to which I refer in my story, ends with the lines: "Too many words, / but precious."

In *Into the Weeds*, the book she wrote in response to being asked to write about why she writes, Davis cites Ashbery approvingly. When asked to deliver the Charles Eliot Norton Lectures at Harvard to explain his poetry, Ashbery admitted in the first lecture that "he felt his poetry *was* the explanation," and went on for the whole five lectures talking about other, minor poets whom he thought were under-appreciated. In *Into the Weeds*, Davis does the same thing, writing about a handful of other writers – Knut Hamson, J.A. Baker, George Sturt – as a way of approaching the main question, why she writes, from a slant. Just as, in the story "Glenn Gould," she writes about the Canadian pianist in a way that seems to have little to do with the subject of her story, which is the breakdown of a couples' marriage, but somehow provides the same emotional tension as the breakdown.

Lydia Davis is as well known for her translations as for her own writing; she has translated Proust, Flaubert, the Dutch writer A.L. Snijders, and the Swiss writer Peter Bichsel. In a blog in which she discusses her translation practice, she writes that she began translating Proust's *Du Coté de chez Swann* before she finished reading the novel in the original, "since it was by then a long-standing habit, or practice, not to read a book before beginning to translate it." This revelation startled and fascinated me, because I do the same thing when I am translating. Often, I set the book down midway through and begin working on the translation, except that I've always felt that was something I shouldn't admit to, like watching *The Mary Tyler Moore Show.* I read the novel in French until I feel that it's time, as Davis puts it, "to do something about it," at which point I go back to page one and begin the laborious and absorbing business of "remaking" the work in English. Mostly just to see if I can do it.

In the case of "Ministry to the Dying," I began writing the story before I finished reading Davis's original. I read enough to capture her voice, made a note of the key images with which she worked – the letters from her friend Mitch, details from the life of Glenn Gould, watching *The Mary Tyler Moore Show* – then wrote the first two pages of "Ministry." I then went back and reread "Glenn Gould" from the beginning, and saw that Davis had woven details of her narrator's life into the story as well, in fact that was what made it a story in the first place, rather than an essay about Glenn Gould and Mary Tyler Moore. I began to follow Davis's story more closely while writing my own, weaving in the parts of having lived in isolation during the pandemic where Davis wove in the details of her female narrator living with an emotionally distant husband while raising a baby in a strange city.

Davis remembers where she left off reading *Du Coté du chez Swann* before putting it down: it was "about two-thirds of the way through," she says. When I put "Glenn Gould" down and started writing "Ministry," I was about two-thirds of the way through Davis's story, at the point where her narrator walks past "the Reformed Church and Pastor Elaine's house." This image so forcefully recalled to me the circumstances surrounding my mother's death that I had to sit back and take a few deep breaths. Then I closed the book and began to write. It was almost an act of penance, begun without knowing where Davis's writing had taken her, or where my writing was going to take me. My mother died in 2003, very much in the way I describe it in "Ministry to the Dying." I had not been able to write about her death until then: reading Davis's story, being struck by that reference to a church and its female pastor's house, allowed me to see my mother's death as part of a pattern with the other images in her story, and to write about it in a way I had not otherwise been able to do.

When writers talk about being influenced by other writers, this is what they mean: when they read one of those writers, they keep wanting to put the book down and start writing themselves. That is how I came to write these stories.

ACKNOWLEDGEMENTS

No story is an island: all writers owe a debt of gratitude to the writers who preceded them. My own indebtedness is even more palpable, since each of my stories is inspired by a specific work by a particular writer. In all but two cases translators were also part of the conversation, and I wish to thank them, as well.

An earlier version of "It Happens Every Day" first appeared in *Queen's Quarterly* under a different title, and once again I wish to thank James Carson and Steve Anderson for their continued support of my writing.

I could not have found a more skillful and sympathetic collaborator than Deborah Willis, my editor at Freehand. Her task was complicated by the fact that in each of these stories the voice is slightly different, although I hope the underlying tone is my own, and Deborah deftly caught each off note and steered me back with grace and charm. Kelsey Attard at Freehand also improved the text, and saved me from several potentially embarrassing gaffs.

George Saunders's *A Swim in a Pond in the Rain* proved that it was possible to combine fiction and essays in one book, and I am grateful to him for his example. And when Margaret Atwood, ever generous and encouraging, read one of these stories she encouraged me to keep going; she also advised me on the book's title. I am grateful to her for those and much else.

I thank my agent, Marilyn Biderman, for her patience and guidance. She neither groaned nor sighed nor looked longingly out the window when I told her I was working on a book of short stories, and she found the ideal home for this book.

I have lost count of how many times I have thanked my wife, Merilyn Simonds, for her unfailing love and support, for her inspiration, and for everything else that goes into making a life together. And I am very happy to be thanking her again.

As a writer of fiction, Wayne Grady has explored his own mixed-race heritage (*Emancipation Day* and *Up From Freedom*), the often strained relationship between fathers and daughters (*The Good Father*), and now, in *The Cartel and Other Cover Stories*, the creative exchanges between writers of different languages and cultures. His science writing has taken him to the North Pole (*The Quiet Limit of the World*), the Gobi Desert (*The Dinosaur Project*), and to Patagonia (*The Bone Museum*). He is also an award-winning translator of French into English. He and his wife, the writer Merilyn Simonds, divide their time between Mexico and Canada.